BUSINESS BEFORE PLEASURE

Louis placed his hands on Marian's desk, gripping it to lean in closer to her. "You are a gorgeous woman working in a man's business. For the last three weeks I've sat across from you and tried not to show that I notice how beautiful you are. How your lips beckon me every time you flick your tongue across them. I've tried to deny how I feel, but I can't do it anymore."

Marian's eyes widened and she leaned away from him.

Louis stepped around the desk, took her chair and whirled her around to face him. He grasped her forearms and roughly pulled her to her feet and toward him until she stood just inches away from him. Her lips glistened, tempting him not to hesitate, but to do the deed.

"Really, Louis, I'm not falling for this ridiculous attempt to persuade me not to come back," she said, her voice breathy, tremulous.

He smiled. "Good. Because this is not an attempt, Marian. This is for real."

He'd only meant to scare her away, but when she called his bluff, he reacted by covering her mouth with his. Yet the moment he did, all thought of frightening her disappeared.

Dear Romance Readers,

In July of 1999, we launched the Ballad line with four new series, and each month we present both new and continuing stories set everywhere from medieval England to the American West—the kind of passionate, romantic stories you love best, written by the most gifted authors. At the back of each book, we tell you when you can find subsequent books in the series that have captured your heart.

First up this month is **Just North of Bliss,** the second book in the fabulous new *Meet Me at the Fair* series by Alice Duncan. An ambitious photographer thinks he has no interest in a certain Southern belle except for her pretty face—until he learns that love knows no boundaries. Next, Sandra Madden introduces Elizabethan-era siblings *Of Royal Birth* with **A Princess Born.** Everything changes when you discover that you're a princess . . . except the man you love.

Also this month, author Tracy Cozzens presents another fabulous new series called *American Heiresses.* **Flight of Fancy,** the first of five books about the wealthy Carrington sisters, takes readers from New York to Paris to London—and straight into the heart of passion. Finally, ever-talented Sylvia McDaniel begins a provocative new series called *The Cuvier Widows* with **Sunlight on Josephine Street,** in which the wife of a philanderer discovers that she's not her deceased husband's only widow—and she's suddenly prepared for a second chance at love.

From Bourbon Street to Elizabethan England, these are stories we know you'll love!

Kate Duffy
Editorial Director

THE CUVIER WIDOWS

SUNLIGHT ON JOSEPHINE STREET

SYLVIA MCDANIEL

ZEBRA BOOKS
KENSINGTON PUBLISHING CORP.
http://www.kensingtonbooks.com

ZEBRA BOOKS are published by

Kensington Publishing Corp.
850 Third Avenue
New York, NY 10022

First Printing: May 2002
10 9 8 7 6 5 4 3 2 1

Printed in the United States of America

Thanks to Gale Sartain for her constant love and support. I'm so glad you're part of our family. And to my Uncle Vernon who had the good sense to marry her. Sometimes love, the second time around, is the best. Love you guys.

CHAPTER ONE

New Orleans, 1895

Marian Cuvier for years thought her husband kept a mistress and that her marriage to Jean Cuvier wasn't worth the paper their marriage license was printed on. Still, the sight of the man she had spent the last twelve years of her life with—borne two children and made a home for—lying dead on the floor of a bedroom in the Chateau Hotel ripped a sob of anguish from her throat.

"What happened?" she cried, her mind reeling with thoughts of her fatherless children wrenching her heart.

Policemen stood around the body in small groups, ceased their low whispers and glanced her direction, their gazes stern, but curious.

A man half-bent over Jean's body turned and gazed at her, his dark eyes intense. "Who are you, Madame?"

"I'm his wife, Marian Cuvier," she said, starting to tremble from the shock of her husband's death. His body lay twisted grotesquely on the floor, his skin an odd pinkish hue.

Oh God, no matter how much I hated him, I would never have wished him dead!

The man crouching over the body slowly rose to his full height, his brows drawn together in a frown. "His wife is sitting in the next room Madame."

"What?" she asked, not sure she heard him correctly. "I'm Marian Cuvier. I'm his wife. Who are you?"

"I'm detective Dunegan." He gave her a stern look and took her by the arm, leading her from the bedroom.

Unable to resist, she glanced back perhaps for the last time at the still form that long ago had been her lover, and of late an absent husband. She closed her eyes, the image of the handsome man she'd married twelve years ago foremost in her mind. When she opened her eyes she looked toward the detective, not at the corpse who'd never been a good husband.

"Madame, I will ask you again. Who are you? His wife is sitting in the next room."

Confusion rippled through her and she pulled away from the man as they entered the parlor. "That must be his mistress. I am Mrs. Jean Cuvier, we've been married for twelve years."

The hotel clerk, who earlier had summoned her from her house and brought her to the Chateau Hotel, cleared his throat to draw the detective's attention. He leaned over and whispered something to the younger man who glanced again at Marian.

As if she were at a play, she watched from a distance as the scene unfolded before her, a sense of uneasiness holding her in its grip. The body lying on the floor of the bedroom looked like her husband, Jean, who was expected home today. She supposed the corpse littering the floor must be her cold-hearted husband, the man who had visited her bed fewer times than he had the church, which was almost never.

Detective Dunegan gazed at her, his expression one of bewilderment. "My apologies, Mrs. Cuvier. There seems to be some confusion. The hotel clerk confirmed you were indeed married to Mr. Cuvier. If you're his wife, then, who is the woman who was with Mr. Cuvier?"

The detective watched her closely as if he feared she would be overcome by the news her husband had died in a hotel room with another woman. Clearly, the detective had no clue that her marriage existed only on paper. How could she explain that her husband no longer found her attractive? That Louis often sought the company of other women.

Impossible. So she said nothing about the state of her marriage. Let the police figure it out, maybe they could find the reasons why her husband no longer made love to her.

Marian lifted her chin and consciously pulled her shoulders back. Made of stronger fabric than most women, she would weather this storm, just like all the others Jean put her through. She ignored the way her insides began to quiver.

"Perhaps she is his mistress," she acknowledged, her suspicions about Jean realized.

Damn him, did he never think of their children?

The door to the room burst open and a blonde woman dressed in an exquisite, embroidered crepe lisse flouncing with white India silk, hurried into the room. Her heart-shaped face and soft blue eyes looked distressed and her complexion pale. "Where is he? Is he all right? They told me he was ill."

The detective put himself between the young woman and the door to the room where Jean's body lay sprawled.

"Who are you?" Officer Dunegan asked, halting the stylish woman who looked almost like a young girl.

"I'm Mrs. Cuvier," she replied, her face anxious. "I went by Jean's office and they sent me over here. Is the doctor with him?"

"Good Lord, another one?" the detective muttered, gazing at both of them.

"Who did you say you were?" Marian questioned as she stared at this woman in disbelief.

The woman gave Marian a quick disdainful glance. "I'm Mrs. Nicole Cuvier, Jean's wife. Now, where is my husband?"

Marian wondered if she'd heard her correctly. Did she say she was Jean's wife?

The detective glanced at Marian and then at the other woman. "Jean Cuvier is dead."

Marion watched the woman as her trembling hand clutched her delicate throat. Her eyes reflected horror, while her face tightened with shock and her body swayed. For a moment Marian thought the newcomer would faint and she wondered if this whole scene was a bad dream.

"No! No!" the blonde woman cried, tears rushing to her eyes. "Dear God, no. He can't be! Let me see him. Please tell me this is a mistake. Where is he?"

The detective glanced at Marian who stood staring at the scene in front of her, shock freezing her at the woman's outburst. Jean had likely never been faithful, but how many women could one man be involved with? And did he really marry them?

"I'll take you to him," the man said taking Nicole by the arm. "I'm Detective Dunegan, with the New Orleans police."

He led the latest Mrs. Cuvier into the bedroom where the body lay sprawled on the floor. Marian stood in the center of the parlor, not knowing what to do, feeling like the ground had been ripped from beneath her feet.

Two other women claimed to be Jean's wife! The latest wife was young, attractive, and certainly more appealing for Jean to bed than herself. Could the women be lying about their marital status? Yet the newest Mrs. Cuvier certainly appeared the grieving widow, more so than even Marian. If she were lying, she certainly played her part well.

Or could this be some ploy to cover his murder? Extort money? None of this felt real, but it didn't feel like a lie either. Speculation, but possible.

When the detective and the young woman returned, Marian still stood in the same place, the policemen walking a wide path around her as she stood transfixed, staring, stunned by the day's events.

The room filled with the sounds of the newest Mrs. Cuvier's soft sobs, and Marian felt the most incredible urge to comfort her. To shield her from the hurt that Jean could so easily inflict. She shook herself. When Nicole learned of Marian's identity, she would not accept Marian's offer of solace.

"I think we need to remain calm, sit down, and find out what happened," the officer said, his voice firm and reassuring.

Calm? Remaining composed seemed impossible when you suspect your husband had found you so inappetent that he kept not one but two women to stimulate his sexual desires, leaving you to wait for him to return to the home you shared.

"What—what . . . happened," Nicole sobbed, her face streaked with tears. "How did he die?"

Marian gazed with interest at the detective. What did it say about her relationship with Jean that she hadn't even thought to ask that but rather just accepted the fact that Jean was dead.

"Poisoning. We suspect that his wi . . . the woman we found him with poisoned him."

Nicole spun around and glared at Marian through her tears.

Marian gazed back at the angry and beautiful young woman, until she realized Nicole thought she had killed Jean. "Not me. There's another woman."

"What do you mean another woman?" Nicole asked.

"You're not the only Mrs. Cuvier in this hotel suite."

"I don't believe you," Nicole said almost hysterical.

Marian wanted to laugh, but thought it would be cruel and there was already more than enough pain in this hotel room. So instead she remained quiet, let the detective explain the situation.

The detective took Nicole by the arm and motioned for Marian to follow him. They walked into an adjoining room where a girl who looked like she should still be in school sat staring out the window at the horizon, her dark eyes glazed and distant.

"Layla," the detective said, releasing Nicole. "Tell these women how the man you're suspected of killing was related to you."

She turned her oval-shaped face toward the door. Hair as black as night was swept up off her neck in a coiffure that left wisps of curls swirling around her pale face. She glanced at the detective and raised her brows in a disdainful look that was both elegant and disapproving. "I told you I did not kill my husband."

Nicole moaned, the knowledge seeming like a blow to her. "What are you saying? You lie. You can't be married to Jean?"

The girl stared at Nicole, not responding.

"Did you marry Jean Cuvier?" Marian asked gently

feeling more certain that Jean had married each one of them. If Jean had done what she suspected, she had a sudden premonition they were all going to need consoling in the next few minutes.

"Yes," the young girl said, her voice starting to tremble. Her bright red lips pouted.

Marian squeezed her eyes shut, the pain almost overwhelming her at Jean's deception. How could he do this to her? To the others? To their children?

"That can't be. He married me. He's my husband," Nicole said, her voice rising, the pain and hurt audible in her voice.

"And mine," Marian said quietly, as she sank down onto a nearby chair. "I'm Marian Cuvier. I married him twelve years ago at St. Ann's Cathedral."

Nicole turned abruptly and looked at Marian in disbelief. "No. That's impossible." She paused, her face contorted in disbelief. "No. We were married four years ago. I don't understand. He would never do something so horrible."

"And I married him a year ago," Layla whispered, her face turning ashen.

"Impossible. Jean loved me. That's . . . that's bigamy!" Nicole said, shaking her head from side to side.

"Yes it is bigamy. We're all married to the same man," Marian replied, her voice distant and hollow. Her insides were numb. Her mind slowed to a crawl, as she comprehended the situation. "And now we're all Jean's widows. The Cuvier Widows."

Marian shut the wooden door of her house behind her and leaned against it, relieved to finally be home, to her children. For four hours the detective interrogated her before he concluded she had answered enough questions and released her. Now before she could rest, she must finalize the funeral arrangements, notify the family, and the children . . . God, she dreaded telling her babies.

Notwithstanding Jean's bigamies, he would always be her children's father and they loved him even if their parent's marriage had been dead for many years.

Her sister, Claire, walked into the entry hall from the back of the house to greet her.

"Hello, I thought that might be you." Her eyes darkened to an even deeper shade of green. "I wondered where you rushed off to. When I arrived the servants told me you'd gone out."

Claire rattled on, never pausing, her brows drawing together as she watched Marian. "What's wrong? Are you feeling unwell?"

Marian shook her head and walked into Jean's study. She went to the brandy bottle on the Pembroke table. With trembling hands she poured herself a little brandy from the crystal decanter into a glass. Her sister followed her, still prattling on about nothing.

"Good Lord, now I really am worried about you. What's brought about you taking strong drink? You seldom touch alcohol."

"Where are Philip and Renée?" Marian asked.

"They're in their rooms. Philip is studying and Renée is playing with her dolls."

"Close the door. I'm not ready to tell them just yet," she said, her voice quivering.

Claire hurried over to the door of Jean's study, her skirts swishing as she walked across the oriental carpet. When Marian heard the click of the door, she sank down into the leather armchair behind Jean's French Provincial desk.

"What's wrong, Marian? What's Jean done now? Only he can make you this upset," her sister said.

Marian shook her head. The news was still hard to believe. "Jean is dead."

The other woman gasped. "Oh my God! How?"

"This morning a clerk from the Chateau Hotel knocked on the door and told me Jean needed me to come to the hotel." Marian sipped the brandy, the alcohol warming its way down her throat, giving her a boost of strength.

"When I arrived the police were waiting for me and immediately took me to his room. In the suite Jean lay on the floor, dead." She shuddered at the memory of his lifeless body. "Policemen told me he'd been poisoned. They suspect that someone killed him."

"Somebody finally did him in." Claire stood and placed her arm around Marian's shoulder giving her comfort. "Do they suspect anyone?"

"That's the worst part." Marian laughed, but tears gathered in the corners of her eyes. "They suspect Mrs. Cuvier."

"That's ludicrous! You didn't even know he was in town. Did you?" she asked, her eyes growing wide.

"He was due home today," Marian said, and then dropped the social bomb that hung over their heads. "I'm not the Mrs. Cuvier they suspect."

Her sister's face contracted quizzically, clearly not understanding her. "I beg your pardon? What are you saying?"

"There was yet another woman there who claims she's not his mistress. He married not one, but two women besides me."

Confusion then dawning realization crossed her sister's face as she grasped what Jean had done. "But . . . but how? That's against the law. It's . . . it's bigamy!"

Marian laughed, her voice sounding strained in the dead man's study. "Do you think Jean cared he was breaking the law?"

"But two women? Good Lord, how did the man do it and get away with so many wives without anyone knowing?"

"I don't know. I doubt that we'll ever understand Jean's rationale and right now I don't want to feel any sympathy for that man." She took a deep breath. "I know I am the jilted wife, but the woman accused of poisoning him is so young! And neither woman had any idea about each other or me."

She paused, glancing at the furnishings of her dead husband's study. Once, many years ago, she had loved Jean. But something changed him, and in the end she'd only felt contempt for the man she'd married.

"Do you think this woman killed him?" Claire asked.

"I don't know. Of the three, I may be the one who wanted him out of my life the most. Though I could never have divorced or killed the father of my children." She drained the last of the brandy, patted her sister's hand. "Now I have to tell the children. No matter how much of a bastard Jean could be, they loved him."

For a brief moment Marian and her sister simply sat in the confines of Jean's office, gazing around them at the man's possessions, contemplating the change his death would bring.

Claire shook her head. "Bigamy. Even that's more than I expected from Jean." She stood and gazed down at her sister. "I'll inform the servants that the house needs to be prepared for mourning. Have you contacted the undertaker?"

"Yes. On my way home Edward stopped and I made the arrangements. When the police release the body, he will prepare it and bring it to the house."

Claire shuddered. "Do we have to bring that man back into this house? I'm afraid his ghost will somehow get trapped here and he'll bother us in death more than he did when he lived."

Marian shook her head. "He's the children's father. We'll show him respect."

"I will, but you and I both know this is a great day as far as I'm concerned," she turned and walked out the door leaving Marian alone.

Claire had the courage to say the words Marian thought, but refused to acknowledge. Jean had been like a jailer. The marriage she once regarded as a prison sentence suddenly ended and like a prisoner released she was free. She closed her eyes savoring her newfound freedom as a widow. She couldn't be happier.

Louis Fournet leaned against the wall in the home of his business partner and watched Jean's widow speak with her guests. The *real* Mrs. Jean Cuvier wore a black gown that set off her dark hair making it glisten against her pale skin. She appeared the grieving widow, as she made her way through the throng of people, nodding at their condolences, dabbing at her eyes occasionally, and keeping her children close by her side.

Either the woman was an excellent actress or she had indeed loved Jean. The newspapers were full of stories of the two other Cuvier widows, yet wife number one had given old Jean quite a lavish send off.

The mansion on Josephine Street was brimming with guests as Louis glanced around wondering if any of the other "wives" were in attendance. He observed Marian Cuvier as she walked through the mourners, carrying herself in an almost aristocratic manner, her head held high. The scandal had leapt from the front page of the newspapers, shocking Louis with its implications for the business. How could a man do to his wife and children what Jean had done to Marian? Louis felt almost sorry for her.

However, that didn't change his need to sell Cuvier Shipping and with Jean out of the way, selling the business should be an easy conclusion. He would find a buyer for the business, push the paperwork through quickly and then present the widow with the sale. Cuvier Shipping would make her a wealthy widow who could escape the damaging scandal of her husband's death.

"Excuse me," a young woman said, drawing his attention from the lovely Mrs. Cuvier.

"I do not believe we've met. Were you a friend of Jean's?"

The dark-haired older woman gazed at him with questioning green eyes, and Louis was a little amazed at how forward she seemed.

Louis smiled. "I'm Louis Fournet, Jean's business partner."

"I am happy to meet you. Jean spent little time here. We never had the opportunity to meet his business associates."

"Who did you say you were?" he questioned.

"Excuse me. I should have introduced myself. I'm Claire Bienvenu," she said extending her hand. "Mrs. Cuvier's sister."

Louis nodded. "Nice to meet you. I intend to speak to Mrs. Cuvier before I leave. How is she?"

Claire smiled. "She's holding up well. Marian's life has centered around her children for many years now."

Louis noticed the two children at Mrs. Cuvier's side. The boy looked to be about ten years old and the girl at least six. For a moment he felt sad as he realized his own son should have been close to the boy's age by now.

He watched Marian reach down and pat her son on the arm in a comforting gesture.

"Those are nice-looking children."

"They're the only decent thing Jean did in his life," she glanced at him quickly to check his reaction. "I'm sorry, I'm not very good at hiding my feelings for my dead brother-in-law."

"That's quite all right," Louis said thinking maybe he should stand here with this woman a little longer. The more he learned about Marian Cuvier, the better he would understand her.

"So tell me, Mrs. Bienvenu, do you know your sister's plans, now that Jean is gone? Has she said anything?" he asked.

She smiled. "You'll have to ask her about that. I know she would want to meet you. Let me get her."

Before he could respond, Claire walked toward Mrs. Cuvier. He watched the woman approach Marian Cuvier and whisper something in her ear. She glanced up, her eyes meeting his across the room. Smoke-gray eyes, the color of the moss that hung from the cypress trees, met and held his stare. He nodded in her direction. No one would ever have questioned Jean's taste when it came to women.

Marian Cuvier represented the genteel woman who lived a life of privilege. She made a beautiful widow, stunning, in fact. Surely she would want to rid herself of Jean's business. However, her husband's infidelities seriously threatened her position in society and would keep her name in the paper in the months to come.

Most men kept mistresses, but Jean had played a dangerous game of marrying more than one woman at a time and eventually the conquests had cost him his life.

Current gossip said one of the widows had killed Louis's partner.

He watched Marian approach, both children clinging to her waist, their eyes large with grief. She turned her large gray eyes on him and he smiled. "Mr. Fournet, I am pleased to make your acquaintance."

"Mrs. Cuvier," he said bowing over her outstretched hand. "I'm terribly sorry for your loss. Jean was a character that will be hard to replace."

"Thank you, Mr. Fournet, I quite agree."

He chuckled at the memory of the newspaper articles fresh in his mind. "Sometime in the next week I'd like to call on you to discuss the business."

"What about the business, Mr. Fournet? Everything is well, I presume?" she said, her eyes narrowing.

"Everything's fine. I just wanted to discuss some options we have."

She raised her brow. "The reading of the will is tomorrow morning and I'm sure you'll be present to hear Jean's bequests."

"Yes, I'll be there. Perhaps when I call on you next week I could give you a brief report on the current status of Cuvier Shipping," he said, not wanting to mention the fact he intended to sell the shipping company.

"That's an excellent suggestion," she said.

He noted with interest the way her cool gray eyes assessed him as if she were deciding if he was an adversary or a foe. But then again, right now perhaps she felt that any man was an enemy after Jean's betrayal.

"Once again, let me offer my condolences to you and your children on the loss of your husband," he said, with a polite nod.

"Then I will see you tomorrow," she said, and walked on through the crowd of people.

He watched her move away, her back straight, her

head held high, the gentle swish of her skirts tempting. Somehow the quiet temperate woman he imagined beneath that widow's garb appeared sharper than he anticipated. Yet she intrigued him as she moved about the room. A quiet sense of strength seemed to emanate from her.

Somehow he had expected a quiet mousy woman who could easily be convinced that selling would be in her best interest. Unless he'd misunderstood her, the widow was far more than just a pretty face who had been easily deceived by her husband.

Selling the business could take a little longer than he estimated, but he would be getting rid of Cuvier Shipping whether the lovely widow wanted to sell or not.

CHAPTER TWO

Marian picked up her skirts in one hand as she climbed the steps to the office of Drew Soulier, her husband's attorney. At the top of the steps, she put her hand to her belly to quell the butterflies rioting in her stomach. Shouldn't a wife know the details of her husband's estate? Would she have known if she were about to become penniless?

So far, government secrets had seemed easier to uncover than the family financial secrets. A thorough search through Jean's desk revealed only that the man organized nothing and kept no detailed records of the family income at home.

The thought of experiencing another painful truth regarding her husband this week would send her screaming into the street.

"Mrs. Cuvier!" someone yelled.

Marian turned at the sound of her name to see a man

she didn't recognize running down the street toward her, shouting her name.

"Mrs. Cuvier, wait! I want to ask you a few questions!"

She stood, bewildered, on the steps of the attorney's office, unable to move, staring as the man ran closer and closer. The smell of sandalwood tickled her nose and a sense of being surrounded pervaded her.

Behind her, a deep masculine voice said, "I think it would be a good idea if we went inside before that reporter reaches us," which penetrated the fog that seemed to have enshrouded her these last few days.

She turned slightly and glanced up into eyes the color of royalty, a deeper blue than the wisteria that bloomed in springtime. They were so close and until this moment she never realized how tall Louis Fournet stood.

Moving her hand from her waist, she gripped her reticule and turned as he opened the door, bowing his dark brown head toward her as he gestured for her to proceed.

"After you," he said, a smile widening his face, accentuating the dimple that cleft his chin, adding a touch of masculine ruggedness to his otherwise smooth face.

"Thank you," she said, pulling the skirt of her dress to the side as she quickly entered the lawyer's office.

Mr. Fournet shut the door firmly behind her and turned the lock. "I'm locking the door, Drew," he called. "The press knows we're here."

"Quick thinking, Louis," Drew Soulier replied, approaching Marian, with his walk smooth, his face serious. Dark and regal, the man looked like a serious lawyer, except for the twinkle in his green eyes. "Mrs. Cuvier, how are you?"

"I'm fine, Mr. Soulier," she said, and then glanced

about the room. She felt awkward, unsure of what to do.

A slight cough drew her gaze to the two women who claimed to be Jean's wives, each one standing stiffly on opposite sides of the room. Though she expected they would be represented at the reading, she had hoped they would send their attorneys, rather than appear themselves.

They stood awkwardly, not looking at one another, staring off into space. Marian wanted to curse her dead husband for the situation he'd created. Hell wasn't good enough for one who had hurt her and their children so much.

Drew saw her looking at the two women and whispered, "I thought it would be wise for them to hear Jean's last will and testament. But if you'd be more comfortable, I'll send them away."

"No," she said quickly, trying to cover her resentment. "Let us all hear Jean's wishes at the same time," Marian said, her heart cringing with dread.

"All right, as you wish," Drew replied, and turned toward the other women. "Ladies, tea and refreshments are in my office. Please go inside so we can get started."

He motioned them to proceed.

Marian entered the lawyer's office and glanced around the dark paneled room. She turned and watched the women as they entered, the tension in the room almost unbearable. The men seemed poised to step between them in the unlikely event a fight should break out.

Layla entered, her eyes down, refusing to look at Marian, while Nicole walked through the door with her head held high, her eyes red-rimmed as if she had been crying. Jean's death appeared to have shocked them and she wondered if they had really cared for her dead husband.

Drew closed the door enclosing them all together and Nicole nodded her head in Marian's direction. "Mrs. Cuvier."

Marian returned her head bob, then turned her attention to Layla, who stood with her back straight, her eyes staring at a distant object. She looked so young and fragile.

"Mrs. C-c—" Layla stumbled over the name.

"I think it would so much easier if we dropped the formalness and called each other by our given names," Marian said, glancing at each woman.

Layla nodded, "Please, I'm going back to my maiden name anyway."

"I think that's wise," Marian said curtly, trying to remember they were victims, as was she.

A tense silence greeted her and for a few moments her words seemed to hang suspended in the air. Suddenly she realized they were both looking to her and she felt compelled to speak her mind.

"This is an extremely awkward situation we find ourselves in. The press is outside just waiting for us to succumb to arguing over whatever crumbs Jean has tossed our way." She sighed and stared at them. "Ladies, I have no desire to come to blows over a man who deceived me like my . . . our dead husband. I only wish to take care of my children and live in peace without them being tarnished by their father's scandal."

She paused and glanced at each woman. "Keep in mind, I shall certainly do what I must to protect my babies."

Layla let out a long sigh. "I understand. But Jean lied to me as well."

Nicole removed her hat from her carefully coiffed

blonde hair and laid the bonnet on a table nearby. "Excuse me: *I* loved Jean very much. Though I can't help but wonder why he didn't tell me the truth." She took out her handkerchief and dabbed her eyes. "It's so unfair that he died knowing all the reasons he did this but keeping them from us. Surely there's an explanation."

"I'm sure he could give you one, but why do you care? He lied to all of us. If he were alive, he wouldn't tell you the truth. He would just invent some new excuse to protect himself," Marian said, wondering at the woman's blindness to her husband, a man who hadn't cared for anyone but himself.

Nicole shook her head in disagreement, but didn't dispute Marian's comments. "But I loved him!"

"We all did at some time in our life," Marian said, attempting to keep the sarcasm out of her voice, knowing she'd failed, feeling like an idiot because of Jean's betrayal.

"I hated him," Layla stated her voice quivering with emotion.

The room became silent as they all stared at her. She was the one the police suspected. A shiver went through Marian.

"Ladies, we need to get started," Drew said standing beside the door ending their impromptu confessions. "Why don't you all take a seat?"

The lawyer seated the three women in chairs placed strategically apart, while Louis Fournet stood at the back of the room, his hands across his chest, a lock of deep brown hair falling over his forehead. He gazed at Marian and raised his darkened brows in a questioning way. Marian frowned at him and wondered what his look meant.

Drew cleared his throat. "Before I read the will, I

want to acknowledge some facts and let you all know why I invited Louis Fournet. He is co-owner of Cuvier Shipping and for that reason I requested his presence here today." He paused, looking at each of them. "I must clarify my position in this difficult situation. If I had known of Jean entering into any legal act of marriage with Nicole or Layla, I would have advised against such an unlawful arrangement. I knew nothing of your supposed marriages."

Marian felt a sense of relief that at least Jean's lawyer had not been involved in his treachery.

Drew glanced down at the will he held in his hands holding them all in suspense. "According to Louisiana law the only legal marriage the state recognizes is the first one to Marian Cuvier. I'm sorry to say, Nicole, that your marriage and Layla's are not binding and therefore unless he names you specifically in the will, you will receive nothing."

Both women gazed at Drew, their eyes widening, the shock of the news seeming to stun them.

"If you had been his mistress and he'd named you in the will, then you would inherit. But as an illegal spouse you receive nothing unless you're named in the will."

He cleared his throat and turned to Layla. "Jean wrote this will four years ago." He paused and gazed sympathically at the young woman. "I'm sorry, but the will was written before your marriage."

A gasp could be heard. Layla opened her mouth—the words seeming to hang suspended—before she finally said, "I have nothing?" she asked perplexed. "What will I do? Where will I go?"

She stood, her eyes seeming to glaze over. "You don't understand! Jean bankrupted my father's business. My father made him marry me, just so I would be taken care of. Our shipping company had been the family business for over three generations before it was taken over by Cuvier Shipping. I have no means of support. I have nothing!"

Drew swallowed and shook his head. "I'm sorry, Layla. Legally, everything belongs to Jean's estate, including the house and the business."

The girl swallowed and glanced around the room, her eyes wide with disbelief. "I have to leave my home?"

"Yes, it's in Jean's name."

Her eyes pooled with tears as she tried to absorb this startling revelation.

"How long before I have to get out of the house?" she asked, visibly trembling.

"Jean appointed me executor of his will. I'll give you thirty days to find another residence. Is that all right, Marian?" he asked, his green eyes dark with worry.

Marian knew she wasn't supposed to feel sympathy for the young woman, but she couldn't help herself. She hated what Jean had done to all of them.

"Yes, please give her all the time she needs to find another place to live."

"Thank you." Layla stood, her face completely ashen. "I have to leave—I can't stay—I have to think about what I'm going to do. I must get out of here."

Flinging open the door to Drew's office, she ran out into the entry way. A sob echoed in the entry hall as she fumbled with the lock and then yanked open the outside door and disappeared as the door slammed.

"Someone should go after her," Marian said, her voice sounding stilted to her own ears. "We can't just let her go like that!"

Drew stood up and walked to the door. He shouted a young man's name. The clerk came from the back of the building.

"Eric, go after that young woman and make sure she makes it back to the hotel safely."

"Yes, sir."

Drew shut his office door again, and returned to the chair behind his desk.

Marian shuddered, feeling as though some evil had touched her with the realization of Jean's deception. "This is dreadful."

"What about me?" Nicole asked. "The plantation is in my name." Her voice broke and a sob escaped. "We never got around to putting his name on the deed."

"If it's in your name, then your home is your own," Drew said taking a deep breath. "Let's finish this."

He proceeded to read Jean's last will and testament, as Marian sat waiting expectantly for the moment of revelation. The moment when they found out they were wealthy widows.

After several minutes Drew paused and looked at Louis. "Regarding Cuvier Shipping—I entrust the running of the business to my partner Louis Fournet until my son, Philip Cuvier, reaches the age of understanding. My son's guardian, his mother Marian Cuvier, will vote or act in my son's best interest until he reaches the age of eighteen."

Marian glanced at Louis, noticing the tightening of his expression. An unreadable look graced his face, except for one little place above his temple that pulsed with impatience.

Drew finished reading the will and laid it down on the desk.

"That's it?" Nicole asked. "He left me nothing?"

"I'm sorry, Nicole," Drew said, the office silent.

She looked stunned. "But . . . but, I was married to him. I loved him. We were . . ." She jumped up and before anyone could reach her, she crumpled to the floor in a dead faint.

Marian rushed to her side, where Louis joined her. "Get some smelling salts!"

The woman moaned. "No ammonia! I'm all right. Just give me a moment to clear my head. I must have stood up too quickly."

Nicole moved, trying to sit up, but Louis touched her shoulder. "Lie back and give yourself a few more minutes."

She looked up at Marian. "He left me nothing? I didn't dream that part, did I?"

Marian glanced away and swallowed the lump that had risen in her throat. She felt awful for feeling relieved that the bulk of the estate had been left to her and her children. "No, you didn't."

Finally Nicole rose and dusted off her skirt. She glanced around the room and sighed. "I'm going back to the hotel. I can't believe he did this to me. That bastard left me nothing."

"I'm sorry," Marian whispered.

Nicole sighed. She started to leave and then turned to Marian. "Mrs. Cuvier, this must be extremely difficult for you."

Marian nodded. "No more than it's been for you."

"I must be going. Goodbye." The woman walked out of Drew's office, her head held high, her back straight.

When she opened the door to the outside world, the sound of a crowd intruded. Drew went to the window and glanced out at the crowd of reporters who surrounded the front steps vying for attention.

As the door closed, Marian breathed a sigh of relief. She turned and found both men gazing at her, their expressions stunned. "What? Why are the two of you gazing at me like I'm some kind of ogre?"

"Close the door and take a seat, Mrs. Cuvier." Drew's voice was serious, so intense that a shiver ran up her spine. He returned to his desk.

She swallowed, suddenly quite nervous.

"What I didn't tell the women while they were here is that while you are not broke, running three households has certainly put a drain on your personal finances and even hurt Cuvier Shipping," Drew informed her.

"Are you trying to tell me that I have no money? How bad is the situation?" she asked.

Drew stood and walked around the room, his hands in his pockets. "You still have money, but you must be careful until either Cuvier Shipping recovers, or you remarry."

She laughed. "Remarry? You assume too much, Mr. Soulier. I have no intentions of ever remarrying."

Louis gazed at her and she thought she could feel his disapproval and for some reason that irritated her. "Do I need to sell the house? Get rid of the servants? What?"

"No. I would advise you to be conservative. Maybe consider selling Layla's house."

"Not right away. I just couldn't do that to her," Marian said with a grimace. "Give me your definition of conservative."

"It means you have enough money to live on, but nothing extra. Nothing extravagant. No redecorating the house or buying another house. You have enough to live at your current expenditure for a couple of years. By then I hope the business will have recovered."

"What about the business? How is it doing?" she glanced at Louis Fournet.

"Last quarter profits were up, but I don't know how the scandal will affect our customers. We'll have to wait and see," he said.

Marian swallowed, her mind racing with fear. She needed some time to think about her situation, decide what she was going to do. She needed to get away from these two gentlemen and be alone to think.

"I must go," Marian said, standing and picking up her hat and firmly fastening it on her head. "The children will be returning and I don't like to leave them alone with the servants for long."

"Fine. We'll talk more about this later," he assured her. "But I wanted you to know Jean's other domiciles took their toll on your finances."

"Mr. Soulier, everything about my dead husband has taken its toll on my life in one way or another." She took a calming breath. "Now, I really must go."

She hurried into the front office area, the men trailing behind her. A quick glance out the window confirmed her worst fears. Her carriage sat alongside the curb, surrounded by newspapermen. "Good heavens, isn't there any other dreadful news breaking in this city? Now what am I going to do?"

Louis stood beside her, his hands in his pockets, and gazed out the window at Bienville Street. "You're never going to get out of here through that crowd."

She turned and gave him an irritated look. "Thank you, Mr. Fournet, for that brilliant observation. I need to get home to my children."

He raised a brow at her and smiled. "I have an idea. Drew, do you have any more sacrificial law clerks?"

Drew frowned at him. "I think James is still left in the building. Why?"

"Let's send him out to Mrs. Cuvier's driver and tell the man to pull the carriage around back. My own carriage is sitting across the street. Most of the news hounds should follow Mrs. Cuvier's carriage and then I'll take her home."

She glanced at him, an awkward smile on her lips. It really was a good idea. She just hoped it worked. "Thank you."

"Now you're going to have to go through those doors on the far wall, so it appears you've gone to the back of the building while we send James out."

Marian frowned, but did as they told her. In a few moments she heard her carriage pull around back. Shouting voices could be heard in the distance, following it.

Drew hurried into the back room where they'd placed her. "Hurry up, I think we have drawn them to the back."

She ran back into the lawyer's reception area, where Louis stood waiting impatiently for her. "Come on, we've got to get out of here now, before they realize they've been tricked."

Louis opened the front door and the three of them stepped outside. The number of newspapermen had dwindled down to a manageable size, and Drew and Louis hurried her out the door, one on each side.

Marian felt a moment of sheer panic when the reporters turned their greedy gazes on her, seeing their lead story right before their eyes. They began running toward her, like an unruly herd of cattle.

"Mrs. Cuvier? Mrs. Cuvier? Who killed your husband? Can you tell us anything about the will? Did Jean leave the other women any money?" they shouted at her.

"Don't say anything," Drew said sharply as they all but ran down the steps to the waiting carriage across the street.

Drew protected her right side, while Louis kept the reporters at bay, shielding her with his big muscular body. A sense of gratitude overwhelmed her as she realized the risk the men had placed themselves in, shielding her.

When they reached the carriage, Marian was completely winded. Louis handed her up into the vehicle and then climbed in after her. The moment he slammed the door shut, Drew hit the side of the carriage and immediately they pulled away from the curb, just as the other reporters rounded the street corner behind them.

"Good Lord, please don't tell me it's going to be like this until this is resolved. I can't live this way," she said glancing out the window at the reporters who ran behind their carriage.

"No. I think it will become old news in a day or two. At least until whoever killed Jean is brought to trial," he said, gazing out the window at the reporters.

"The trial." Marian shook her head. "How am I going to protect my children from the sensationalism of a trial?"

"Maybe it would be better to tell them than to keep the information a secret," he responded.

She glanced at the handsome man, her new business partner, who sat across from her. "Are you married, Mr. Fournet?"

"No, I'm a widower," he replied.

"Do you have children?"

The corners of his lips turned up in a smile. "No children. So you can tell me I don't know what I'm talking about and to quit making suggestions that affect your children."

"Thank you, you've saved me a great deal of trouble."

They rode along the edge of the Garden district, the warm breeze blowing off the Mississippi making the air damp and humid. For the next couple of blocks they sat in silence, Marian trying not to notice the way his shoulders looked broad and firm beneath his suit coat, how clean his hands were, his nails clipped, the fingers long and strong.

Clearing her throat, she looked away. What was wrong with her? She'd noticed men before, but previously the barrier of her marriage had stood like a wall defending the fort. That hurdle no longer stood in her way, though it made little difference. She had no use for a man, no matter how handsome he appeared.

Finally, the carriage pulled up in front of Marian's home and she breathed a sigh of welcome relief. The morning's revelations had left her exhausted and she still needed to think about her finances.

Louis opened the door to the carriage and stepped out to help her alight. His hand gripped her fingers and held her steady as she descended the carriage steps.

He held onto her hand a little longer than necessary and turned her toward him, before releasing his hold.

"Mrs. Cuvier, regardless of the fact that I know nothing about children, I'm looking forward to calling on you next week regarding Cuvier Shipping."

She paused, staring at him, and tilted her head. "Of course you know nothing of children. Though I do expect you to know my husband's business. I look forward to speaking with you on a subject you're well acquainted with, Mr. Fournet."

He smiled and stepped back up into the carriage. "I shall be well prepared in that case so as not to disappoint you."

A smile spread across his face and then he winked at her, before shutting the door and driving away.

Marian frowned and watched the carriage pulling away, wondering why he winked. Did he think he was being flirtatious or just trying to lighten the mood? The last time a man flirted with her she had been poised on the brink of motherhood and certainly still serious about her vows of matrimony. He must be trying to lighten the mood, but still there was something about Mr. Fournet that she didn't quite trust.

In a quaint courtyard café on Rue Royale, Louis met Daniel Comeaux, a gray-haired gentleman who had been a friend of his father's for many years. Louis had met the man only in social settings, but today he met him for lunch with the express purpose of doing business with him.

"Louis, you're looking well. How's your father?" Mr. Comeaux asked as he sat watching Louis from across the table.

"He's well, thank you."

"I haven't spoken with him much since I shut down the mill and moved to New Orleans. I don't get to spend much time with him anymore."

"He still says you handled his sugarcane better than any mill he's ever used before or since," Louis responded.

The gentleman smiled contentedly. "When you enjoy what you do, you hope the people you're working for reap the benefits."

"Papa always did," Louis replied.

"And the plantation? It's doing well?" Daniel asked.

"Yes, my brother is more or less in charge, with my father overseeing things. They had a record crop last year," Louis informed him.

"Splendid. I guess you've heard that I'm retiring and trying to sell the mill. It's way past time for me to retire. I think I've earned some time to spend with my grandsons and my wife. I'm going to do some traveling and just enjoy life for a while."

"Yes, my father mentioned your decision not to

reopen the mill. That's why I wanted to meet with you. Have you sold your business yet?"

The man looked at Louis puzzled. "No. Why?"

"I'm interested in buying your company."

"But I thought you were a partner in Cuvier Shipping."

"I am. But with your business I could tie in with my family's plantation and help not only them, but their neighbors, just as you've been doing for years."

The man gazed at Louis, sizing him up. "Does your father know you want to do this?"

Not wanting to disappoint his father if he were unable to buy the business, Louis had decided not to tell his father until the deal was complete.

"No. Before I left home, he tried to convince me to stay at home and work on the plantation. He kept telling me there was plenty of work, but I didn't want to be my brother's lackey."

The man chuckled. "You were much younger then."

Louis grinned. "Yes. Now I see this as an opportunity to work with my brother and father again. But I want to do it on my terms."

"That's understandable." The man picked up his wine glass and sipped from it. "Do you have the capital to finance the business?"

Stalling for time, Louis picked up his own wine glass and sipped. The alcohol soothed its way down his throat. "I own half of Cuvier Shipping and I intend to sell the business as quickly as possible. That's where my capital will come from."

The man laughed. "Don't you think you're going to have a hard time selling now that Jean has not one but three women going after his money?"

"No, according to law only the first wife owns part of the business. The other two received nothing."

"Damn! Didn't they know about the other women?"

Louis shook his head. "Apparently not. It seems Jean kept them in different cities. The day he died was the day they found out about one another."

"Damn shame." Daniel shook his head. "Couldn't you borrow the money from your father? I'm sure he'd be happy to help you."

"Probably. But I'm thirty-five years old and I want to do this without my father's help. Call it my foolish pride, but I don't want his money," Louis said, the memory of his father telling him he wouldn't amount to anything still vibrated through his head even after all these years. "In fact, I would appreciate your not saying anything to my father about our conversation."

Daniel nodded and sat his wine glass back down on the table. "Okay, let's meet with my lawyer and we can draw up the specifics of the sale. In the meantime, I'll give you several months to sell Cuvier Shipping."

Louis smiled and held out his hand. "It's a deal."

The older man glanced at his hand. "You're sure this is what you want and that you'll be able to sell the shipping company?"

"There won't be any problem selling Cuvier Shipping," Louis said, thinking of how Marian would probably jump at the chance to sell the business and bring in money to replenish the family coffers.

The older man shook his hand and then lifted his wine glass. "Here's to a quick sale of Cuvier Shipping."

Jean had been dead for almost two weeks and the newspapers had yet to forget about the three women. After the incident with the newspapermen, Marian had kept her children home from school. The thought of her babies surrounded by a crowd of men shouting questions left her shivering with fright. Soon there would be some new scandal to report and hopefully the newspapers would forget about Jean Cuvier's wives and her children could return to school. But until she thought they were safe they would stay home.

Marian looked up from her correspondence to see a servant in the doorway.

"Mrs. Cuvier, a Louis Fournet is here to see you," the maid announced.

"Thank you, show him into the study. I'll be right there," she said. The servant nodded her head and backed out of the doorway.

Marian stood and brushed a piece of lint from her black skirt. She wore the color of mourning in deference to her children's feelings, not because she was honoring Jean's memory. Philip and Renée would know the truth regarding their father soon enough, but for the time being she would protect them and their memory of Jean.

Pulling her hem aside, she made her way down the hall to the study.

As she entered the room, Louis Fournet stood, his back to her, gazing out upon Josephine Street.

"Good morning, Mr. Fournet," she said, standing behind him. He turned and glanced at her, his dark blue eyes assessing her with a look that reminded her of warm, lazy, summer days. The warmth of that look seemed to linger, spreading through her.

"Mrs. Cuvier, I hope you are well and have recovered from our carriage ride the other day?"

"Of course, though I still worry about newspapermen. I do hope this dreadful business dies away soon." Oh God, how could she have used the word "dies" in the same sentence as Jean's scandal. Inside, Mr. Fournet, must be laughing at her.

He smiled showing even white teeth, the cleft in his chin prominent. "There will be some other event to take their attention away soon enough. But today I came to show you I'm more knowledgeable in regard to business than I am to children."

"Oh yes, now I remember. We were talking about children that day and you made a suggestion that I found rather lacking in merit."

He shrugged. "What can I say? I'm a widower, not a father. You seem very close to your children."

"Yes, I am. Please take a seat and tell me about my husband's business. I want to know everything." Marian sat across from her new partner. A man she had yet to decide she could trust.

For the next thirty minutes, Marian listened as Mr. Fournet described how the scandal that had jolted her life was also wreaking havoc on the shipping business that might save her from having to remarry. The business that was going to support them in future years and keep her son's inheritance alive had seen a reduction in customers since Jean's death.

After Mr. Fournet finished speaking she sat gazing at the polished and distinguished looking, dark-haired man. Was his character as good as his appearance?

"So what are your suggestions, Mr. Fournet? You've told me the negatives, now what do you consider the solutions?" she asked, watching his expression closely.

He stood and walked across the room to the bookcase and then turned to face her, leaning against Jean's liquor cabinet. "Considering the fact that Mr. Cuvier's extra households have put such a drain on your family's resources, I would suggest that we sell the business and end our partnership. This way you would have a healthy bank balance once again and I would be free to consider other business pursuits."

Marian sat back for a moment, stunned by his suggestion. When she spoke she tried to make light of the situation, yet couldn't be more serious. "I knew you wouldn't like having a woman partner, but I certainly hadn't expected you to try to get rid of me so quickly. Shame on you, Mr. Fournet."

He chuckled. "Mrs. Cuvier, I feel honored to have the responsibility of having you as my partner. This decision has nothing to do with working with you, but rather what's best for you and your family. And considering that you need the money, I think it's the only solution."

Would it be better to sell the business, she wondered?

Marian gave him her best "be-at-ease" smile while she contemplated his response. Somehow it felt wrong. It was as if he was telling her what he thought she desired to hear, when actually his solution was just the opposite of what she really wanted.

"In the will, my husband asked you to continue the business for his son. Why will you not do as he asked?"

"Under different circumstances, I would do what Jean requested. But Mrs. Cuvier, selling the business would ease your financial burden. You wouldn't have to worry anymore," he answered her.

"Worry is a part of life. And though it would ease my financial situation temporarily, I would have no way of producing an income," she reflected. "What happens when that money runs out?" she asked, listening to her instincts telling her that somehow his advice was all wrong.

"The money you could make from the sale of the business should last you for many years. If you invest it, your family would never have to worry about money again," he said, walking across the room toward her.

"But you told me today that the scandal has tainted

just about everything and that business was slow. How do you know that we can sell the business and get its full value right now? I would think that now would be a terrible time to sell."

"A new buyer could change the name and then they wouldn't be attached to the scandal," he countered.

"This company has been Cuvier Shipping for many years, it's not going to lose its reputation overnight."

She watched his face and saw something that looked like surprise reflected in his eyes. He stepped back and took a seat in a chair. He leaned forward, his arms resting on his knees as he observed her for a few moments, making her feel uncomfortable.

"Do you think we should wait?" he asked.

"You yourself said that in time there would be another scandal to draw the public's attention away from the Cuviers." She took a deep breath. "Mr. Fournet, the shipping business is my primary source of income. You heard the lawyer say that I must watch my finances closely. If I sell this business, I lose my source of income, my son's inheritance, and I would probably be forced to remarry someday." She shook her head. "I'm sorry, but I'm willing to take a chance that Cuvier Shipping will rebound. Of course you mentioned other business pursuits. Perhaps you are wanting out of Cuvier Shipping, Mr. Fournet?"

"No." He looked across the room at a portrait of Jean on the wall, not quite meeting her gaze. "If you are willing to stay and fight this battle, risking your family's prosperity, then I could never leave until I knew you were secure."

Marian suddenly had the uncanny sense that Mr. Fournet was not being totally honest with her and she wondered what about. "Mr. Fournet, in the last few weeks my life has changed more than all the years I've been an adult. I've found out my husband was a liar, a bigamist, and he kept me in the dark regarding our financial situation." She took a deep breath. "Therefore, I think it would be wise of me to get to know the shipping business before I make any decisions. I intended to wait several weeks before I approached you, but I think now is the time to let you know of my plans."

She smiled at him and leaned forward just enough to get his attention. "I plan on becoming very involved with Cuvier Shipping. How else can I know how to help my son, if I don't know the business?"

She watched his eyes widen, and then she pressed on. "Though I know it's highly improper for a lady, I intend to take Jean's place."

Marian wanted to laugh at the stunned expression on his face. "Mr. Fournet?"

He blinked, his eyes wide with surprise. "You have caught me totally unprepared."

"It seems the logical step if I am going to make sound business decisions."

"Really, Mrs. Cuvier, I think you're overreacting. I can bring daily reports to you if you'd like, but the shipping business is no place for a lady. Need I remind you that you are in mourning? It's improper for you to leave the house, let alone go to work each day."

"Thank you for your kind consideration, Mr. Fournet. I'm sure some people will be appalled at my complete lack of propriety, but I am wearing black out of deference to my children. I owe Jean nothing." She smiled, watching his stunned expression. "Regardless, starting Monday morning, I have every intention of taking Jean's place."

"Mrs. Cuvier, this is unheard of! A woman in your position with children should be at home. If you want to help the business, I suggest you stay at home and not bring any additional scandal on Cuvier Shipping."

She raised her brows at him. "What are you afraid of, Mr. Fournet?" She paused. "I sense you want to sell the business—I want to keep it intact. You've mentioned other business pursuits, which make me leery of your reasons for recommending that I sell. I've already been deceived at the hands of one man. What makes you think that I'm going to trust you and your judgment?"

He stared at her for a moment, clearly offended. "You have just questioned my integrity, Mrs. Cuvier. I understand your not wanting to trust me, but there is more to running a business than just showing up. A woman has no place in a shipping office."

"I will be there on Monday, Mr. Fournet," she said straightening her back, the smile on her face frozen into place. The tall grandfather clock ticked in the silence, the steady rhythm the only sound in the study.

Louis Fournet stood. "I would ask that you reconsider, but I think you've made up your mind."

"Yes, I have," she said sharply.

"Then I shall expect to see you on Monday. But I warn you, you will not find the place one where a lady feels comfortable. But it is your choice, not mine. And if Cuvier Shipping goes under, please understand, madam, that you will be blamed. Not by me, but by the sailors along the river."

"Cuvier Shipping will not go under, Mr. Fournet. My share will not be sold. What you choose to do with your part is up to you. But I will be showing up for work on Monday to look after my son's inheritance and to protect our way of life."

"Monday, then," he said with a polite coldness that Marian found oddly amusing.

He stood and walked from the study. Marian followed

him to the front door. Opening the wooden door she glanced at him. "True to your word, Mr. Fournet, you are well versed in shipping."

"And you, madam, should stay home with your children where you belong," he informed her sternly.

She nodded her head, noticing his rigid posture, his flashing blue eyes. She'd certainly put a bug under his collar.

"True, but circumstances prevent me, so I shall take matters into my own hands."

"If by chance you change your mind, I will be greatly relieved. And we can act as if this discussion never took place."

Marian nodded and smiled. "We may pretend this discussion never took place, but I will be at the office Monday morning," Marian said with certainty.

She shut the door, leaned against the wooden portal and sighed. What in the world had she just done? Yes, she was doing what was necessary to protect her children, but she did hate stepping into a man's world.

"You're going to go to that awful shipping office? Have you lost your mind?" Claire said, with about as much grace as a gossip spreading a piece of juicy scandal.

Marian glanced at her older sister and wished for the hundredth time that she had just a little more tact. "Who can I depend on to be honest with me regarding the financial state of the company that will be paying my bills?" She took a deep breath. "I know it will be hard. I'm going to be scorned for working almost as soon as my husband was put in the ground. I hate to leave my children, while I work a job where I will be looked upon with contempt."

"Hire someone, Marian. Sell the business. If you must work, at least find a job where there are women," Claire said with disgust.

"You would have me sell the company that I own a portion of and go to work for someone else, just so that I obey the dictates of society?" Marian said, her voice rising.

"Yes. At least it would be accepted. You wouldn't be creating even more of a scandal than we're already involved in. Think of your children and how even more shame is going to hurt them."

"I have. We must have a roof over our heads and food on the table. Cuvier Shipping has always provided that for us. It will continue to do so," Marian said.

"Marian, people will talk."

"I don't care what people say." Marian shook her head. "Jean may have been a dreadful husband, but he left this business for his son and I intend to make sure that Philip receives his inheritance. My son will own his father's business someday."

"You are still as stubborn as when we were children," Claire said. "I hope for your sake you know what you're getting into. Working down at the riverfront with an office full of men is not going to be pleasant. Promise me that you'll be careful, that you'll always have Edward pick you up in the carriage."

Marian smiled. "I'm not sixteen anymore. You know I'll be careful."

"I don't know why I waste my breath on you sometimes. You'll do whatever you've set your mind to." Claire shook her head. "You will have to tell me all about how your first day goes with the handsome Mr. Fournet."

"Yes, well Mr. Fournet left here today very annoyed when I told him I would be at the office on Monday.

Somehow his reactions made me wonder if he was hiding something."

"Like what? I thought he came by to discuss the shipping company?"

"Yes, but he also recommended that I sell the business. Somehow I don't know if I trust my new partner. He's handsome to look at, he's charming, he's smooth, but there's something about him that makes me want to be cautious."

"That's only because of Jean. If he hadn't been Jean's partner, then you would have more confidence."

"I don't think so. In some ways, Mr. Fournet reminds me of Jean. He's a charmer, a flirt, someone who makes you feel like he has everything under control. And maybe that's what frightens me the most. Jean obviously could control very little in his life. Now I wonder about the handsome Mr. Fournet. Is he any different from Jean?"

CHAPTER THREE

From her carriage window, Marian saw the docks were teeming with activity. The sun shone bright in the early morning sky and the sounds of shouting as the men loaded the boats reverberated through the air. Before she was ready, the carriage came to a halt and Marian wanted to tell Edward, her driver, to turn the vehicle around and take her back home. But she refused to give in to her cowardice.

With her knees trembling beneath her black skirt she picked up her reticule and stepped out of the carriage. Edward helped her to alight as she gazed up at the brick building wondering what she could expect inside.

"What time shall I return madam?" Edward asked.

"Five o'clock will be fine," she said, and walked up the steps to enter the building where her husband had conducted his business.

The sound of the carriage pulling away wrenched at her, but she didn't call him back. With trembling hands she opened the door. She could do this, she reminded herself and stepped into the shipping office.

Inside the reception area a counter ran eight feet across the room, with desks scattered throughout the airy space behind the bar. Men glanced up from their work, staring at her, their eyes questioning as she entered the room. *What was she doing here?*

A large scruffy man with a week's beard and a worn cap on his head stood at the counter, leaning against it. His dark eyes gleamed at her, a wrinkle appearing between his brows.

"A little early in the morning to be gettin lost?" he taunted her, his accent heavy.

"Excuse me?" she said. "I'm not lost. I'm looking for Mr. Fournet."

He laughed. "Now I understand, darlin'. He's gone to the back for a moment, but don't fret. He'll soon return."

She frowned, feeling uncertain as to the man's reaction.

"Tell me darlin', what do women see in Mr. Fournet, that they don't see in me? I may not have his fancy looks, but I know how to treat a lady decent," he said, his eyes raking over her. "And you in mourning, too. Shame on you."

Feeling more vulnerable than she cared for she took a steadying breath. She glanced at the river man in his rugged waterproof boots, his worn cap, and sleeveless shirt that revealed his deeply tanned arms. Though normally she would have ignored him, maybe it would be better to attempt to be polite, but curt. He could be a customer or even an employee.

"Yes, I am in mourning," she said, in a short clipped tone, resisting the urge to run for the door. "Mr. Fournet and I are business acquaintances."

"Now don't be gettin' yourself all riled up. I just thought you might have been one of Mr. Fournet's lady friends since you're pretty enough for the gent and all dressed up to boot," he said pointing to the material of her dress. "Around here ladies and gents aren't usually seen until much later in the morning."

Marian wished Louis would appear. She felt so uncomfortable standing here talking to this sailor, while everyone in the room looked on. It wasn't proper, but she couldn't turn and walk away.

"Mr. Fournet's gone back to get me money." He rambled on. "So what you be doin' down at the docks?"

She paused debating whether to be honest with the man and then decided she would not hide the reason for her being here from anyone, not even the sailor.

With a lift of her chin she told him, "I'm starting work here today."

He frowned. "You? I think you have the wrong building, lady. This is Cuvier Shipping."

"Yes, I'm aware of that."

Just then Louis Fournet came rushing around the counter slightly out of breath. He saw her and frowned. "Mrs. Cuvier, I hoped you would take my advice and stay home."

"I said I would be here and I am," she said defiantly.

The noise in the outer office suddenly ceased and everyone including the sailor stared.

Mr. Fournet shook his head. "Just let me pay Captain Paul and then I'll be right with you."

"Certainly," she said, feeling more and more uneasy as time went on. The urge to run out the door grew stronger, yet the carriage was long gone and there was Philip's future to consider.

Louis turned to pay the ship's captain but his eyes

were fixed on Marian and his stare made her hands sweat.

"So you're Jean Cuvier's wife?" the captain finally said staring at her hard.

She gave him a haughty look. "Yes, I am."

"Why's a woman like you comin' to work in a man's business?" he asked with a sneer. "You should be home mournin' your husband."

"I'm here to learn the shipping business," she replied pulling her shoulders back and raising her chin. What did the man know about the loss of a cheating husband, the fear of your children starving and your son's losing his inheritance? Did he think she'd be here if she had a choice?

The man made a disgusting snort. "You're wastin' your time. Women have no head for business."

Marian glared at the sailor. "Then I guess you're in trouble, as I intend to help Mr. Fournet run Cuvier Shipping."

The room grew silent enough to hold prayer service, until Louis broke the stillness.

"Paul, your money," Louis said, handing the man an envelope.

The sailor took the envelope and jammed it into his pants pocket and strolled out the door, giving Marian a parting glare. Was this how her days at Cuvier Shipping would be? Unaccepted by everyone, a struggle every day to find her place in a world dominated by men? She wanted to cry, but refused to show any weakness.

Louis watched the captain walk out the door. He ran his hand through his hair and released a long breath. Marian's first morning at the office was beginning exactly the way he'd feared. He resisted the urge to slam his fist down on the counter, knowing the pain would outlive the pleasure. Just what he needed, a woman helping him run a business he wanted to sell!

He'd watched the exchange between Marian and Paul, hoping that the sailor would frighten the widow and send her running. But Marian held her ground like an embattled army, refusing to surrender. While Paul had stuck to his guns to the end, he'd been as effective as a popgun. Quiet and gentle were not words used to describe Marian Cuvier. She could take care of herself and he'd do well to remember this interesting facet of this woman.

Several days of sitting in an office, not being accepted would surely break down her resistance. He just needed to bide his time and Mrs. Cuvier would soon want nothing to do with the shipping business and would hurry home to her rightful place in life.

Marian turned and glanced at Louis, her face looking strained. "Well, I must say I'm starting off on a positive note. I can't wait to see how the rest of the day unfolds."

He tried to hold it back, but the chuckle that bubbled up from his chest refused to cooperate and he laughed out loud at her wry acceptance of how her day had begun. "Welcome to Cuvier Shipping, Mrs. Cuvier. Come around the gate and I'll introduce you to the rest of the staff."

"I'm glad I've made your day entertaining," she said walking through the open gate and into the back office area.

"Indeed you have, though I had hoped you would come to your senses and stay home."

She looked beautiful, with flushed cheeks against the paleness of her complexion. Her dark hair piled high on her head showing off her long and graceful neck. He frowned at the observation. Just what he needed to be noticing on her first day in the office. All the desirable places on her neck to place his lips.

With a shrug she strolled past him, her black skirt brushing against his legs. "Staying home was not possible. I knew I had to be here." She glanced around the office. "Where is my husband's desk?"

Louis frowned at her. "Jean had his own office, which someone else has since taken over."

"Then I suggest you have him removed, so that I may occupy that space," she said, in such a way that he knew it would be useless to argue with her.

"You're definitely going to be popular with the employees," he remarked, shaking his head reminding himself to let her sink her own boat. "Follow me and I'll show you around and then take you to Jean's office."

She followed Louis through the office area, while he pointed out where different people who worked for the business sat. It was still early enough that most employees had yet to arrive. When they stopped in front of her new office, a man sat at a desk scribbling in a leather-bound ledger.

"Henry," Louis called. The man glanced up. "Mrs. Cuvier, this is Henry Chatham, our accountant. Henry, I'd like to introduce you to Mrs. Cuvier, Jean's wife."

The man jumped up and hurried around the desk. "Nice to meet you, Mrs. Cuvier. My condolences regarding your husband."

"Thank you," Marian replied, glancing at Louis expectantly.

"Henry, Mrs. Cuvier is going to be taking Jean's place." The man's jaw dropped and Louis couldn't help but smile. "We're going to need Jean's office for her."

"But . . ." he glanced up at Marian, his face reflecting the surprise Louis's announcement had brought.

"If you'd be so kind as to vacate his office, then I can move in," Marian said with a smile.

The man frowned. "Mrs. Cuvier what . . . what are you going to do for us?"

Marian shrugged. "I'm not certain yet. Mr. Fournet is going to teach me the business."

There were a lot of things Louis would like to teach her, he thought, *none of which had to do with shipping, but rather a different kind of exploration.* Marian Cuvier's curves were definitely an interesting attraction that his eyes were naturally drawn to. The thought caught Louis off guard before he could put a halt to the wayward idea. She hadn't been here an hour and already he was thinking about things he had no business considering.

Jean had been his partner and Marian was the dead man's wife. It wouldn't do to become involved with the pretty widow, especially considering the brief time she would be here.

"Henry, if you'd move your work out, then I'll get Mrs. Cuvier settled in here," Louis said.

The man sighed, clearly not happy with this turn of events. "I'll start packing."

Before lunchtime, Louis had Marian ensconced in her own office and given her a tome to read called *The Merits of Trade in the New World.* The book was large enough to occupy her for quite some time and keep her busy and out of his way, at least until he took care of some pressing issues.

All morning a steady stream of employees casually strolled by the office, gazing upon the Widow Cuvier. Business would be slack today, because of the constant foot traffic in front of her office. Not to mention the employees that flowed continuously into his office asking questions regarding the widow.

At first he'd been polite and explained that Mrs.

Cuvier would be in the office for a few days. Or at least he hoped that's all it would take before she'd become discouraged and give up this foolish notion of working in her dead husband's place.

"Excuse me, sir. I have some papers that need your signature," his clerk said, stepping into his office and disrupting his thoughts.

Louis glanced up and frowned. "Leave them on the corner of the desk and I'll sign them."

Jon peered out the doorway, across the way to where Marian sat reading the book. "What's she doing here?"

The frustration that had been building for most of the day engulfed him. "Hasn't everyone filled you in yet? She's taking Jean's place."

His voice came out louder than he expected and he saw Marian glance up at him, a quizzical look on her face. Not only did he get to show her around, but their offices were located directly across the hall from one another. Unless their office doors were closed, they could see each other at any time.

Just what he needed, to look up and see Marian's smile. The woman could be pure vinegar one moment and then suddenly with just one look, have your nerve endings standing up and taking notice. And he'd already taken more notice of the widow than he considered wise. After all, he still intended to sell the business.

"Sorry, sir. I've been out of the office most of the day."

Louis shook his head. Now he was taking out his frustrations on his employees. "No, I'm the one who should apologize. It's not your fault."

"No need, sir." The young man all but ran from his office.

Louis bent his head and tried to work once again. If he continued to disregard her, would she take the hint and leave? Yet to overlook a beautiful woman in his direct line of sight was difficult at best. Several days of avoidance should do the trick and Mrs. Cuvier would never darken his door again. Until the sale he hoped for would bring them together one last time to sign the final papers.

A shadow fell across his desk and the smell of lilacs alerted him that she had walked into his office. He glanced up and felt as if his insides were being squeezed. For a moment he wanted to reach out and touch her skin to see if it were as smooth to the stroke as it appeared. Annoyed for taking notice of her complexion, he gave himself a mental slap. It would be better to avoid sensuous ideas involving the widow.

She smiled. "I'm finished for the day."

He shook his head, the frustration of the day once again rearing like an ugly sea serpent's head. "Mrs. Cuvier . . . may I call you Marian?"

"Since we're going to be working together every day, I think that would be a good idea," she responded, with a smile that left him stunned, but only irritated him more because she was both cheerful and beautiful.

"Marian, do yourself a favor, stay home tomorrow. There's no need for you to come in here every day like this. I give you my word that your part of the business will be fine," he said, his voice sounding sharper than he intended.

She tilted her head. "But Louis . . . I can call you Louis?"

"Yes."

She smiled. "Louis, it's very necessary that I come in here and work each day. Maybe it's not my share of the business I'm concerned about, but yours? After all I will be here looking out for mine."

"Damn it, woman!" he shouted, jumping up from

his desk, startling her. At the sound of his voice, some women would have run for the door or at least broken down in tears at his outburst. But not Marian, who just took one step back.

"I have tried to keep my patience with you, but I don't know how to help you to understand," said Louis. "You've disrupted the office, upset the employees, and totally confounded this whole place. Have some consideration and stay home so that at least a small measure of work will be done! You are not needed here."

Her eyes grew wide and dark and furious. And then she turned on him. "Don't you curse at me! Get accustomed to seeing me at the office, Mr. Fournet. I own part of this business. I'm going to protect my interest. Get used to seeing me every day."

She whirled around and walked out of the office, her black skirt swishing angrily as she left, her head held high.

Louis glanced out and saw everyone watching her as she proceeded toward the door. One steely look sent the employees quickly back to work.

He slammed his fist against his desk. "Damn!"

A more stubborn female he'd never met!

Marian had spent the whole week at Cuvier Shipping. She couldn't say she'd really worked; instead, her time had been spent reading a large book on shipping that had just about put her to sleep. She had cleaned her desk three times. Her knowledge regarding the shipping business was about the same as when she'd walked in the door.

They were paying no heed to her, hoping to push her out before she even got started. Since his temper tantrum that first day, Louis had hardly spoken to her.

And while his ignoring her somehow stung, she was determined not to give up. It would take more than a lack of attention to drive her out.

Today would be different. Sometimes taking matters into one's own hands was called for and this could be one of those times.

She walked out of her office and down the hall to where Henry Chatham, the accountant, sat working on the books. If no one would teach her the business, then she would work her way backwards through the ledgers. She would use the files and whatever else she could to teach herself. Just because the men in the office were united against her, she would not let them stop her.

"Excuse me," she said clearing her throat to draw Henry's attention.

He glanced up at her as if she had two heads and six arms. "I'm looking for the general ledger."

"Uh," he glanced around nervously. "I know it's around here somewhere, but I don't see it right now. How about if I bring it to you?"

"That's fine. I'll expect it on my desk in ten minutes," she said, before turning and walking away.

She suspected the leather bound book that kept all the financial records for the company was not really missing. Henry just didn't want to share the information.

Ten minutes passed and when Marian looked up from the newspaper she sat reading, Louis stood in her doorway, filling it completely. He wore a dark suit with a white shirt that contrasted with his bronzed skin. His dark blue eyes gazed at her, warm and intense, causing a shiver to trail along her spine.

"Handsome" wasn't the word to describe him. His looks were rugged, with broad shoulders and muscled forearms, though his lazy, confident gaze drew her to him. He was the first man in years whose appearance she'd taken notice of, and Louis's certain smile told her he knew she'd observed him.

"Yes, Mr. Fournet?" she asked trying to ignore his self-assured grin.

"Louis," he replied.

"What can I do for you, Louis?" she asked, her honey-sweet voice emphasizing his name.

He smiled. "I hear you're looking for the general ledger."

"Yes," she replied.

"Why?" he asked, his brow raised.

"Because I am part owner of this company and I intend to find out what's going on," she said sweetly. "Now, you can tell Henry he has an additional ten minutes before I fire him."

Louis laughed. "Behind that innocent face and all that black silk is quite a spitfire I'd say."

She shook her head. "No, just a determined woman who, no matter how much you push her, is not going away."

"Not yet anyway," he replied smiling congenially.

"Not ever," she returned sweetly, wishing she could take her eyes off his full lips, wondering what they would feel like to kiss.

Jon barged into the room. "Louis, Priscilla Morgan is here to see you."

Louis glanced at Jon and then again at Marian. "I'll tell Henry to bring you the ledger. Excuse me, I have more pleasant matters awaiting me."

He turned and walked away and she couldn't help but watch the way he strode across the room with a determined step. Yet when she spoke with him, he seemed more playful than serious. Which was Louis Fournet, the serious businessman or the playful bachelor? Or some randy combination of both?

A few minutes later, the balding accountant strode into her office, a big ledger in his hand. "Mr. Fournet said to bring this to you."

Marian smiled at the accountant and took the ledger from his hands. "Thank you, Henry. I appreciate your promptness. And I know that you realize if you ever question my authority again, it will be your last day with Cuvier Shipping."

The man frowned, but nodded. "Yes, ma'am."

Marian watched him as he hurried out the door. She sighed and turned her attention to the ledger. Taking a sheet of paper, she made some notes as she flipped through the ledger to see who Cuvier Shipping was doing business with.

Ten minutes later, Marian heard the soft trill of a woman's voice and glanced up from the accountant's book to see a woman with a full figure, who had tumbling blonde curls, and a soft angelic face. Priscilla Morgan was everything that men adored in a woman.

She watched Louis laughing and talking with the pretty woman, participating in a flirtatious ritual that amused Marian, yet made her sad. He leaned toward the woman telling her something for her ears only and Marian couldn't help but wonder what it would be like to have a man's attention. So many years had passed without even a flirtatious smile from her husband. Had they ever been this enamored with one another?

The woman smiled coyly at Louis and Marian watched him respond to her banter with his own teasing response, just as Jean once reacted to her so many years ago.

Louis responded like her dead husband. They had been business associates and friends who had much in common. And the very fact they seemed alike should be enough to keep Marian's thoughts off the dark-haired man with the bewitching blue eyes, perhaps too much like Jean Cuvier.

Marian returned her attention to the ledger and tried to concentrate on the names and figures before her eyes. Each time she heard the woman's laughter, the words seemed to blur on the page as her concentration shifted to the people across the hall.

Why couldn't she just block their laughter from her mind? Why did the woman's voice seem more like a purr that made Marian's heart ache? With a sigh she returned to the ledger page, more determined than ever to learn all she could about Cuvier Shipping. Her focus had to remain on the company and her children, not her Don Juan of a business partner.

Louis sat staring across the hall feeling morose as he stared at Marian Cuvier. Silk-wrapped and smelling of lilacs, the woman with her stubborn will of iron had entrenched herself in Jean's office these last weeks. Nothing seemed to bother her enough to send her running home and losing this battle between them was maddening.

He hated losing any battle.

Worse, little-by-little Marian seemed to be charming and winning over the men who ran Cuvier Shipping. Slowly she had managed to break down their resistance and he could see subtle changes in their attitudes and even in their language. He hadn't heard a swear word ring out in the office in over a week.

At first he scoffed at her attempts to bribe the men with fresh baked goods each morning. They were smarter than to let their stomachs lead their minds. Now he was considering donning an apron and bringing in a full-course meal, just to show them they were being bought off.

But then this morning as he walked in, he'd overheard a conversation between Marian and Henry. She'd been talking to him about his wife and children. She'd called his wife by name. Until that moment, Louis hadn't even known his accountant was married!

And that wouldn't have been so surprising, but he'd overheard her do the same thing with the new man, Sean. Maybe it was coincidence that she knew Henry's wife's name, but with Sean the only way she could have known anything about his family was if she'd asked.

She was getting to know the employees, finding out about their personal lives, even going so far as to bring a baby gift to Joe, a new father in the office.

Hell, he didn't know half the employees' first names, let alone who their wives and children were. Like a politician running for office, her campaign to undermine him and make him look bad was working!

Then there had been her frequent diggings through the files, doing research, or so she claimed. He had nothing to hide, just the same her investigations were driving him crazy. What could she be looking for?

For the thirtieth time that day he caught himself staring across the way at her. Past five o'clock on a Thursday afternoon, only a few employees remained. Marian sat sifting through some papers.

Sitting across from her, staring at all that dark hair twisted up off her graceful long neck, imagining what she looked like beneath the black gown that encased her body, and wanting to dispel the sadness he sometimes saw reflected in her gray eyes, was making him uneasy. How could he work with her for the next few months, until he sold the business?

Maybe he could scare her away. What would a woman

like Marian be afraid of? Somehow he had to convince her to stay home or he would take advantage of that cherry red mouth. The realization caused him to smile at how easy the answer seemed. There was one thing he'd wanted to do almost since the day he first met her, and it would certainly send her running. Suddenly he stood, unable to wait any longer.

Louis strode across the hallway, his steps sure and even, until he found himself standing in front of her desk. "You're still here. Why?" he asked.

She glanced up at him, her face an innocent mask. "I was just trying to finish up the last of the ledgers I've been going through. Very interesting what our customers transport on our boats."

He shrugged and then leaned across the desk. "Marian, I need to talk to you."

"Can it wait until tomorrow?"

"No. It must be now," he demanded.

"Okay, let me just finish this ledger and put it back."

He reached across the desk and shut it for her. "Now!"

She gazed up at him, her eyes widening at his urgency. "What's wrong?" she asked.

Louis placed his hands on her desk, gripping it and leaned in closer to her. "You are a gorgeous woman working in a man's business. For the last three weeks, I've sat across from you and tried my damnedest not to show that I notice how beautiful you are. How your lips beckon me every time you flick your tongue across them. I've tried to deny how I feel, but I can't do it anymore."

Her eyes widened and she leaned back away from him.

Louis stepped around the desk, took her chair and whirled her around to face him. He grasped her forearms and roughly pulled her to her feet and toward him until she stood just inches away from him. Her lips glistened, tempting him not to hesitate, but to do the deed.

"Really, Louis, I'm not falling for this ridiculous attempt to persuade me not to come back," she said, her voice breathy and tremulous.

He smiled. "Good, because this is not an attempt, Marian. This is for real."

He'd only meant to scare her away, but when she called his bluff, he reacted by covering her mouth with his.

Yet the moment he planted his mouth over hers, all thoughts of frightening her disappeared. The sensation of her mouth pressed against his, her breasts crushed against his chest, sent delight spreading through him. Right where he hadn't anticipated feeling anything for Marian Cuvier.

He sampled her warm, soft lips, suddenly intent on exploring this surprising new sensation. She didn't resist him as his tongue began a careful exploration of the fullness of her lips. The sweet taste of her mouth left him craving for more than just the taste of her. And as the reason for the kiss vanished from his mind, he was tempted to further his study of her mouth as he savored Marian.

She sighed the sound deep in the back of her throat, just before she pushed him away. She leaned away from him, her eyes wide with dismay as she covered her mouth with her hand.

"Oh," she gasped.

Then before Louis could recover from the kiss and gather his wits about him, she jumped up from the desk. She grabbed her reticule.

"I . . . I must go. Edward . . . is waiting," she said, her voice breaking up.

"Marian," he called, still a little stunned by the impact of her kiss.

"I . . . Goodbye!" she said, and ran out the door.

Louis stood there, shocked. What just happened? He'd kissed her, but somehow something more than just the pressure of their lips had taken place. Marian's response confused him, but even more his own reaction shocked him. He liked kissing Marian. He liked it so much he wanted to do it again. But Marian was his business partner, not someone you wanted to play with and then send away.

A heavy sigh escaped him. Maybe kissing the widow wasn't such a good idea after all. Maybe she just reversed the situation and he should be the one running scared.

CHAPTER FOUR

Marian returned to the office the next morning, although with some reluctance. Louis's kiss the night before awakened all kinds of thoughts and images. Things that she hadn't thought about in years. Feelings she had buried, once it became evident that Jean would no longer be frequenting her bed.

The pleasure that burst inside her at feeling Louis's lips against hers had surprised and frightened her. She sat behind her desk and touched her fingers to her mouth, the memory of his kiss still fresh in her mind. So many years had passed since a man kissed her, let alone made her feel passion. Surely her response yesterday had been an accident. If he were to kiss her again, she would probably feel only the texture of his lips and nothing of the pleasure. Whatever reaction he'd evoked yesterday afternoon had been a mistake.

An enjoyable mistake, but doubtful it could happen again or should. Certainly he'd resorted to trying to frighten her away and when she saw him today she would act as if the kiss meant nothing.

"Good morning," Louis said, standing in her doorway.

Her heart leapt within her chest at the sight of the man who kept her dreams troubled last night. How long had he been standing there watching her?

He leaned against the doorframe looking like temptation . . . with a hangover. Dark shadows circled his bloodshot eyes, his complexion a pasty shade of white.

"Someone mentioned you brought croissants and coffee," he said, with a weak smile.

She blushed, not quite meeting his gaze, unable to look at his full lips without remembering how they felt.

"They're on the table. Help yourself."

He moved slowly to the food, poured himself a cup of coffee and picked up a hot croissant. Seeing a chair beside her desk, he sank down, making himself cozy, like he wanted to settle in for a nice long chat.

How could he just come into her office sit down as if they were old friends, after he had behaved so brazenly toward her the night before?

Marian kept working hoping he would get the hint and go away. He sipped his coffee and moaned.

"The brew is strong, but it didn't have that effect on any of the other men who stopped in this morning," she said, not looking up.

"My head is killing me," he answered solemnly.

"I noticed you don't appear your usual chipper self this morning. What's wrong?" she questioned innocently, knowing he suffered.

"I was bit by a malt-bug last night," he replied.

"Never heard of the little beast. Must be pretty bad," she said, not feeling any sympathy for the handsome man.

He shook his head at her and tried to smile. "I can tell you don't go out very much. It's not a real bug. It means I had too much to drink."

"From the looks of you, that wasn't hard to discern. I just don't have any sympathy for you."

Furtively she glanced at his mouth, trying not to stare, wondering again why his kiss had aroused her long-denied body. The memory of those luscious lips covering hers and the feel of his tongue running along her outer lips caused her to jump up and walk to the coffee pot. With shaking hands she poured the hot brew into a cup.

He acted as if nothing had transpired between them yesterday, like it was just another day at Cuvier Shipping. She had wanted to be the one who acted so nonchalant about their kiss. But somehow she felt like he was doing a better job and that left her frustrated. He had started this, not she.

"I usually don't do this," he said.

"Do what?" she asked, returning to her seat behind the desk. "Have coffee and croissants?"

"No. Drink to excess," he grumbled.

"What changed?" she asked bluntly. "Did you have a case of bad conscience that you were trying to rid yourself of? Or did you need a dose of courage to come back and face me this morning?"

He stared at her, his eyes growing wide with surprise at her less than subtle attack. He opened his mouth to speak, but before he could reply, they both heard a female voice calling, "Mr. Fournet, where are you?"

"Damn!" he said, spilling hot coffee over his trousers as he jumped up at the sound of his name.

He glanced around the room, and then slipped behind her office door, just as the woman came into view.

"What are you doing?" Marian softly hissed at Louis, stunned by his behavior. "Are you insane?"

"What does it look like? I'm hiding," he whispered.

She shook her head. "Aren't you a little old to be playing hide-and-seek from women?"

"That's easy for you to say. You don't know Jane," he said motioning her to lower her voice.

Marian leaned forward across her desk, so he could hear her better. "If you don't want to go out and see the woman, then why don't you tell her, instead of acting like a child and disappearing?"

"Jane can be . . . clinging."

"Please! Mr. Fournet, a man with your experience with women should know how to handle this type of situation by now."

"My experience?" he questioned. "I'm no Lothario. I admit I like women, but no more than any other normal man."

"Normal men don't hide behind office doors when they have a visitor," she admonished, resisting the urge to laugh at him.

He shook his head. "Just do me a small favor. Go out there and tell her I had to leave for a while and that I won't be back until the year 1900."

She stared at him from her desk, the cup of coffee in her hand. He wanted her to lie for him after he had refused to help her learn the shipping business. After he'd made it very clear she was not wanted in this office. After he'd kissed her, clearly trying to scare her away and then acted as if nothing had happened.

"Why should I?" she asked.

He paused and smiled at her, turning on the charm that came so naturally to him. "Just do this as a favor to me."

Charm had little effect on Marian. Jean's charm had

left Marian immune to the effects, but Louis hadn't recognized that fact yet.

She gazed at him over the rim of her cup, wanting to refuse but realizing there were other ways to handle his request. Standing, she pushed her chair away from the desk and walked around it.

"All right, I'll help you. After all, you've been so welcoming and helpful to me since I came here," she said, hurrying out the door trying to hide her smile.

Louis frowned suspiciously, sudden realization making him nervous.

"Wait," he hissed.

He peered through a crack between the door and the frame and watched Marian approach Jane, who stood looking in at his office.

"May I help you?" she asked the young woman.

Tall and graceful, Jane Fitzwilliam was on the prowl for a husband and she'd decided Louis was her mate of choice. The grand prize was to be a trip to the altar, but Louis had already visited the inside of her bedroom and had no desire to go to church with her.

"Do you work here?" the woman asked.

"Yes, I'm Marian Cuvier."

The woman's eyes grew wide at she recognized Marian's name. "I'm looking for Louis Fournet."

"Is there anything I can help you with?" Marian asked.

"No. I need to speak with Louis."

"Didn't the men up front tell you?" Marian asked her voice filled with concern.

"Tell me what?" Jane questioned.

"If you're a friend of his I'm sure he would want you to know," Marian said with sympathy.

"What are you talking about?" the woman said, beginning to look worried.

"Well, I don't know how to say this. It's rather an indelicate subject that normally I wouldn't discuss, but since you're his friend, you should know," Marian said, taking Jane's elbow and drawing her closer to the door.

Oh God, what was she doing? he wondered.

"What's wrong? Is it Louis?" she asked.

"There's been an accident," Marian said, a solemn look on her face.

"Accident? What kind of accident? Is he hurt?"

How could he stop her? She intended to ruin him. Yet if he went running out there, he would look like a fool. But if he stayed behind the door he feared what Marian's next words would be.

The woman had a mean streak in her!

Marian leaned closer to the woman. "I only know because I overheard the men talking about—what happened. And even then I didn't get all the details. They hushed when they saw me listening."

Jane leaned forward, closer to Marian, whose voice was just loud enough that Louis caught every word.

"Seems like he was hurt," she said, pausing, her face a frown. "You know . . . down there."

How could this get any worse? Louis thought as he watched Marian ruin him.

"No," Jane gasped. "How bad is he?"

Marian half closed her eyes and shook her head. "Bad."

He was going to wrap his hands around her throat and slowly choke her. The liquor had obviously dulled his brain for him to ask Marian to speak with Jane!

"The men said that the doctors don't know if he'll ever be the same. It's doubtful he'll ever have children." She paused, stumbling with her words. "Because . . . because, well, these things can be so uncertain."

Oh God! It was bad enough his head was splitting,

his mouth tasted like cotton, and his stomach was riding the high seas, all because he'd gotten drunk trying to forget the feel of her lips against his. All because watching her every day for the last three weeks was driving him to distraction. How could such a simple plan to drive her from the business have gone so wrong? And now look what she was doing to get even.

She had just told one of the biggest gossips in town that he had been—damaged. Up to now he'd enjoyed a very active sexual life, which now seemed to be ending.

The brunette backed away from Marian, her hand on her mouth. "Oh, dear! What a shame!"

Marian nodded her head. "I didn't want to say anything, because it's just something you don't talk about. But I thought *you* would want to know."

The woman blinked her eyes rapidly and shook her head sadly. "You're right, it's certainly something I could never discuss with him."

"No. We just need to remember him in our prayers."

Louis almost groaned as a bout of nausea gripped him. If the sickness from his hangover hadn't held him in its grip, he would have come around the door and strangled Marian.

"Oh yes," Jane said. "I'll be sure to put his name on the prayer list at church."

Oh God, what kind of illness would she list by his name? Eunuch?

How could he get out of this mess? How could he prove to Jane that he was a complete man? And did he want to go to the trouble?

"Should I tell him you came by, madame?" Marian asked.

Jane glanced around the office uneasily. She wrinkled her forehead in a frown. "Maybe it would be better if he didn't know that I visited."

Marian nodded her head. "Good idea. It's such a shame."

"I'll say. Thank you so much for telling me."

"You're welcome. Shall I walk you to the door?"

"Please."

The two women disappeared from sight and Louis banged his head against the wall behind the door. He must not underestimate this woman again. Marian didn't get even, she got ahead. And, worst of all, she'd done it at his expense.

She returned a few moments later, a satisfied smile on her face.

"I did everything that you asked," she said, at his look of pure frustration.

"Yes, I heard what you did," he said. "I'm certain that Jane won't be returning to the office again."

Marian shrugged. "Pity, I rather enjoyed talking to her."

"Maybe you can tell her when I'm healed," he said taking a deep breath to calm his annoyance.

A blush spread across Marian's face. "Oh, no that's a delicate subject that ladies don't discuss."

"I can see that," he said, his voice rising until his head throbbed.

"Any time you want to hide in my office, I'd be happy to speak with your lady friends for you," Marian said, with a wicked smile.

He gave her a look that would have halted a sensible person, but not Marian.

"Don't worry, you won't be here," he said, his voice low and irritated.

She smiled. "We'll see who lasts longer, Mr. Fournet. It's going to take more than a kiss to send me running out the door."

"And more than rumors of an accident for me," he said, and walked out the door, slamming it behind him.

Several days later, Marian laid the morning paper down on her desk and wanted to cry. Another sensational story about Jean's murder appeared on the front page of the newspaper. Since his death, there were few days that went by that an article did not appear regarding his murder or the other Cuvier Widows, as they were called.

Now the papers were saying that the arrest of Layla was imminent and claiming she murdered Jean.

The police claimed they had found a motive, though Marian doubted the girl had had the courage to kill Jean. She didn't know who killed her husband but Marian felt relieved Jean was gone.

Jon rapped on her door. "Mrs. Cuvier?"

Marian glanced up. "Yes?"

"There's a young boy here who says he's your son," the man said. "He's bleeding, Ma'am."

She jumped up out of her chair, pushed past Jon and ran out of her office, down the hall. This week was Philip's first week back in school and when she'd sent him off, she was afraid that newspapermen would hound him.

She saw her son standing at the front door, his head down, his knees skinned, and his left eye swollen. His clothes were torn and dirty as if he'd been rolling in the dirt. *Who had done this to him?*

"Philip," she cried. "What happened? Are you hurt?"

She knelt down beside her son, her black skirts billowing around her and the boy.

Philip glanced at her, his face dirty and tear-streaked.

He blinked, trying to hold back the tears. "I . . . I got in a fight at school. They sent me home."

"Oh son! Are you hurt?" she asked, as she pushed the hair back away from his forehead to check the area where he received the blow.

"No," he said dejectedly. "My eye aches, but that's all."

Noticing for the first time that everyone in the office was watching them, she stood and took him by the arm. Not releasing him, she proceeded to walk him back to her office. Once there she sat him in a chair. She walked over to the bowl and ewer she'd brought from home and poured water onto a small towel, which she used to dry her hands.

Walking back to her son, she knelt in front of him and glanced at his face. Gently, she washed the scrapes and bruises on his knees and elbows.

"Why were you fighting, Philip? You've never been one to cause trouble," she said, as she gently washed his face.

He looked away and shrugged his shoulders. "I don't know."

She folded the towel and wiped his face, her heart aching for the boy she loved with all her heart.

"Philip, I know you wouldn't get into a fight without a good reason. You can tell me. What happened?"

He wouldn't look at her. "I guess I got mad at what some kids were saying."

Marian's heart ached as she gazed at her boy. "What kind of things were they saying, Philip?"

The boy shrugged, trying so hard to hide his pain. Restlessly he kicked his feet. "It's okay, Mother. I took care of them."

She swallowed, he was trying to protect her, afraid he

would hurt her feelings. "Were they saying things about your father?"

She walked over to the bowl and rinsed the towel out and then came back to her son.

Philip glanced away, unable to meet her gaze. "I'm not going to let them say those things."

She dabbed tenderly at his swollen eye with the wet towel. "Sometimes people do things that hurt their families. But that doesn't mean that they love their children any less."

"Did you love Daddy?" he questioned, taking her completely by surprise.

The query touched her. She gazed at her son, her heart overflowing with love. He was growing up and she wanted to protect him from the ugly truth about his father, but the world was not going to let her.

"I loved your father very much at one time. I would never have married Jean, if I had not been in love with him," she answered truthfully.

"Did you love him when he died?" he asked.

The question tore at her heart and she wanted to lie, but couldn't.

"I cared for your father, but somehow we lost our love for one another. But that does not mean that we didn't love you and your sister. Your father loved you. And I love you and Renée, with all my heart."

Her son's lower lip trembled.

"The kids at school called papa a bigamist. They said that means he married other women. That he didn't love you or me. They lied!" he declared vehemently.

Marian brushed the hair away from her son's face and smoothed his brow with the damp towel. "I wish I could protect you and your sister and keep the truth away from you, but I can't. Your father did indeed marry two other women."

With his hands he thrust her away from him. "No!" he yelled. "You're lying! My father would never do that."

Marian resisted the urge to take her son in her arms and rock him like she had when he was a small child. She wanted to comfort him, to take away the pain she knew he felt, but she could only be there for him.

She pulled up a chair and sat down beside him. She tried to take his hand in her hand, but he pulled away.

"Philip, you loved your father. Regardless of what anyone says about him, you love him and you miss him. He made mistakes in his life, but his love for you was always constant. Remember him for the man he was to you and the way he loved you. Don't let anyone's opinion tarnish your love for your father."

"Why did he have to leave us? He should have stayed," he said trying not to cry, the tears hovering near the surface.

"If he could have stayed here with you and me and Renée, he would have. He didn't have a choice, Philip, so don't blame him for leaving." She sighed. "I know you are hurting right now, but try not to blame your father."

He glanced up at her, his tears momentarily gone. "Are you mad at me?"

All mention of his father's other wives vanished from his talk. For a moment, Marian thought of explaining more to the boy, but then decided to let it alone. If he had questions, she would answer them, but why not let him get used to some of the truth, rather than giving him more than he was ready for?

She should reprove him for fighting, but her heart wasn't in it. So much had been thrust upon the boy all at once, not to mention the fact that he grieved for his father.

"Fighting solves nothing. I won't punish you this time,

but don't do it again. If your friends start to taunt you about your father, just walk away. They really aren't your friends."

A noise drew her attention and she glanced up from her son. There in the frame of the doorway stood Louis, watching her with Philip. His face held an odd expression, his eyes filled with sympathy. For a moment she wondered, How long had he been standing there in the doorway? How much had he heard?

Louis's heart wrenched at the sight of Philip, dusty, beaten, with scraped knees and an eye that was rapidly swelling. He remembered those days of his own bygone youth, when he'd tangled with someone in the schoolyard.

His own boy would have been about the same age as this boy by now. Quickly he pushed the thought from his mind. There was no sense in dwelling on the past, especially when it hurt.

Marian was staring at him, her look questioning.

"They told me Philip came in hurt and I wanted to make sure he was all right," Louis said meeting Marian's gaze.

She glanced at her son, whose head was bowed. "I think he's going to be fine."

The boy looked dejected and angry at the world. Louis had heard just enough to realize what happened. The boy had gotten into a fight at school because of his father. Louis felt the urge to take him and give him some fighting lessons that would cure the other boys from picking on him. But instinctively he knew that Marian would not appreciate his efforts.

"I know your carriage isn't due until five o'clock. If you'd like, I can take you and the boy home now, in my buggy," he said, wanting to do something to help Marian and the child.

Marian contemplated him for several moments and then glanced at her son.

"Thanks, I think that is a good idea," she said. "I'll spend the rest of the day at home with my children."

He nodded his head. "I'll met you at the front door."

Less than five minutes later, Louis helped her and young Philip into his buggy. He climbed in and picked up the reins. He called to the horses and they were soon on their way.

Passing the river docks, a bird flew overhead squawking a lonesome cry that was barely heard over the cries of the men yelling to each other as they loaded the boats. The boy sat between them, quiet and withdrawn. Louis felt sorry for the kid and wanted to cheer him up.

"Philip, is this your first black eye?" Louis asked, trying to make light of the subject.

"Yes, sir," he replied, sullenly.

"Most boys remember who gave them their first shiner. My brother gave me mine. Of course my father thought we shouldn't have been fighting in the first place, and made us clean the animal barn as punishment."

"Nasty!" the boy said, with some interest.

"Yeah, we hated it," Louis told him.

"How many brothers and sisters do you have?" asked Marian.

"I have an older brother," he replied. "He runs my family's plantation."

"Why didn't you stay on the plantation instead of deciding to go into the shipping business with my husband?" Marian asked.

Louis shrugged. "My father and my brother were

doing just fine running the plantation together. There was no challenge, except in getting along with them. I didn't want to do their dirty work. So I took my inheritance and came to New Orleans to make my fortune. That's where I met Jean."

"You knew my father?" the boy asked.

"Yes, I was his business partner," Louis replied. "Maybe your mother could bring you to the shipping office sometime and I'll give you a tour of the place. We could even go out on one of the boats and see a shipment start off for some far-off destination. Would you like that?"

"Yes!" the boy said loudly, his eyes growing large in anticipation, a tentative smile on his face.

It was the first smile Louis had seen on the boy's face and it pleased him that he'd managed to draw it out of the kid.

Marian turned and stared at Louis, frowning slightly, yet her gray eyes were surprised. His easy manner with her son had astounded her. He smiled. The wind teased wisps of her hair about her lovely face.

He swallowed and glanced away. It would not do for Philip to see Louis's desire for Marian. Philip wouldn't recognize Louis's longing for his mother as the simple flirtation Louis knew his lust to be.

"Hey look, we're right here at Tony's," said Louis. "How about we stop for an Italian ice? It would cool us all off."

"Would you like that, Philip?" Marian asked.

The boy glanced with longing at the outdoor cafe and then at Louis, his eyes so much like Jean's. "All right."

Leaving the buggy at the curb, Louis helped Philip out then he reached up to help Marian alight. His hands encircled her waist and he lifted her out. When he placed her on the ground, her eyes met his.

"Thank you," she whispered.

"My pleasure," he said indulging his gaze in the depths of her gray eyes.

He took them into the courtyard where a water fountain babbled from a cherubic angel, the water splashing down over rocks into a pool. Lantana bloomed in pots in the courtyard, with crepe myrtle growing along the sides.

Louis seated them at a table and ordered the ices.

They sat there awkwardly staring at one another, the boy watching him with interest.

"I remember you," he said finally. "You were at my father's funeral."

"Yes, I was," Louis replied, as the waitress served the Italian ices.

"My mom is working with you now," the boy said.

"Yes, she is."

"Do you like her?" he questioned.

"Philip! What a question to ask the gentleman! You don't ask that kind of question," Marian scolded.

"It's okay, Marian. Of course I do, Philip. She's a nice lady. Awfully smart, too." Louis glanced over at Marian and noticed her cheeks were flushed and her eyes bright in the afternoon sunshine. She spooned the ice between her full lips, while he tried not to notice that her mouth was more tempting than any chilled dessert.

If the boy hadn't been there, he would have considered trying to kiss her again. Just to experience the velvet and sweetness, with a hint of orange Italian ice.

"If you like her, then why don't you want her in the office?" young Philip asked.

Louis was taken aback. While he sat thinking lustful

thoughts about the boy's mother, Philip surprised him and he didn't quite know how to answer him.

"Philip! What's gotten into you?" said Marian.

"It's okay, Marian." He paused.

"Where did you hear that?" Marian asked Philip.

"You told Aunt Claire he didn't want you there."

Marian looked at Louis with an apologetic smile. "I did."

"Philip, the business your father and I ran has no women in it. It's not that I don't want your mother there, it just isn't a place for a woman. One day you'll understand. I'm trying to look out for her."

"Oh," the boy said, and once again delved the spoon into his Italian ice, somehow satisfied with Louis's response.

Marian glanced at her son and then at Louis. She raised her brows with a questioning look. "And Philip, I'm trying to look out for our family's interest, since someday you will take over. Until then, I'm going to take your place."

The child glanced at the adults like he knew something wasn't quite right, but didn't understand exactly what.

Louis pushed away the niggling feeling of guilt that suddenly appeared. He had to have the business. Marian Cuvier would marry a wealthy man to take care of her and then he would have his new business. He would not give up until he won this battle. He needed the capital from Cuvier Shipping.

CHAPTER FIVE

Exhausted, Marian reclined, putting her feet up on the footstool in her sitting room. The afternoon had been spent with both of her children, playing games, catching up on their schoolwork, and just being with them. The problems of Cuvier Shipping had been left behind and for a little while, she'd been just a mother.

She hoped the time together would help Philip come to terms with his father's death. She worried about her son, but didn't quite know how to help him. One moment he seemed a little boy and in the next moment he tried to act a man. Since Jean's death, he'd fluctuated between sad and angry, lashing out at anyone in his path, including his mother.

Marian closed her eyes, reveling in the silence. It seemed like forever since she'd just laid back with her feet up. Cuvier Shipping consumed her time and for the first time she understood some of Jean's moods. At night she came home exhausted, with her mind reeling from the information she gained researching the files. The clientele was large, money matters complex, and the volume of work staggering for such a small company. As the female partner, she received very little respect.

Yet for the first time in years, she felt invigorated and challenged, and more determined than ever before to show Louis Fournet and the men she worked with that she could lead this company. Just until her son was old enough, then she would gladly relinquish the control to Philip and Louis.

Her mind conjured up images of Louis sitting across from her laughing and talking to Philip, smiling at her, making her feel warmer than the afternoon sun. He'd treated her son well today, going out of his way to cheer Philip's spirits and offering to show him his father's company.

Today for the first time she'd even felt like there was progress between the two of them. Though part of her wondered if it was because of Philip, the other part just wanted to accept Louis's behavior at face value. Maybe he was softening toward the idea of her working in the business? Or maybe he thought Philip needed a man's influence. Whatever the reason, he certainly seemed congenial and she'd enjoyed the time they spent together.

"There you are," Claire said, coming into the room. "I wondered where you'd gone to."

"After I said good night to the children, I decided to sit down and relax a bit," Marian said opening her eyes to look at Claire.

"Hard day working with the men of Cuvier Shipping?" her sister asked, smoothing her skirt as she sat on the fainting couch in Marian's sitting room.

Marian chuckled. "Actually, today went rather well and that surprised me."

"What was different about today?" she asked.

"Louis was nice to me and to Philip."

Claire raised her brows at Marian. "Not our Mr. Fournet? The one determined to rid Cuvier Shipping of you?"

"Yes. He brought Philip and me home when he realized that Philip had come from school. Then he took us to Tony's for an Italian ice. He even offered to take Philip on a tour of Cuvier Shipping, which excited the boy."

"What's the man after now?" Claire asked, a frown wrinkling her forehead. "Maybe he's decided if ignoring you doesn't work, that he'll go through Philip to convince you to stay away."

"No, I don't think so, he was quite different when Philip was there," Marian said, remembering the way Louis had reacted to her son.

"I'd be very careful letting him get near the boy. Philip is much too vulnerable right now."

Marian didn't pay her sister any mind. "I caught Louis standing in the doorway, watching me doctor Philip. He looked almost sad as he gazed at the boy. Maybe I imagined the look, but he seemed different today. He went out of his way to treat Philip and myself nicely. He seemed genuine. Almost a different person."

"You must be careful, Marian. He's going to try a new tactic to get to you. If you're not careful he'll use his charm to try and persuade you to stay home where 'women belong.' "

Marian laughed. "Oh Claire, you're such a cynic. I realize I need to be careful of Mr. Fournet. He's already tried several different tactics. Why, just this week, he kissed me, in an effort to frighten me away!"

"What?" Claire asked, her eyes growing wide.

"Don't worry, I handled him and his penchant for creating trouble. I don't think he'll try that one again."

Pity, she thought. His kiss had been intriguing and Marian couldn't help but wonder if she might enjoy a second chance at a taste of his lips. Just one more time to see if the first kiss was a fluke or if there was something about a man's kiss she'd never noticed before. Certainly she couldn't remember reacting so pleasantly before.

"You're going to bring even more scandal down on this house, if you don't give up this foolish notion of working alongside those men," Claire admonished.

Marian gazed at her sister, peeved at Claire's attitude. She was so concerned with what society thought.

"I'm accustomed to scandal. It's poverty that frightens me." Marian paused. "Unless you want me to start taking in sewing or become some man's kept woman?"

"Hardly. I'm not against what you're doing, I'm just worried about the effects on the children."

"I worry about them too. But food and shelter are a priority," Marian said realizing that since Jean's death, they all depended on her to take care of them, even her sister in some ways.

For a few moments only the sound of the mantel clock ticking its soothing rhythm could be heard as Marian sat, her mind returning to Louis's kiss.

Marian sighed and leaned her head back, gazing up at the patterns on the ceiling. "Do you remember when we were little girls and we dreamed of the day we would marry?"

"Yes," Claire replied, wistfully.

"Do you think marriage ever turns out for anyone the way little girls dream of weddings and husbands?"

Claire stared off into space a moment. "Can't think of anyone I know who has one of those storybook kind of marriages. I don't think I took into account a man's need for nights at the club or their sweaty feet. Not to mention the fact that love seems to last for only twenty minutes a week for most men."

"Where did we get such idealistic dreams of marriage?" Marian asked, with a laugh.

"For the answer to that question, I think you'd have to go all the way back to Eve." Claire gazed over at her sister. "Why so pensive suddenly? Did Louis's kiss make you long for marriage?"

Marian laughed. "Hardly. Though I must admit to being quite shocked. It's been years since any man has kissed me like that. It was naughty, but oh, so nice."

"Marian! You sound as if you need to reconsider marriage."

"Why? What's the purpose of me marrying at this stage in life? I can have all the benefits of living alone and if I should desire a man—I'm a widow. Old enough to know the consequences, young enough to still take chances."

"You wouldn't!" her sister said, shocked.

"Depends on if the right man came along," she proclaimed, sitting up and gazing at her sister. "With all the poems and love songs that have been written, don't you wonder if there is something to love that we may have missed?"

"I don't know." Claire stretched her legs the length of the fainting couch and leaned her head against the cushion. "Love that's fresh and new is exciting. It's only when you cease to be a person and are merely a wife, that suddenly it's no longer any fun. It's not that I've missed out on love. It's just been so long since a man kissed me and held me in his arms."

The image of Louis wrapping his arms around her suddenly appeared and Marian felt her breath quicken.

Their kiss had been awkward and he hadn't really held her. So how would his full embrace feel?

"I know," Marian acknowledged with a soft sigh. "I know. I had forgotten about passion until Louis's kiss."

"Well, it looks like he left a lasting impression," her sister said.

"It's been so many years."

She sighed and wondered if she could feel that way again.

Marian sat at her desk, gazing at the empty office across from her. A week had passed since Louis kissed her in an attempt to run her off and still they were at a stalemate with neither one of them winning out.

Well past noon, Louis had yet to show up for work and she wondered what he could be doing. While she knew his whereabouts were none of her concern and she should not worry, she could not help but wonder where the man could be hiding.

The thoughts went round and round in her head, while she tried to trace back journal entries to see who the company was paying. This week she'd learned that shipping manifests were long and incredibly dull, and her mind kept wandering back to the image of the man across the hall.

Feeling his mouth covering hers, his hands gripping her, feeling his lips moving against hers, intruded more often in her thoughts than they should. And now along with that image came the burning question of how would she feel with his arms wrapped around her? Would it be comforting and soothing? Or wild and wanton? Or was it possible to have wild, wanton, and soothing all in the same embrace?

Doubtful. And she shouldn't really consider the question. After all she would never experience his embrace, so why torture herself with wondering? But still, the thought intruded.

The sound of shouting startled her and she jumped from behind her desk. What was that?

"Get him in here, now!" yelled a man, the silence when he finished deafening.

Hurrying to the door, she glanced out, half-afraid of what she would find.

"What do you mean Mr. Fournet is not here! I told him if this happened again, we were through! I mean to tell him just how much he's cost my company with this damn lost shipment!" shouted the man.

An irate customer wanted Louis and she was here alone!

Marian walked down the hall, her feet carrying her toward the counter, while her thoughts seemed rattled and she shook nervously. She didn't know what she would do, but she must face this customer.

What if he refused to speak with her because she was a woman? Ridiculous, she could convince him. For the sake of Cuvier Shipping and Philip, she had to.

As Marian approached the reception area, she felt like she was headed to the gallows. Her heart pounded inside her chest and her palms sweated, but she knew she could not stand by and do nothing.

As the co-owner, she was the one to take this man's complaint, but she didn't know what she would tell him.

"Sir, I promise you I would not hide Mr. Fournet from you," Henry Chatham said, his voice rising with growing frustration. "I wish he were here to handle your complaint."

Marian reached the counter, her gaze taking in a red-faced man who towered above her. Brown eyes snapped in anger, his pupils were large and dark. She swallowed the butterflies that seemed to rise from her stomach.

"You tell that French bas—"

"Excuse me, is there a problem?" Marian asked, her voice soft, but firm.

The large man halted, seeming almost ready to explode with rage, as his face turned an even darker shade of red at the sight of her.

"Damn yes, there's a problem. Just who the hell are you?" he demanded.

Marian swallowed, drawing on a reserve of strength she hadn't known she possessed. She pulled back her shoulders, lifted her chin, and met his angry gaze.

"I'm Marian Cuvier, part owner of Cuvier Shipping. Can I be of service to you?" she said politely.

"If you weren't no damn woman, I'd give you the chewing that Fournet deserves," the man bellowed.

"I'm sorry, I didn't catch your name," Marian said, ignoring his comment about women, though she wanted to kick him in the shin. Somehow she felt like he was still swearing at her, though only in polite tones.

"Morgan! George Morgan of the St. Martin Sugar Refinery."

Marian recognized his name from the ledgers.

This man was no ordinary customer, he was their largest account. He controlled one of the largest sugar plantations in Louisiana, not to mention the fact that he also had a business that moved coffee and bananas around the United States.

He was their largest account and she had to somehow calm down the customer and retain his business.

"Nice to meet you, Mr. Morgan. Would you like to come back to my office where I'd be happy to discuss any problems you may have with your shipments?"

Her even tone and offer of help took the sting right out of his anger as he stared at her, stunned.

"Ma'am how's a woman going to help me?"

She smiled, thinking a woman could do so much for him. "I'm Jean Cuvier's widow. I own half of this business. You have my guarantee that I will work out some plan that will make you happy with Cuvier Shipping again, Mr. Morgan."

Where moments ago there had only been the sound of shouting, now silence filled the room as he stared at her, along with all the other men in the room. For a moment she thought he was either going to yell at her or laugh, she didn't know which. The fear that they were about to lose their biggest account almost overwhelmed her.

Mr. Morgan glanced around at the men who stood gazing at them. "Well one thing I can say for you, you're the only one who has offered to help me. The rest have been scurrying out of my way, including this swamp rat behind the counter."

"Then you're willing to sit down and discuss the problems?" she asked, putting her shaky, perspiring palms together to hide them.

"Hell yes, I'll discuss them with you. But I'm going to expect some improvement. You're not going to just mollify me with talk and no action," he bellowed.

"Fair enough. Let's see what we can agree to." She held open the gate for him. "Shall we?"

Marian could feel every eye in the room on them as they walked down the hall toward her office. For the first time since she'd started working at Cuvier Shipping she felt like she was in a position of power. For the first time she was going to actually do something beneficial for the company.

A bird squawked overhead at Louis as he looked over the ship's manifest before they departed. He had spent the morning down at the docks speaking with several of his boat captains hoping to resolve some issues before he came into the office. The process had taken longer than he'd expected and several times, quite unexpectedly, the image of Marian had crossed his thoughts.

Yesterday, he'd seen her as a mother and realized just how important her children were to her. Hearing her say the words didn't have the effect that watching her with Philip had. She brought to mind his own mother and he'd been reminded of what he was missing in life. Once he'd had his own family and he sometimes dreamed of having a son or daughter again.

Spending the afternoon with Marian and her son, Philip, had been enjoyable. Watching her spoon Italian ice into her mouth had been quite a sensuous experience, one that wakened his senses and left him feeling a little unsettled.

The widow Cuvier was an attractive woman, who he was learning had a will of iron and packed a powerful kiss that startled him.

For some reason he'd held the notion she would be easy to get rid of, and now he was beginning to doubt that even dynamite could loosen the woman from her grip on Cuvier Shipping. She could still be sitting across the hall from him while he tried to arrange the sale of the shipping company without her knowledge; because he was determined to sell the company, with or without her.

Louis stood, notebook in hand, as he checked off items on a shipment bound for England. The pungent odor of bananas and coffee, along with river smells surrounded him, though he hardly noticed.

"Mr. Fournet! Mr. Fournet!" a voice shouted across the way at him. Jon, his office clerk, came running toward him, looking harassed and out of breath.

Louis walked across the dock, meeting him halfway. "What's wrong, Jon?"

"It's . . . it's George Morgan, sir," he said with a gasp.

"Of St. Martin Sugar Refinery?" Louis asked.

"Yes, he's at the office, shouting obscenities at Mrs. Cuvier. He's furious."

Fear sparked through Louis at the image of Marian being threatened by this man.

"Damn!" Louis said, tossing the notebook to the Captain of the vessel about to leave, his attention focused on Marian. Certainly she was no shrinking violet, but the thought of anyone mistreating her bothered Louis more than he cared to think about. But think of her was all he could do while he hurried to her.

As a satisfied customer, George Morgan was often difficult, but when angry, he could become threatening. Poor Marian was probably in tears.

Louis ran the short distance to his buggy and jumped in, picking up the reins, he looked back at his clerk. "Get in Jon, or get left behind."

"I'm hurrying," Jon said, jumping in.

Louis snapped the reins across the horses' backs, sending them off in a rush. Anxious, he drove the horses hard those few scant blocks through the crowded streets to the office.

"How did this happen?" Louis asked.

"Mr. Morgan came looking for you. He chewed out Henry, until Mrs. Cuvier came up front. I didn't stick around to see any more. I knew you'd want me to come get you, so I ran to the docks to find you."

Louis pulled the buggy up in front of Cuvier Shipping and glanced at the building.

"Thank you, Jon." He set the brake and jumped out of the buggy. "Take care of the horses."

Sprinting up the steps, Louis yanked open the door

and hurried inside. The door slammed behind him and everyone glanced up. The men smiled at him and all started talking at once.

"Hey boss, we knew you'd show up."

"Where is he?" Louis asked, glancing around the office, certain he would still be in the lobby area.

"Mr. Morgan is with Mrs. Cuvier, in her office."

Oh God, he thought as he took off down the short hall. As he neared her office he heard laughter. The sound caused him to pause as he came to her office door. He looked around the corner and watched her for a few moments.

She smiled at George, her head tilted as she told him something that Louis couldn't hear.

George started to laugh, his voice light and carefree. The man had never been this relaxed and friendly with Louis. In fact, he'd been rude and obnoxious, his language vulgar, every time Louis dealt with him. Yet he was their largest account. Revenue from St. Martin alone paid for at least three ships out of the ten they had traveling the seas. George Morgan was not someone they could afford to make angry.

Louis backed away from the door, slowly easing his way back down the hallway, not wanting to disturb Marian. God, he hoped that she wouldn't promise their profit away, but whatever she'd done, from the tableau he saw going on in her office, it appeared she'd just saved their largest account.

He breathed a sigh of relief. His fear for her safety eased. Mr. Morgan appeared actually to be enjoying himself. Reeling a little from the rapport Louis had just witnessed between the two of them, he went back to the lobby and sank down into a chair.

Henry came rushing over to him. "Mr. Fournet, what was happening in there?"

Louis glanced up at him still in shock. "They were laughing."

"What?" said Henry, his eyes widening in disbelief.

"They were laughing like old friends," Louis said bewildered.

Henry looked shocked. "You should have seen them earlier. She just gave him one of those cool looks she has and settled him right down," Henry said getting excited. "She was as calm as the eye of a hurricane, and then swept him along to her office, as if she did this every day."

The accountant shook his head. "I have never seen a woman quite as cool as that one. You should have seen her. George was ranting and raving, while she just stood there like they were chatting about the weather."

"How long have they been in her office?" Louis asked, beginning to realize how this would affect the way the men saw Marian.

"Getting close to an hour. It took Jon over thirty minutes to find you."

Henry walked away and then one of the shipping clerks came over. "Mr. Fournet, is Mrs. Cuvier all right? The men say that she's still talking with that bastard."

"She's fine, Charles. I checked on her."

"You missed a mighty good show, Mr. Fournet. She didn't back down an inch, but took him back to her office like she was inviting him to tea. You should be glad you weren't here."

"Why's that?" Louis asked.

"We would have lost the account. He planned to show you how much money he'd lost and then never do business with us again, besides giving you a good tongue lashing."

"Yeah, I heard about the tongue lashing."

For a moment, Louis felt a touch of jealousy. Marian

had not only calmed the man, she suddenly was someone the employees looked up to, all because she'd saved their biggest account.

He heard her laughter and glanced toward her office. The two of them were coming down the hall talking like old friends.

When they reached the foyer, Marian saw him standing over at the side.

"Louis, you've returned," she said, and then turned to their customer. "Mr. Morgan, did you still want to speak with Louis?"

The man glanced at him, his brows drawing together in a frown. "Louis, it's a damn good thing you weren't here earlier or we wouldn't be doing business together anymore. But Mrs. Cuvier has straightened everything out and guaranteed my shipments from here on out." He glanced at Marian. "She's an excellent addition to your staff and I want only her handling my shipments from here on."

A sliver of apprehension attached itself to his spine. What had Marian promised this man? "Certainly, Mr. Morgan."

The customer turned his attention back to Marian. "I enjoyed our meeting very much and next time I'm in town, I hope that you will let me escort you to lunch."

"That would be my pleasure, Mr. Morgan."

Louis felt ill. Obviously her sense of grace and charm had easily persuaded the man.

George Morgan tipped his hat and strolled out the door. Louis couldn't help but wonder how this would affect Marian's stature in the company.

It didn't take long to find out.

The men in the room surrounded Marian, clapped

her on the back and congratulated her as if she were one of them. This was the damage Louis realized that George Morgan had done. The ruin of his carefully built world where Marian was left in the cold.

Once again he was losing this little chess match they played for control of the business.

"Marian, may I see you in your office?" he asked.

Everyone glanced at him, his sharp tone indicative of the feelings that seemed almost to overwhelm him.

The two of them walked into her office and Louis shut the door with a decisive click.

She started to pace the small office.

"Oh, Louis, I'm so glad you weren't here. I was so afraid at first, but then I realized it was up to me to handle this situation. I just went out there and decided I would do whatever is necessary to make him a satisfied customer," she rambled on, apparently not noticing his mood.

She turned and faced him, a funny expression crossing her face. "Is something wrong?"

"What did you promise George Morgan to make him keep his business with us?" he asked. "You do realize he's our largest account?"

Marian glanced at him quizzically. "Yes, I know that. I've come across entire ledgers with the name of his company on them."

"So what made him decide to continue with Cuvier Shipping?" he asked again.

She took a deep breath, sat down behind her desk, and gazed at him with frosty coolness. "I told him that I would personally oversee his shipments and make sure that as our most important customer his shipments would have priority over our other customers. Then I told him if I promised a date and didn't make it, we would refund three percent of the total shipping cost."

"You did what?" Louis shouted. "That's absurd."

She held up her hand. "In exchange, I also told him that he would be required to pay his invoices within sixty days and if he were late, he would be mandated to pay us an additional three percent of the amount due."

Louis, who was ready to explode, felt like someone had punched him in the stomach. "Why would you offer this? Weather could delay the shipments."

"No. I put in a clause that we could not be penalized for any weather-related delays." She shrugged. "When I looked in the journals, I saw he was usually ninety to one hundred and twenty days late in paying us. So I thought if I offered more incentive, just maybe we would get our money quicker. And for an account his size, that could be a lot of money for us."

Louis stood there not knowing what to say. How could he argue with her for generating more money for them and saving their largest account? But by God, he felt so irritated he wanted to yell in frustration.

He'd lost some of the control of Cuvier Shipping today to a woman!

"Mrs. Cuvier, in the future all discussions with customers on the terms of their shipments will be held when both of us are present. Do you understand me?"

She raised her brows, giving him a haughty look and turned up her nose at him. "Certainly, Mr. Fournet. I understand completely. But, of course, both partners must be in the office."

"I'll keep that in mind," he said, and walked out the door, holding tight to his self-control.

The woman was driving him crazy. Those flashing gray eyes and that saucy mouth of hers beckoned to him every time he saw her and he wanted to taste her before he yelled at her. Hell, he wanted to yell at her just because he needed to taste her again and was unable to.

CHAPTER SIX

Louis hated losing. Marian's voice echoed in his head and he thought he could hear her saying, "Checkmate!"

In his office, he sat morosely staring at the empty room across the hall, the waning light throwing shadows on the wall. Marian had gone home for the evening along with everyone else. Only Louis and Henry remained and Louis knew that Henry would soon be leaving him alone with his pensive thoughts.

No matter what he did, Marian thwarted his every move or somehow managed to overcome whatever obstacle he threw in her path, and generally frustrated him no end.

When he'd seen the other men congratulating her like a conquering war hero, he'd known that no longer would she be looking in from the outside. With her quick reaction in saving their largest account, the men had accepted her, and now even wanted to protect her.

When had she become a dues-paying member in the office?

Though Louis had to admit she'd certainly earned her way by digging through the old files, looking through ledgers and finding the original shipping manifests. And he couldn't deny that her resolution of George Morgan's problems this afternoon had been a feat that not only would bring in their money quicker, but also let the customer think he was getting a deal.

But she was still a woman and her place wasn't here. In any case, he made the decisions, not her, so she could pack up her optimism and take it home to the children. He still intended to sell this business.

But, what could he do now? He could continue ignoring her, kissing her, and doing everything in his power to send her packing, but what would it gain him besides a raging erection?

The widow is a beautiful woman, and he respected and admired her, but nevertheless the sale of Cuvier Shipping would come through. Marian Cuvier wasn't budging and every day she seemed to set down more roots than a willow tree. No matter what he did, she was ensconcing herself in the business more and more. And he damn well didn't like it.

Henry peered in from the doorway, his eyes widening with surprise at the sight of Louis.

"Mr. Fournet, you're still here?"

Louis scowled at his accountant; as if he never stayed late!

"I'm *thinking,*" Louis said, his tone as grumpy as he felt.

"It's been quite a day. Mrs. Cuvier certainly keeps things interesting around here," Henry said, with a nod of understanding.

"Yeah, you could say that." Louis paused, needing

someone to confide in. "You know, I've done everything I could to get her to go home and give up this foolish idea. But she just doesn't seem to budge. And now she's more engrained than ever before in this company."

"Mr. Morgan would be upset if she weren't here to handle his account," Henry gently reminded Louis. "Maybe you should just agree to let her be the other partner. After all she is Jean's widow."

"She's one of his widows. And shipping is a man's business. Men should run it," Louis said, not bothering to hide his dissatisfaction.

Henry shrugged. "Jean had heirs and bequests: and he named her in his will as his son's guardian."

Louis glanced up at Henry, surprised by the older man's defense of Marian. "I would give Marian her share of the profits."

"Of course," Henry said glancing away, his mouth turning down. "A woman's 'place is in the home,' not working in an office full of men."

"Damn right it is," Louis said, determined to prove he was right.

"You've told her you feel this way?" Henry asked.

"She doesn't care. I've tried to get rid of her but the men are beginning to acknowledge her."

Leaning against the doorframe, the accountant levelled his gaze at Louis. "What are you going to do?"

Louis laughed, his tone more a pathetic whine. His current ploys were not getting him anywhere. After the scene today, the men had most definitely accepted her. Only he and Henry Chatham were resisting the influence of Marian Cuvier. And he wasn't too certain that Henry wasn't ready to give in to her persuasive personality.

Perhaps the time had come to resolve this problem in a different way. Maybe it was time to use Marian's skills to his advantage. Maybe, just maybe, it was time to let the lady think she was in control, though of course he would never relinquish any of the power.

She didn't understand the scope of the business and most clients wouldn't agree to working with a woman. Yet if he let her believe she was an equal partner in the company, Louis thought, she would be more likely to agree to his future plans for the business. While actually she would be no more than a puppet and he would be the puppet master.

All the while he would be trying to sell the company and its assets.

He smiled once again, feeling powerful. The time to solve the problem was upon him and suddenly Louis knew just how to resolve the dilemma of Marian Cuvier to his satisfaction.

After a lengthy pause, Louis glanced up at Henry. "In answer to your question, I'm going to do the only thing I can do. Accept her. And give her a real taste of what working in this business is all about. Then we'll see if the lady still wants to be a partner in Cuvier Shipping."

Marian walked into the office the next morning, thinking about her children, who had only two weeks left of school before vacation. For the first time in their lives, she wouldn't be home with them for the summer. Normally, they traveled to Virginia to see her family, but this time they would be home alone with the servants and visiting with their Aunt Claire, while Marian spent her days at Cuvier Shipping.

"Good morning, Mrs. Cuvier," one of the employees said as she walked through the main office.

Startled, she stuttered, "G—good morning."

For the first time, she had been greeted pleasantly. Up to now she was met with little more than snickers or glowering glances.

Jon smiled at her, waved and called, "I put some mail on your desk."

"Thank you," she said, stunned at his friendliness.

As she walked through the room, greetings were called out to her, along with smiles and nods of hello. She did her best to return them though she felt astonished at the responses.

"Good morning, Mrs. Cuvier," a slightly balding man said, blocking her path. "I have to tell you that you handled Mr. Morgan very well yesterday. I was impressed."

"Thank you," she said. "All I did was help our customer."

"Some customers are easier than others. Mr. Morgan has always been difficult. You did a good job," he said, and walked away.

Before she could make it to her office, she was stopped twice more by employees telling her how well she handled Mr. Morgan.

Her co-workers this morning were warm and accepting and she almost wondered if she had come to the right office. Did this mean they had now recognized her as an employee?

She put her satchel down on her desk and took off her hat, carefully hanging it up on the coat rack she had brought from home. Little by little, she had been bringing things from the house on Josephine Street to make her office more livable.

An envelope with her name scrawled across the front lay on her desk. She picked up the missive and glanced at the handwriting, not recognizing the penmanship. It was written on the finest quality paper and she wondered who it could be from. The envelope's square size looked more like a card than an actual letter and obviously had been hand delivered.

Picking up her letter opener she sliced open the envelope with quick curiosity. She pulled out a handwritten card with the initials GM engraved on the front. Quickly she scanned the card and dropped it on her desk.

She went to the window and glanced outside at the people hurrying by on the sidewalk, her mind on the dinner invitation she had just received from George Morgan.

The tone of the letter seemed casual, though she feared the invitation was more personal than related to business. George Morgan's heart may well be free, but a very thick gold band around the fourth finger on his left hand proclaimed him married.

No doubt Mr. Morgan thought that the Widow Cuvier would be in desperate need of company. She feared he thought because of Jean, she would be a loose woman, which she found amusing. Accused of being stiff and rigid by Jean, their marriage had never been warm.

A rapid knock on the door silenced her thoughts and she turned to see Louis standing in the doorway. A gracious smile lit his face and she couldn't help but be cautious. Always wary of the charming turn of his lips, Marian watched him guardedly, unable to ignore the way his white shirt and dark trousers accentuated the blue of his eyes.

"Good morning," he said.

"Good morning," she replied, her response not as enthusiastic as his because she remembered his irrational anger of yesterday. Could she expect more today?"

She moved away from the window to sit behind her desk and glanced at him expectantly.

He sat down across from her, settling in like he intended to stay a while. A smile played on his lips. What was there about this man that drew her? Yet she couldn't trust him.

"Yes?"

"I heard from Capitan Mike last night that the *Ithaca* is loaded and ready to leave. We're a week behind on the shipment for The United Fruit Company, but we could make up that time with good weather."

She raised her brows. What reasoning prompted him to volunteer this information?

"All right," she said.

"Also one of our steamships is being repaired. Seems the good Captain Marshal hit a sandbar," he said. "It should be out of commission for probably three or four weeks. This is his third accident in six months and I told him one more time and he was gone."

"Why would he be having so many accidents? Does he have trouble seeing?" she asked. "Or is it possible the man drinks alcohol?"

"Hmm," Louis said. "I never considered there was a reason behind his accidents, just that suddenly he'd become prone to disaster. I thought he was being careless, but maybe something else is awry."

"Might be worth asking the hands if they've noticed any changes in the last six months," she said, responding to Louis, still wondering what he was doing in her office and telling her this information.

She took a deep breath to relieve the tension she felt in her shoulder blades and breathed in the tempting aroma of sandalwood. The spicy smell of his soap was delicious and she felt her pulse quicken as she listened to him continue about their customers.

"I also negotiated a contract with that new broker,

Jim Florin, and we should get some business from him soon," Louis said.

Louis never just came into her office and sat and talked with her about customers or employees like this. What brought about this change? Imparting this type of information he was treating her like a real owner, one that he accepted.

Could the incident yesterday with Mr. Morgan have gained his respect? Certainly the confrontation changed the way the employees in the front of the office viewed her. Louis must have also been affected.

"Why are you telling me this?" she finally asked, staring at him, feeling very suspicious and unable to keep from inquiring another moment.

He shrugged. "What do you mean? I thought you would like to know what's going on."

"I would, but you've never been forthcoming before," she said, gazing at him. "So why is it different now?"

She watched him squirm uncomfortably in the chair across from her. For a moment she believed he really felt awkward. But then when he looked up and stared into her eyes, she saw the mischief dancing in his gaze and couldn't help but be on guard. There was something in that gaze she never could trust.

"I'm giving up," he said.

"What do you mean you're 'giving up'?"

"You're my new partner," he said, not looking at her directly, but patting his leg with a nervous hand. He glanced up, gazing at her as if he was surprised that she would inquire about his actions. "I had wished you would just let me buy you out, but you obviously want to hold onto the business. So, I'm accepting your position within the company. You're my new partner, for now."

For a moment, Marian sat back astounded, feeling a little distrustful. "What changed your mind?"

"Yesterday. The employees were all talking about what a great job you did handling Mr. Morgan and it's obvious you saved the account."

"But last night when I left, you seemed angry with me."

Louis nodded. "You're right. That was last night. Today I'm not angry."

"What's changed your attitude?"

He shrugged. "Last night I wasn't ready to accept you. I thought about it some more and I guess I just grew accustomed to the idea."

She raised her brows at him and slowly smiled. "So does this mean that we're going to work together for the good of Cuvier Shipping?"

He smiled, but his eyes didn't change. "Yes."

Marian could hardly contain her happiness. Finally they were going to quit fighting each other and get down to real business.

She wanted to throw her arms around his neck, but feared how he would take her spontaneity. So instead she sighed with relief. While she knew there may still be difficult moments, at least they were making progress. "Thank you. I'll try to do a good job."

Louis shrugged one shoulder, his face impassive. "That's up to you. It's your company, too."

Marian felt as if someone had released the chain that had been tied around her ankle, releasing her from a heavy burden. Hopefully they would get along better now that they were working together, rather than against one another.

"I realize that I know very little about this business and you've been doing this for years." She paused and gazed deeply into his eyes wishing she could see his thoughts. Would he take her seriously or would he scoff at what she wanted to ask? "Would you teach me everything you know about how this company operates?"

For a moment he sat there and returned her stare as if he were unable to move. Then he slowly smiled and reached out and patted her on the arm. "Of course, Marian, I'll teach you everything I can about Cuvier Shipping."

"Thank you!" she said, and breathed a big sigh of relief. Things were going to be fine. "I'm so happy we're going to be working together."

"Yes, me too," he said, but his gaze didn't meet hers and his tone seemed cool.

She picked up the envelope and handed it to Louis. "I received this invitation this morning. I think it would be wise if we both attended the dinner."

Louis quickly scanned the card, frowning.

"Since his account is our largest, I think we should go together," she said. "You could guide me in handling this man. He is quite forward and I still have so much to learn about this business."

Louis laid the card back on Marian's desk. "It probably would be a good idea for me to go with you. This way we'll be seen together."

She smiled. "Thank you, Louis. I'm sure I'll learn so much from you."

"I'm certain you will," he said, the corners of his mouth lifted in a smile.

Marian felt like she had won a small victory, yet she still had her doubts about which side Louis was on. Sometimes a certain glance left her uneasy. Something about him wasn't quite trustworthy, at least not yet.

* * *

On Monday of the next week, Louis walked into Marian's office early that morning and announced, "Gather what you need. We're going on a learning excursion."

"A what?" she asked, annoyed that he just bounded into her office and expected her to drop everything.

"I'm taking you down to the docks to see how Cuvier Shipping operates," he explained. "To understand this business you need to see it from start to finish."

"Oh," she said looking bewildered. "But the docks. Do I need to go see men loading our boats? I've been down there before."

"If you want to understand how the business works you'll come with me. After all, this is what we're all about."

She gazed at him, a frown furrowing her forehead. "It's not that I don't want to learn, it's just not a place I feel safe."

He smiled. "Don't worry. You'll be safe with me."

"Somehow your reassurances don't make me feel any better." She sighed. "Give me five minutes and I'll meet you up front."

"Jon is bringing the carriage around, so hurry."

Marian cleared her desk and closed with a snap the journal she was working on. She picked up her hat and pinned the bonnet in her hair and then grabbed her reticule, heading out the door.

She met Louis at the front door and watched as his eyes roamed over her and then returned to the top of her head, where her favorite bonnet sat perched. "Are you going to wear that thing?"

"What's wrong with my hat?" she asked him.

"It has feathers in it. We're not going for a stroll, mind you."

She raised her eyes heavenward, trying to see the pointed brim of the mauve hat that sat at an angle on her head.

"I rather like this hat."

"Suit yourself. Reminds me of a pink chicken."

"Never seen one myself. Do you get these visions often or just when you've imbibed too much?" she asked.

He turned and gazed at her, a coy smile of mischief on his face. "Oh, I do think I'm going to enjoy spending some time on the docks with you."

She smiled. "Is the buggy here?"

"Yes," he said, the word clipped short.

"Then let's go."

"Yes, Ma'am," he said holding the door open for her as she strolled out into the warm sunshine.

When they reached the buggy, he helped her into the vehicle, climbed in after her, and took the reins from Jon.

He thanked the man and slapped the reins gently on the back of the horse as the buggy began to slowly roll down the street. They were within blocks of the docks and often Marian passed them on her way to the office.

As they traveled down the road, the horse's hooves clop-clopped against the stones in the road.

"Tell me exactly what you're going to show me today," Marian questioned, noticing the way the wind tousled his short brown hair.

"Well, I thought first I would introduce you to the crew of the *Natchez* and the ship's captain. I thought the captain could explain to you what his crew does. Afterwards, I thought we might have lunch somewhere before returning to the office."

"All right," she said. Even though he had agreed to teach her all about the business, she was still wary of his motives.

They turned the corner onto Canal Street and she could see by the merchandise piled on the wharves that the port of New Orleans was extremely busy.

Different colored flags stood beside the piles of merchandise and cargo. Marian stared at the men who bustled around tossing sacks of grain and heaving bundles of cotton onto the ships.

"What are the flags for?" she questioned.

"That's how the stevedores, the men who load and unload the ships, locate their cargos. Each company has its own flag and that guides the stevedores to where the cargo is either waiting to be loaded or needs to be transferred to the warehouse," he said pointing out the workers who were carrying large sacks on their heads.

"I know our principal cargo is sugar and cotton, but there has to be more here than just those crops," said Marian.

Louis leaned closer to her. "These bags that man has on his head are filled with coffee beans. Then there are the banana boats that come in from Latin America and one of our newest customers, The United Fruit Company, is about to vie with Mr. Morgan for the top spot in our company."

Marian turned and stared at Louis, the question that had troubled her most recently on her lips. "From the looks of the docks, I'd say business is booming. Then, why do you seem eager to sell Cuvier Shipping?"

He pulled on the reins until the buggy came to a halt, and he set the brake. Then he turned to face her. "The industry is going through some changes. Since the war, the docks of New Orleans have been in pitiful shape. The dockage fees are higher than in the larger ports, and we're no longer a main port for business; Plus the steamboat is dying. The twentieth century will be upon us soon and I want to do something different."

She felt a trickle of fear and for the first time wondered if she were doing the right thing by holding tight to the family business. Yet how could she trust Louis to tell her the truth? Could this be just another tactic to scare her into staying away from the business or, even better, into selling everything to him?

"Well, from all the cargo I see, things don't look that bad."

"You're absolutely right. But you've just had your first lesson about shipping. Now let's go meet Captain Pool and let him give you your second lesson."

Louis climbed down from the buggy and came around to help her alight. As he went to lift her out of the small vehicle, she felt a sharp tug on the bottom of her skirt as she tripped, For a brief second she was afraid as she felt herself falling. Then Louis caught her and held her tightly as her body slammed full into his arms, her breasts smashing against his chest, her face mere inches from his.

A feeling of safety overcame her as she gazed up into blue eyes that shone brighter than an early morning sky. Feeling his chest beneath her own beating heart was warm and somehow right.

"Oh my," she said, unable to look away, feeling breathless as she stared deep into those fathomless blue eyes.

"Are you all right?" he asked, his deep voice tender.

"Yes," she managed to say as she lingered for just a moment, the feel of his embrace warm, comforting.

With a start she realized her skirt draped from the buggy to herself, exposing the back of her limbs in an embarrassing exhibit of pantaloons.

She stepped out of his arms and tried to pull down the offensive garment, but the snag was out of her reach leaving her exposed to the men on the docks.

The sound of catcalls resounded and Marian felt her face begin to flame. She had just made her entrance into this manly world in a definitely unique way. One that wouldn't win her acclaim for her talented business skills, but rather for her more earthy gifts that she'd obviously never known she possessed before.

Realizing her problem, Louis stepped forward, blocking the view of her lace pantaloons from the men on the dock.

"Get back to work," he barked at them in a voice that brooked no argument.

Then he leaned around her, unhooking the hem that had become snagged.

With her cheeks burning with embarrassment, she brushed the skirt back into place and lifted her chin. "Thank you."

"My pleasure," he said, his blue eyes wide, his pupils dancing with a mischievous light, though he was gentleman enough not to mention the fact that every man on the dock, including himself, could now describe, in colorful detail, her undergarments.

She took a deep breath and slowly released it to gather her wits, while he stood waiting for her.

He held out his arm. "Shall we?"

"Of course," she replied, still feeling somewhat unnerved by her ghastly exhibition.

They walked to the waiting boat where men loaded bags of coffee beans on a flatboat barge and gawked at the sight of a woman. The dockworkers' language was coarse and colorful as they shouted to one another, until they realized a lady stood in their midst.

"I thought we had only steamships?" she questioned.

"No our fleet has both steamships and flatboats. The steamers are slowly disappearing and we needed the flatboats for the smaller loads we haul up and down the Mississippi.''

''Oh,'' she said feeling like there was so much she didn't yet know. Jean had never shared any details of the business and she felt so inept. But she would learn everything she could, even down here on the docks. Even at the risk of almost falling on her face or exposing her limbs.

Then she saw the man who had greeted her the very first day she had appeared at the office. ''Oh no, that's Captain Paul. I thought you said we were meeting Captain Pool?''

''Pool, Paul.'' Louis frowned. ''The name's are so similar. I forgot. I'm sorry, it slipped my mind about your earlier meeting. If you'd feel more comfortable with someone else, we could do this another day.''

Marian gave Louis a quick glance. Had he really forgotten about their previous meeting or could this be a new tactic to frighten her away?

''Not a problem. I'm sure we'll get along just fine,'' she said, determined that before she left this boat, Captain Paul would be her friend.

They crossed the gangplank, the sound of their footsteps echoing against the wood.

''Mrs. Cuvier,'' Captain Paul called. ''Welcome aboard.''

Well, at least he wasn't calling her darling, she thought as she stepped on board the rocking flatboat.

''Thank you,'' she said trying to find her balance on the moving deck, the feel of Louis's strong hand beneath her elbow lending support. If she distrusted him so, why did the touch of his hand feel so comforting?

''So what are you here to learn?'' the Captain asked.

''Everything that you think I should know. I want to

understand the business from beginning to end," she replied, her voice growing excited at the prospect. "And I hope that you'll be your bluntly honest self."

The Captain grinned. "I always am, Ma'am. This time, though, I'm not suffering from a bloody awful hangover."

"Good. I'll remember to ask next time how you're feeling. You can be quite nasty, Captain."

He smiled and then begin to explain to her the different deck hands and their rank and file onboard, and how each hand was responsible for a certain job on the boat.

Captain Paul strode across the deck and Marian gingerly followed him, Louis at her side, touching her elbow with his fingertips when he thought she needed a steadying hand. Captain Paul described the different parts of the boat, making clear what starboard meant and what a masthead was, how most days the sails were what got them down the mighty Mississippi. He then went on to explain about the different cargos and how the larger ships traveled up the coastline into either Charleston or Boston ports.

After the man had talked for over thirty minutes, Marian glanced at Louis who stood beside her frowning.

For some reason, he didn't appear pleased.

"Well, Ma'am, I don't know what else to tell you. I could spend a lot more time givin' you the tiny details of a voyage on this here boat, but some things are better experienced. Mr. Fournet should take you out for a ride sometime in one of the company boats," said Captain Paul.

"That's an excellent idea. I would love to today, but I've already taken up so much of your time," she said.

"Can't do it today, Ma'am, as we need to shove off

here in a few minutes. I see the boys have finished loadin' and we must be gone."

Marian smiled at the Captain. "You know we may not have gotten off to a great start, but you've been downright gracious to spend all this time with me. I really do appreciate it, Captain Paul."

"My pleasure, Ma'am."

"Well, we best be going so that you can get underway." She started for the gangplank that led back to shore. "Come on, Louis."

"So long," the Captain called.

Marian reached the gangplank and walked across it to dry ground. Louis stayed close to her side.

She smiled at him. "This was a great idea, Louis. It's turned out to be a wonderful day and I've learned so much about the business. I even made friends with Captain Paul now!" She paused and noticed he didn't seem quite as happy. "Thank you."

"You bet," he replied, tartly.

She glanced at him and noticed the tightness around his mouth and eyes. "Are you all right?"

"I'm fine," he responded. "We need to get back!"

That afternoon Louis sat in his office feeling grumpy, unable to believe the woman had turned an outing planned to be uncomfortable for her into a wonderful day. Even when her skirt had gotten caught on the buggy, she'd somehow managed to make that appear as nothing to get upset about. Didn't women get the vapors anymore? What happened to the females who were timid and shy and fainted at an unmentionable word?

Marian never had appeared embarrassed or the least bit intimidated. And somehow she'd made friends with the meanest captain in his crew. Louis hated what he was doing and how he was acting, but if he wanted his dream, he had somehow to daunt her interest in the business.

"Mr. Fournet, may I speak with you?"

Louis glanced up from the papers he was reading on his desk, and noticed the man standing in the doorway. It was after five o'clock, and most people had already left for the day. He glanced across the hallway and noticed that Marian was gone.

"Come in," Louis said. He motioned to the man to sit across from him. "What can I do for you?"

"My name is Richard Vanderhorn and I am the leader of the United Dockworkers Association, here in New Orleans."

Louis felt his body stiffen at the mention of the new union that had recently been formed.

"We're contacting all of the shipping companies that we do business with to let you know our demands. We don't want a work stoppage, but most of us haven't had a raise in years and we work six, sometimes seven, days a week."

The man held his cap in his hands, twisting it nervously as he sat stiffly in the chair across from Louis.

"The men have asked me to let you and the other owners know that we'd like a ten-cent-an-hour raise, with a week's paid vacation a year, and paid holidays." He paused. "We don't feel like we're asking for much, but we're serious. If our demands are not met, then we will walk off the job in thirty days."

Louis sat back in his chair and stared at the man he felt was trying to intimidate him. He let the man wait, while he stared at him. In the last five years, unions had sprung up all over the city.

"What makes you think I have the money to give

every man a raise? Plus a week off and paid holidays?" He leaned back. "You're talking a hundred workers and thousands of dollars. If your workers haven't noticed, we aren't receiving as many shipments as we were before the war. The docks are in bad shape and most people are now shipping directly into Boston and Charleston rather than New Orleans."

"We have families, sir."

"I understand and I sympathize. But business is decreasing and until the city decides to restore the wharf we're losing out to other cities that have better docks." He paused. "I suggest you go back and tell your men that they should be thankful they have their jobs."

The man drew himself up. "I'll go back and tell them what you said, but I can tell you they're not going to be happy. I'm sure this won't be the end of this."

"That may be, but my business doesn't have the money to give to you and the other workers."

"Cuvier Shipping is the second largest shipping company in New Orleans. I find it hard to believe that you can't give your workers a ten-cent pay raise," he said.

"I can't do it without letting some of them go," Louis said.

The man shrugged and Louis felt certain he didn't believe him. They sat there in silence a few more moments and finally the man stood.

"I appreciate your time. Good day, Mr. Fournet."

"Good day," he said, and watched him walk out of his office.

A strike. Damn, but that's all he needed was labor problems to complicate the selling of this company. Worse, if Marian found out, she'd probably give the man exactly what he was asking. Maybe it was a good thing she'd already gone home for the day. This little matter fell into the shadowy area that Louis kept from his partner. Marian need never know about the union leader's visit.

Maybe the business would be sold before any strike could be called.

CHAPTER SEVEN

Louis stared across the table at Marian and watched the candlelight shimmer on her pale skin. From the moment he'd first seen her this evening, he'd found his eyes returning again and again to the woman he'd never really examined before tonight. Certainly he'd noticed her beauty, but this evening she no longer hid behind her matronly image and widow's weeds. Tonight an elegant gown wrapped around her figure, framing her full hips and trim waist in such a way that he wanted to skim his hands over her shapeliness.

She appeared graceful, almost regal, with her hair dressed high on the top of her head, a few curls soft and tempting around her face. The unexplainable urge to release her midnight tresses and tangle his hands in all that hair, or better yet entwine them together in her silken mass of curls tempted him. Since the first time he met her, she had worn only black dresses, her hair carefully coiffed in a more dowager style than the way she looked tonight. Still, just once, he'd like to see her with her hair down, loose and flowing around her.

Tonight, the widow's black garb was gone. Dainty white lace curved around her delicate throat crossing over her breasts in a teasing display of cleavage that drew his gaze and every other man's in the building.

He didn't know much about women's fashion, but Marian's dress flaunted her figure to womanly perfection. And Louis had the job of keeping wayward George Morgan under constant surveillance this evening. Instead of a business dinner, he felt more like a duenna protecting an innocent charge. Though being married to Jean Cuvier certainly couldn't leave Marian naïve, she didn't appear to be accustomed to the flirtatious games George engaged in.

An old fuss budget, married, yet known for stepping out with single ladies who lived on the fringes of society, George Morgan's taste in women obviously included widows. And Marian's defiant show of backbone had whetted the man's sexually charged appetite.

George raised his champagne glass in a toast, dragging Louis's attention from the pearly swells of Marian's breasts. How do you protect a woman when she is in even greater danger from yourself?

"To Mrs. Cuvier, whose beauty and charm are both a delight and a temptation," George said, his eyes ogling her bosom. Louis wanted to toss his champagne in the man's face to cool him off.

Louis promised himself he'd feel that way if it were any woman. Mr. Morgan had a wife and, until death did them part, his eyes had no business straying to Marian's décolletage or his hands to her slender waist.

Where could Mrs. Morgan be this evening?

"So, George, why didn't your wife join us tonight?"

Louis asked, doubting that George had extended his wife an invitation.

The man directed his annoyed gaze at Louis, a frown on his weathered face. "She wasn't feeling well and decided to stay home and rest."

"Pity. I hoped she would join us tonight. Mrs. Cuvier would enjoy meeting the charming woman you're married to," Louis said trying to remind the man of his marital status, though vows probably meant little to him.

"Yes, sometime I'll bring her." He turned his body toward Marian, shutting Louis out. "Tell me Mrs. Cuvier, why did you take over your husband's position in his company?"

Louis shook his head, determined to protect Marian from this old geezer, who he could tell wanted more than just a business relationship with his partner. He watched as George leaned toward Marian and picked up her hand, giving the appearance of listening intently.

"After Jean died, Louis tried to convince me to sell, but my son is only ten and I wanted to save his father's business for him. I felt I needed to be involved, to stay in touch with the business until my son is old enough to take over," she explained.

"Don't you trust Louis?" he asked.

Marian glanced at Louis and their gazes locked as he wondered what her response would be. How could she trust him? They had been adversaries almost since the moment they met. Their agreement to work together was yet new and fragile.

She smiled and discreetly pulled her hand away from George, picking up her champagne glass. "It's not that I distrust Louis. By being involved, I know that my interests in the company are protected."

She grinned at Louis as if to say, *I had you worried for*

a moment, didn't I? Her gray eyes were clear and luminous and twinkled at his obvious discomfiture.

He breathed a sigh of relief. She'd responded brilliantly without saying she distrusted him, but she hadn't said she trusted him, either.

George laughed. "Very smart of you. Louis is a good manager, but looking after your own interests is indeed the best. You strike me as a very intelligent woman, Mrs. Cuvier."

"Why thank you, Mr. Morgan." She set her glass down, and he picked up her hand again.

Intelligent wasn't a word most women wanted to be associated with, but Marian responded favorably.

He bowed over her hand and pressed his lips to her fingers, which he held in his large hand. "Mrs. Cuvier, you're a bright woman and I'm honored you're handling my account."

Louis felt ill watching the older man fawn over Marian, though she didn't appear to discourage his attention. She must realize that George's attempt at charm would conclude with an attempt to seduce her! Hell, Louis had used the same tactics often enough himself. A lot of women enjoyed the flirtatious compliments and hand stroking. The next step would be to get her on the dance floor with him, then into a carriage with him, and from there wherever or whatever the woman was willing for.

"Would you care to dance?" George asked.

Louis cursed to himself. He intended to ask her to dance and while they were on the floor, he would enlighten her as to George's maneuvers. After all, she'd been married to Jean for over twelve years and he doubted that during that time she'd even considered another man. She may be susceptible to someone like George, who would soon have her in a nice little lover's cottage, meeting her twice a week because his wife didn't understand him.

"I would love to," Marian exclaimed.

George jumped up out of his chair faster than most twenty-year olds. He moved Marian's chair back and Louis watched with dismay as George took her hand and led her to the dance floor. Louis stared at them waltzing around the floor, George's lusty gaze focused on Marian's cleavage. He held her closer than Louis liked and when his hand slid below her waist, Louis stood. One more inch and George would find himself dancing on his butt. Just then, Marian pulled back, forcing George's hand back around her waist.

Louis eased back down in his chair still ready to jump to her rescue. This was the reason women were not in business. They tainted a man's thought processes and created problems of jealousy and possessiveness that didn't belong in the workplace. If Louis had met George for dinner alone, none of this would be taking place and he wouldn't be ready to tell his largest account their last shipment with Cuvier Shipping just left the harbor. Marian was not a permissive woman for George to maneuver into his bed and Louis wasn't going to sit back and watch him try.

At the end of the dance, the couple strolled back, laughing, to the table, where Louis sat scowling at the two of them.

"More champagne?" George asked Marian.

"Oh no, thank you, I can't. One glass is more than enough," Marian said breathlessly.

"How about you, Louis? You look like you could use some more refreshment," he said.

Louis raised his brows and returned the man's gaze. George had noticed his displeasure. "Thank you, I think I will. So George, tell me how your sugar mill is doing.

I hear that most plantations are closing their mills and moving toward centralized mill operation."

This was Louis's dream: owning a mill where all the plantations in the area brought their sugar cane to refine and sell. He would buy their crop, mill it, and ship it down river.

"We've been considering it, but so far we're still operating our own. It could be that I close it down in the next few years. It's expensive to run, and letting someone else have that part of the business seems to work for a lot of plantations," he said to Louis.

Instead of George focusing his attention on Marian, maybe now they could discuss their business interests. The waiters brought their food, placing the steaming platters before them.

"How are your children doing since their father passed away?" George asked turning his attention once again to Marian as he speared a bite of his steak.

Marian glanced down at her hands and then up at George, her eyes big and shining luminous gray in the glow from the lone candle on the table.

"Philip, my son, has had some problems, but he's doing better. For the first time, he got into a fight at school." She shook her head. "Mothers don't quite know how to handle fighting."

"He's a boy, Marian."

"Fighting never solves a disagreement, but he let his temper get the best of him. I hope that next time he'll think before he jumps into a situation with his fists."

"Never stopped my sons," George acknowledged.

"I want my son to use his brains to solve his problems, rather than his fists."

George laughed. "Spoken like a woman."

Louis didn't know how much longer he could sit here and listen to George's honeyed phrases and watch the philanderer pursue Marian. He wasn't jealous; he simply had too much pride to watch her be treated like a prize worth taking.

And she was a prize. Intelligent, beautiful, kind, and caring, Marian would be a man's full partner in many ways. As her business partner, he could barely stomach the old man gawking at her bosom, trying to charm his way into her bed.

"How about your children, George? Are your sons still living at home?" Louis asked, once again hoping the subject of his family would help the man see reason, though George's family had never slowed him down before.

"No, my boys have all grown up and moved away, except for the oldest one who is helping me with the plantation. I'll have to bring him in to meet you, Marian."

"I'd love to meet your son and your wife too," she said, eating the last of her fried shrimp.

"How about dessert, and then we'll take another spin on the dance floor," George said, pouring more champagne into everyone's glasses, not asking this time.

"Dessert? No, thank you," Marian said and Louis felt a sense of relief.

George glanced at her. "Now don't tell me you're watching your figure. From what I can see, it looks just fine."

Louis bristled at the man's remark.

"George, how was your steak?" Marian asked, obviously trying to divert the old man's attention.

"I get the hint, Mrs. Cuvier. But I have to tell you, I may be sixty years old, but I'm not dead. And I'd have to be dead not to notice what a fine looking woman you are," he said as Louis ached to wipe the man's smile away with his fist.

"Thank you, Mr. Morgan. You food will get cold if you don't eat," Marian said pointing to his almost untouched plate.

Louis breathed in and slowly released the cleansing air from his lungs, hoping it would clear the rage he felt while trying his best to let Marian handle this situation. One more crack like that and Louis feared he would be defending Marian's honor with his fists.

"Would you care to dance, Marian?" Louis asked needing to speak with her alone.

"Yes, I'd love to," she said, throwing down her napkin.

He pushed back his chair and offered her his hand. She rose slowly from her chair and took his proffered arm. They walked to the dance floor and began to waltz.

"You know he's trying to seduce you, don't you?" Louis questioned, not wasting any time or holding back any punches. He had one waltz to convince Marian to conclude her first business dinner.

"Louis, don't be ridiculous. He's being friendly, maybe a little too friendly, but actually I blame that on the champagne." She shook her head. "I may have had a wee drop too much champagne myself."

"Don't Marian," Louis said, stronger than he intended. "George has turned his charm on you and he will probably offer to take you home and then in the carriage he will make his move to get you into his bed."

Marian stared at him with surprise, and then began to laugh. "Don't be ridiculous."

"I'm not," he said his voice rising.

She gazed at him a moment, her face showing surprise. "I think you're jealous, Louis."

"Now who's being ridiculous?" he said, with a chuckle that felt forced. *He wasn't jealous, was he?*

"George Morgan is our customer. I'm being nice to him because he's our client. I'm having a great time tonight and for the first time in a long time, I feel well . . . pretty."

"Damn, Marian. What do you mean, you feel pretty? You're gorgeous. You're beautiful. You deserve someone a lot better than George Morgan."

"I'm not looking for a man." She smiled at him. "You are full of surprises tonight. I bought this dress especially for this dinner and I think you didn't even notice."

"Oh, I think every man in here noticed," he replied.

She giggled, closed her eyes, and moved with the music. "I don't want George Morgan, but I'm having such a lovely time tonight. There's really no need for you to worry about George seducing me. Remember I'm the woman whose husband married two other women, just so he wouldn't have to . . ."

The music ended and she opened her eyes. "Oh my, no more champagne for me."

What had she meant to say? Why did she think Jean had married other women? Just when things were getting interesting, the music ended and she realized what she'd been about to reveal. He watched her orienting herself on the dance floor, the spell obviously broken.

"Come on, let's finish our dinner and then I'll take you home," he said reluctant to let her go, enjoying her in his arms.

She stepped out of his embrace and glanced at him as they walked off the dance floor. "Why are you so worried about me?"

"I'm not. I just don't want George to—"

She smiled, reached up and patted the side of his cheek, her humor restored. Her hand felt warm and silky against his skin and the sudden contact had him taking a sharp breath to hide his reaction.

Suddenly he didn't want to return to the table.

"Don't worry, Louis. Nothing will happen. You're taking me home," she said her gaze sparkling with amusement.

He shook his head realizing he'd been unable to convince her, while trying to break the spell she'd cast upon him. "This is why women are not involved with business. If this had been just a dinner for two men, it would be over by now. I wouldn't be worrying about how to protect you."

"Oh, that's so sweet, Louis. I never would have thought you would want to protect me." She laid her hand on his arm. "Don't worry. As for your nasty comment about women in business, I'm going to let it slide tonight because I don't want to spoil my good time. But I'm warning you, don't say it again during working hours. Now try to enjoy the rest of the evening without worrying about Mr. Morgan."

Louis stared at her, stunned. Didn't she understand?

They arrived back at the table and Louis pulled out Marian's chair, but before she could sit down, George took her by the hand.

"Come on, let's dance," he said, and whirled her out on the floor.

Marian laughed at the older man's antics and Louis realized she seemed more carefree than he'd ever seen her. In the last two months he had watched her go from being completely shocked at the death of her husband to fighting mad trying to protect her place in the business. Tonight for the first time he had seen her actually enjoy herself and have fun. Tonight for the first time he'd seen her in clothes other than that dowdy black and she looked more beautiful than he thought possible.

Tonight he'd found her irresistible and though he

knew any attraction between them was doomed, he realized he wanted her for himself, at least for one night.

A week passed and since the dinner with Louis and George Marian had received flowers with a note from George, telling her what a wonderful time he'd had that night. The sight of that bouquet of flowers still bothered Louis and he'd resisted the urge to jump up and throw them out.

Just as Louis predicted that night, George did indeed offer to take Marian home. But Marian had had the good sense to refuse George's offer, saying Louis and she had come together, which wasn't a lie.

Somehow she'd fallen asleep in the carriage on the ride home and leaned her head against his shoulder as she slept. The sight of her nestled so trustingly against his shoulder had stayed with him all week and left him feeling oddly warm and protective at the same time.

His imagination had taken the widow home and peeled the clothes from her luscious body and taken her to bed, though his mind knew the fantasy was impossible. Work and pleasure should remain separate if at all possible, he kept reminding himself.

A rapid knock drew Louis's attention to the doorway of his office. He glanced up to see his father standing there gazing at him with an affectionate expression on his face.

"Father?" Louis said jumping up from his desk to come around and give his father a handshake and a partial hug. "What brings you to town? Everyone all right at home?"

"They're all fine. I had to come up here to meet with the banker regarding building a new barn for the plantation. I thought I'd drop in and see how you are."

"I am well. Have a seat," Louis said directing his father to a chair on the other side of his desk. "How long are you going to be in town?"

"I'm returning home tomorrow. Just a quick trip. Tonight, I'm having dinner with Daniel Comeaux and thought that you might join us."

"I think that's possible."

"Heard about that nasty business with your partner Jean Cuvier. You're still involved with the business, I see. Is it all yours now, boy?"

Louis shook his head. "No, Mrs. Cuvier still owns her husband's part of the business, though I doubt she'll be involved much longer. Right now she still thinks she can help the business, I hope she comes to her senses soon."

"Mrs. Cuvier?"

"Yes," Louis said. "I have to give her credit, she's not just any woman, Father. She's learning the business and seems eager to do her part. But I'm hoping she'll give up this foolish notion soon."

Louis felt a moment of shock at the realization that he had not only defended Marian, but also spoken highly of her. And his words were true, Marian never shirked her duties and spent hours combing through volumes to learn the answer to a problem she encountered.

His father snorted with disapproval. "Seems to me if she'd paid more attention to her husband, he wouldn't have married two other women."

Louis shook his head. "No, it wasn't that way at all. Jean didn't know the meaning of the word fidelity."

There he went again, defending Marian to his father. The image of her in the carriage dressed in all her finery came to mind and he'd remembered thinking on the way home, he understood why George Morgan had pursued Marian. Her unique beauty enticed him more than that a girl of eighteen and though he'd thought her beautiful before that night, she'd outshone all the women he'd ever known.

"Speaking of marriage, remember Emily Fratenburg?"

His father's question jerked Louis back from his thoughts of the way Marian had looked that night. "Yes, we were in the same class at school."

"She's just come back from Europe. She's home to stay. And she's unmarried. Lovely too, from what I hear."

"That's nice," he said uninterested.

"You should come home and maybe we could invite her to dinner," his father suggested.

"Maybe."

A moment of silence filled the office and Louis watched his father's face turn serious.

"Louis, Anne has been gone for ten years. It's time you found yourself another wife and moved back to the plantation."

For the first time, Louis noticed how his father's once dark hair had turned silver, making his sixty-five years apparent.

"We've talked about this before. It's not that I don't want to get married. I just haven't found anyone that I want to spend the rest of my life with," he acknowledged.

"You married Anne."

"Yes, but she died. Since then there's been no one else whom I want to marry."

It was true. He would like to get remarried, settle down, and have a few kids. But so far he'd not met any woman who really intrigued him or made him feel compelled to marry.

The image of Marian dancing in his arms, laughing

and teasing him came to mind. He felt a stir in his heart at the memory and quickly pushed it away.

His Father took a deep breath and sighed. "I didn't come here to argue with you. I mainly wanted to make sure that you were well, that this scandal of your partner's hadn't hurt your business."

Louis shrugged, hating to admit this to anyone, including his father, "Business is down some."

"Did you see the article in this morning's paper?" his father asked.

"No, I haven't had time to read the morning paper yet. What did it say?"

"The writer certainly made Jean out to be less than a gentleman. I'd say they all but made him into some kind of miscreant."

Louis frowned, thinking every piece of bad press hurt his chances for selling the business. "Jean is gone. The business will recover and we'll make enough to keep it going."

"Shame," his father said with a sigh. "I know it's selfish, but I kind of hoped you would tell me you were coming home to work the plantation with your brother and me. You know your brother wants you to be his partner."

Louis shook his head. "Neither scandal or marriage is going to bring me back home. I'm thirty-five years old and I want my own business."

"As your father I want you to come home and be a part of the family operation." He sighed. "Come see Emily and then maybe you'll change your mind."

"Maybe I can get home in the next month and then you can invite Emily over for dinner. I'll let you know."

Though Louis knew without hesitation he had no interest in Emily and doubted he would return home anytime soon, yet somehow he felt sorry for his father and tried to appease him.

Marian stuck her head in the doorway. "Louis, have you seen last month's financial statement?" She put her hand to her mouth. "Oh, excuse me, I didn't know you had company."

"It's all right. Come in and let me introduce you to my father," Louis said watching with interest as his father rose to meet Marian for the first time.

They shook hands and said the niceties while Louis remembered how it had been to feel Marian in his arms, the buggy ride home, and the way her head fit the curve of his neck, the smell of magnolias that permeated her hair.

"Nice to meet you, Mr. Fournet. What brings you into town?"

His father smiled graciously at Marian. "I had some business I needed to handle and I wanted to check on my youngest son here and see what he's been doing, since he rarely comes home."

Marian nodded her head.

"Yes, I'm afraid your son doesn't strike me as the family type. He seems more suited for convincing businessmen they need his services and occasionally acting as a chaperone," she said, with a mischievous laugh as she winked at Louis.

Louis felt his father's eye upon him as he watched the exchange between Marian and himself.

"Well, I must run. I hope to see you again soon, sir," said Marian.

"Thank you," he said, and observed her walking out the door, her skirts swishing as she departed.

After she left his father turned to face him and raised questioning brows. "Nice *and* beautiful. A good combination."

Louis shrugged. "She's a recent widow, Father."

"And you're a widower."

"What time shall I meet you for dinner?" he asked trying to change the subject.

"Eight o'clock will be fine. About your trip home. Why don't you bring Mrs. Cuvier just in case Emily is no longer available?"

Louis smiled at his father. "You just don't give up, do you?"

"Of course not, I'm your father. Only I can give you this kind of abuse."

Louis smiled at his father, knowing the old man had gotten ideas about Marian.

Marian spent Saturday afternoon reading over the last quarter's financial statement, the realization of her economic uncertainty and her responsibilities suddenly very clear and frightening. Cuvier Shipping was their livelihood and must be successful or they would quickly go broke.

The numbers for the last month since Jean's murder were pitiful. The fear of closing the doors of Cuvier Shipping almost overwhelmed her, making her frantic with worry.

Upon realizing their dreadful fiscal outlook, she sent a message to Louis to visit her at home as soon as possible.

Just when she'd given up on him stopping by, Edward, her manservant, announced his arrival. Dressed in a rose floral silk dress, she greeted him, pacing the floor in the family room.

"Where have you been?" she asked trying to keep the sharpness out of her voice, knowing she failed miserably.

He gazed at her with his brows raised, his blue eyes

seeming to laugh at her, as she stood there a nervous wreck, the hour late. She watched his gaze slide down the simple dress, taking note of her apparel. When his look returned to her face, a smoldering shadow lingered in his eyes that reminded her of hot, muggy nights spent restless and hungry.

She took a deep breath and reminded herself that this tuxedo-clad man, who liked to chase women even more than her dead husband had, was her business partner.

"May I remind you it's Saturday night. I'm a bachelor and I want to have some fun." He paused. "I've been with men all week. Tonight, I want to be in the company of a woman."

Marian bristled. Just the sort of thing that Jean would have said.

"I've been waiting for you all afternoon. Didn't you get my message that I needed to speak with you right away?"

"I was busy. I didn't receive it until I returned home."

She continued her pacing, her arms crossed across her chest, her mind working frantically to resolve the problem she'd uncovered.

"I'm here. What's wrong?" Louis asked standing in the doorway twirling his hat in his hand.

"Come in and shut the door. No one else needs to know about this," she said with a frown.

Louis closed the door and stood in front of it, his arms crossed over his chest, leaning against the closed door. *It wasn't fair, Louis was so handsome, so debonair and so much like her dead husband.*

"I'm waiting," he said impatiently. "I have a party to attend."

She turned on him exasperated. "I'm terribly sorry to disturb you, but I thought you might want to consider that we have lost over a fourth of our customers since Jean's murder was on the front page of every newspaper in Louisiana. Our profits are way down and the newspaper continues to publish articles on Jean's immoral character. I'm so afraid we're going to lose more business. What are we going to do?"

"Whoa! Take it easy, before you have a case of the vapors! Slow down and let's take these one by one."

He stepped into the room, crossing to where Marian stood. "Let's start with the simplest. Are you referring to the article just printed a couple of days ago?"

"Yes, I think we all agree, Jean was a bastard of the worst sort, but the man is dead and I just wish they would quit writing about him. It's destroying Cuvier Shipping. It hurts my children."

Louis shook his head. "It's not going to end until after there's a trial for his murder. I'm sorry, Marian, there's nothing I can do to stop the press." He took a deep breath. "But I have a friend down at the newspaper who owes me a favor. He's going to write an article on how Cuvier Shipping is changing with the times and about the new direction we're taking toward the twentieth century. That should help our image and bring us more business."

She gazed at him stunned. "So you've already handled that one?"

"Yes. It should be out sometime next week."

Jean had kept everything to himself. She had not been included in any of the decisions regarding the two of them, but lived with his choices. He'd never involved her or even kept her informed. And now Louis had not involved her in the newspaper article.

"As for losing more customers, I sent a letter out just this week to all of our clients saying basically the same thing that the article will say. In the letter, I tell them how important their business is to us."

"Oh. That's a good idea. How did you sign the letter?" she asked, trying not to get upset, feeling more and more like Jean's ghost had invaded Louis's body and continued to make all the decisions, excluding her.

He gazed at her, his face looking quizzical. "I signed them."

"Did you include my name?" she asked.

He looked sheepish. "No."

"Perfect," she said, sarcasm dripping from her voice. "Let's not include the new partner."

He ignored her remark, but took a step back and walked across the room. "I looked at the financial statement sometime last week. I've since taken steps to get us new business and I feel we should recover in the next two or three months. Eventually we'll recapture our losses."

For the last five hours she'd paced the floor worrying whether they were going to survive her deceased husband's reputation, while Louis had already taken steps to ensure the continuation of the company and was out having a good time. Would including her in these decisions have been so difficult? Or just like Jean, had he deliberately kept her in the dark regarding his decisions?

An overriding fury gripped her as she stared at the handsome man standing there in his evening clothes, looking like a man on the prowl.

Just like Jean.

"I have two other questions," she said, her voice calm, her words precise. She glared at him, her eyes saying what she wasn't quite ready to say. "When you and my husband were partners did you discuss the decisions you made regarding the business?"

Louis took a deep breath. "Look, I made these evaluations before I accepted you as my partner. That's why I came in and spoke with you about all those other matters the other day. I was trying to remember everything that's happened and tell you, so you'd know."

"Well there were several important ones you missed. I've just spent the afternoon worrying about how I would feed my family," she said, her voice rising.

"Marian, I can help you. Let me buy the business from you. All you have to do is say the word and I'll buy you out." He stared at her. "You could put all this behind you and concentrate on your children again."

"No! I don't want to sell," she said curtly. "I want to be included. You weren't going to tell me these things, just like you didn't tell me about Jean's other women!"

The room grew silent. Marian stared at Louis. For several moments silence filled the room as he looked at her, shocked by her outburst.

"I didn't tell you about the statement because at the time I hadn't accepted you as my partner." He shoved his hands down in the pockets of his tuxedo. "And I didn't know that Jean married those women. I knew he cheated on his wife, but I didn't know you at the time and frankly his affairs were none of my business."

Marian felt the tears swell behind her eyes and knew she couldn't break down and cry. Not now. Not while Louis stood there watching her.

She turned away from him and walked to the window. "I'd like you to leave now."

Her request was calm and cool and perfectly under control, but she didn't know how long she could remain this way.

Out of the corner of her eye, she saw him take a step toward her and then stop. He stood, uncertain, and then he turned to go, but when he reached the door, he paused with his back to her.

"I'm sorry about Jean, Marian. What he did to you and the other women wasn't right. You deserved to be treated much better." He opened the door and paused for a moment. "I'm sorry I didn't tell you about the financial statement. It didn't occur to me. I'll try harder."

She heard the door click behind him and she burst into sobs. He reminded her so much of Jean. His lack of communicating, his way with women, even the way he laughed sometimes. But thank God, he wasn't Jean. For Jean would never have apologized.

Yet the apology almost made it worse, because somehow it made her like him even more. And she didn't want to be attracted to another man. Not now. Not ever. And especially not her business partner.

CHAPTER EIGHT

Marian stood before the townhouse door, feeling foolish. She shouldn't have come. What if the woman wouldn't speak with her? What if the blonde just wanted her to go away?

Marian took a deep breath and raised her hand, forcing herself to knock on the door. The argument with Louis had forced her to realize that the questions revolving in her head since Jean's death would not disappear until she spoke with one of the women Jean married, maybe both. She needed answers to these questions or go crazy wondering.

A servant opened the door. "Yes?"

"Could I speak with Mrs . . . could I speak with Nicole?" Marian asked. "Tell her its Marian Cuvier."

The servant's face went ashen.

"Please wait in the parlor while I see if she's accepting visitors," the servant said ushering Marian into the house.

He took her into a small room off the entryway of the town house and shut the door. A few minutes later, the door slowly opened and a very pale Nicole walked in. For a moment, the two women stared at one another, their gazes locked as they took measure of each other.

"I . . . I need to talk with you," Marian said.

"Please sit," she invited.

Marian glanced around at the small sitting room where a loveseat and two chairs were placed in front of a fireplace.

"I'll order us coffee," Nicole said stepping into a room off the sitting area.

Marian sat in one of the chairs and glanced at a copy of a Rembrandt painting, which graced a wall over the small fireplace.

Nicole stepped back into the room, her long skirt flowing gracefully behind her. Her manners were elegant and ladylike as she sat on the loveseat across from Marian.

Her blue eyes gazed at Marian with a gentle regard. "How can I help you, Mrs. . ."

"Please, Marian."

Nicole smiled warily. "Sorry, it just feels so awkward."

"I understand. I'm sorry if I've disturbed you by coming to your home."

"Oh, no. But I would suggest that when you leave, you take the back way and be cautious. There's at least one pesky reporter who continues to hound me. There's no need to give them any more gossip."

"Yes, we're still having problems with reporters ourselves," Marian acknowledged.

The room grew silent with only the sounds from the street filtering through an open window that looked out onto a courtyard. A bird trilled a song celebrating the warm sunshine, an odd contrast to the chilled atmosphere in the room. Marian gazed at the young woman, noticing the dark shadows beneath her eyes, her complexion pale, and she wondered if she were ill.

"Are you feeling any better?" she asked, hoping they would warm to one another, before she asked the personal questions she needed answered. The stilted atmosphere made it even harder to ask for the information she sought. "You haven't fainted again, have you?"

"I'm better," Nicole said. "I'm going home in the next few days and I think that will help me more than anything."

A lengthy silence ensued as the two women sat there, Marian not knowing how to bring up the delicate subject.

She cleared her throat. "I guess you're wondering why I came here today."

Nicole looked up and nodded. "Yes."

"I—I need to speak with you about Jean," she said blurting the words out, uncertain even now if she should talk with Nicole about her dead husband. But who else could understand her fears and her concerns about what Jean had done? "You seemed to care for him a great deal."

"I loved Jean. He made me happy," the woman said, her gaze unwavering as she stared at Marian as if daring her to dispute the statement.

Marian stood and began to pace the floor. "I'm sorry this is so difficult. Most people would question my sanity for asking you, a woman he married, but I thought that maybe you could help me. There's no one else."

Marian wrung her hands as she paced the floor. "I feel so betrayed. Not because I loved Jean. My marriage to Jean had been over for a long time, but because—my life with Jean could have been better."

Nicole watched Marian and her eyes filled with distrust. "I too feel betrayed."

"My marriage didn't turn out like I expected. It was not what I dreamed of as a young woman." Marian sighed and walked to the window, gazing out at the beautiful courtyard, not really seeing anything. "I can't help but wonder what went wrong. What did I do to make him seek other women?"

"Marian, you and I both know that men don't need a reason to seek out other women. It's accepted for them to have a mistress," she said. Nicole folded her hands in her lap. "Tell me, if you didn't love Jean, why did you marry him?"

Marian sank back down in her chair and took a deep breath. "My father knew Jean's father and arranged my marriage. I was barely nineteen on the day we wed."

The maid knocked and entered carrying in a tray with a small coffeepot and two china cups, and carefully set it on the small table in the center of the room. Nicole poured Marian a cup and handed it to her. The china pattern had delicate pink roses painted on the side with the rim outlined in gold.

When they both settled back, Marian continued. "Shortly after we married, we moved to New Orleans where Jean took over Cuvier Shipping from his father. I soon became pregnant with Philip and while our life together held no passionate love, I assumed we were happy. Not long after our second child, Renée, was born, I noticed a change in Jean."

She sipped from the cup. "He lost interest in our children, in me, and remained home for only short periods of time. He stopped coming to my bed and when I tried to confront him, he avoided my questions or refused to tell me why he no longer wanted me. I begged him at least to spend some time with the children. They needed him. He never would tell me why he no longer came to my bed." Marian took a deep breath. "I soon realized there must be another woman."

She glanced at Nicole. "I don't know what I did that drove him from my bed to yours. I don't know why he couldn't love me, but he didn't. You said you didn't know he was married, but did he ever tell you anything that could help me understand what happened to our marriage?"

Nicole sat there, her cup and saucer balanced in her hand, staring at Marian, her face showing no expression yet her eyes were brimming with tears. She took a deep breath. "Marian, he never said anything about you. I didn't even know you existed until that morning we all met at the hotel room."

"I know. I came here hoping that something you could tell me could help me to comprehend what happened. I just want to know why."

Nicole sat her cup down, put her head in her hands, resting her elbows on her knees. A tear trickled down her cheek and she quickly wiped it away. "I'm not even sure anymore that I knew the real Jean. How can I help you when my own life with Jean appears to be a lie? I thought we were happy. I thought he loved me, but he married Layla."

Marian resisted the urge to move to the young woman and comfort her. "I'm sorry to upset you. I've dwelled on this for weeks and I needed to speak with someone who could help me to understand what I did that drove him away. I thought you might know."

"No, he said nothing about you, Marian, to me. The worst part is he's dead and we can never ask him why he did this. I'd simply like to know why he lied."

"We'll never know his reasons for betraying all of us. I long to put all this behind me, but it's hard when you don't understand the reasons why. When your husband doesn't love or want you, it does things to your confidence as a woman," Marian said, her hands tightly clasped.

Nicole raised her head her eyes searching Marian's. "Oh Marian, you can't know what Jean's reasons were. You're a beautiful woman."

Marian shrugged. "I don't feel beautiful or desirable. I feel like a matron past her prime, while Jean married two much younger women." She paused. "Sometimes I hate the two of you for what you've done to my life. But then I realize it's not your fault, but Jean's. And then I hate him."

"You're not past your prime. As for hating Jean and us, I can't say I haven't felt many of the same feelings. And once I loved him so much."

"I came here with the hope that maybe together we could finally understand Jean, but you're just as confused as I am." Marian said.

Nicole shook her head. "Nothing makes sense anymore. I don't understand how Jean could be the man I loved and yet betray all of us." Nicole turned her tear-filled eyes to Marian. "For over four years I've been trying to get pregnant. Every time he came home, we talked about what our son or daughter would do with their life."

A tear trailed down her pale cheek. "The day he died, I came into town so happy and excited to tell him—I'm pregnant, Marian. I'm pregnant, unmarried, and Jean is dead. What do I do now?"

"Thanks for meeting with me," Louis said to the attorney, Stephen Hudson, who sat across the table from him in his tiny office located two blocks from the wharf.

"I need to know how the sale of Cuvier Shipping is coming along."

"I'm sorry, but with all the bad press lately, I haven't had many people express an interest," the attorney said. "A year ago, I could have gotten you a good price for this business, but today with all the news surrounding Jean's death, I don't know. It may take some time."

"I have another business interest that I'm pursuing, I don't have a lot of time. Three months at the most. Have you checked with one of the larger shipping companies?"

"No, I always start with my contacts and then progress from there. I didn't realize there was an urgency," Mr. Hudson said.

"Well there is," Louis said pushing away the guilt he felt at arranging the sale behind Marian's back.

"Are you willing to take less than what the business is worth, just to sell it?"

"I might," Louis acknowledged thinking about how Daniel Comeaux planned to retire soon. He didn't want that mill to slip away from him. He needed the mill to turn it into the large-scale operation he had planned.

"Give me a week. I'll speak with several people I know in the business and see what happens. I'll send word to you, if I should hear anything."

Louis started to rise from his chair. "All right, but I'm willing to make a really good deal on this company if I can get it sold." He paused just before he left the office. "There is one other thing. Mrs. Cuvier is in mourning for the death of her husband. Please don't disturb her with the details. Direct all inquiries to me."

"Of course, Mr. Fournet. Women aren't very logical when it comes to business decisions anyway. I will contact you as soon as I know something."

"Thank you," Louis said and walked out of the office.

After Louis found a buyer, he would convince Marian that selling was in her best interest. She could find another business for her son someday.

Marian and Claire strolled down the street, their parasols shading them from the late afternoon sun. Marian's thoughts kept returning to Nicole. She was expecting Jean's baby and Marian felt sorry for the young woman and her unborn child. Marian had sought Nicole out to see if she could tell Marian anything that would help her to learn why Jean married Nicole and Layla. Also to help her understand why Jean had sought other women, but the answers to Marian's questions seemed to have been buried with Jean. Nicole was just as hurt and betrayed as Marian, if not more.

"You're certainly quiet today," Claire said as they walked away from the last dress shop they'd visited.

"I've had some things on my mind today is all," Marian replied, not about to reveal Nicole's confidence to her sister. "I went to see Nicole today."

"Whatever for?" Claire asked.

Marian shrugged. "I needed to understand why Jean married her and Layla. I knew he didn't love me, but still I needed to know if Nicole knew of a specific reason why he no longer found me attractive."

Claire turned toward Marian, her brows drawn together in a frown. "You're being ridiculous. It had nothing to do with you personally. Jean only thought of himself. What did she tell you?"

Marian shook her head. "You're my sister, you're prejudiced. My life with Jean left me feeling unattractive, unappealing, and matronly. I know I'm not as thin as I once was. I did put on some weight when I had the children, and I'm not a girl of eighteen anymore, but

I don't think I'm so ugly that a man would be frightened of me."

"Dear sister, you are being ridiculous. Think of the man you married. He was a bastard."

"Yes, even Nicole I believe is beginning to realize that Jean wasn't the nicest of fellows. She feels more betrayed than I do. And I believe she has reason to feel that way. After all, if the man you thought you were happily married to died and you found out that you weren't even his legal wife, but wife number two out of three! I can understand her feelings."

Claire shook her head. "I don't think it's good for you to become friends with his other wives."

"We're not friends. But she and Layla are the only ones who understand even a fraction of how I feel regarding Jean."

"You hadn't loved Jean in years, it's not your fault he found two other women," Claire reassured.

"It's odd, Claire, I just want to understand how this happened and why. If I know why then it can never happen to me again."

"Oh tosh! You're being silly. Jean made his choices in life. Good riddance, I say."

"I wish it were that simple," Marian said thinking of Nicole and her unborn child and her own fear that she was so unattractive that her dead husband sought other women to slake his desire. Jean's only legacy was of pain and heartache.

The two women continued down the street on their way to a favorite restaurant. The face of the maitre d'hôtel brightened at the sight of them and he hurried over to greet the two sisters.

"Mrs. Cuvier and Mrs. Bienvenu, how nice to see you again." He smiled. "Your favorite table is available. Would you care for it?"

"Thank you," Marian nodded and followed him to the little table situated close to the fountain in the courtyard. Water splashed down the stone statue, the gurgling noise peaceful and soothing.

After they ordered, Claire glanced at Marian. "You haven't mentioned Mr. Fournet in days. I miss your tales of his attempts to rid the office of a woman."

Marian sighed and wished her sister weren't quite so perceptive sometimes. She hadn't spoken to Louis since the night he'd come to the house at her bidding and they'd gotten into that terrible row.

"I haven't spoken to him in several days. I didn't go into the office today."

"Why not?"

"I wanted to see Nicole and then . . . I don't know. I wasn't quite ready to face him. We had an argument the other night when he came to the house."

Claire put her menu down, her eyes questioning as she gazed at Marian.

"It was partly my fault."

"I don't think you'd say anything vile to the man. So what new trick is he up to?"

"Actually he's been rather nice to me of late. You remember how Jean never included me in any of the decision-making for our family?"

"Yes, as his wife your place was to be seen and not heard."

"Yes, well, Louis made some business decisions and forgot to tell me about them. I became upset even though he had made most of these resolutions before he accepted our partnership. I just kept thinking that his actions were exactly like Jean's. And then I mentioned the fact that he'd known about Jean's other women and never told me about that either."

"Did you really expect him to?" Claire asked. "I mean

men take up and cover for one another just like women do. So don't you think your expectations were unrealistic? Did he even know you then, Marian?"

"I know. You're right. Louis didn't know me and he said that Jean's affairs were none of his business. I thought it through later and realized I had overreacted, but I didn't want to go back and tell him," she admitted.

As she had stood there that evening staring at him in his tuxedo, she'd realized just how much she was attracted to this handsome man she shared a business with and she could think of nothing worse in this world at that moment.

"So what are you going to do?" Claire asked.

Their food arrived and spared Marian from having to answer right away. Claire waited for their waiter to walk away and then repeated the question, not giving up on obtaining Marian's response.

"I'll go back to the office tomorrow. I just took today off." She sighed, her memory of his apology still amazing her. "And I guess I now owe him an apology. Do you know he actually told me he was sorry about what Jean had done to me and the other women? God, I was so mad at him and I didn't want to like him, but he apologized and it—few men have ever done that to me."

Claire smiled. "Are you certain you don't like Louis a little more than you're letting on?" She laughed. "I haven't seen you this animated about a man since grade school."

"Oh please, Claire! Don't start this. I can honestly tell you that my intentions are to remain unmarried and focus on this business and my children. I am not going to be involved with a man again."

"You know it's really all right if you wanted to. You

married Jean so young. If you found the right man and married for love this time, it could be different."

"How can you say that? Haven't you been listening? I don't want another man in my life again. And besides I couldn't keep Jean interested in me, how would I keep a man like Mr. Fournet attracted?"

Claire looked at her. "You know Marian, I don't think the problem was with you, but rather Jean. You could have danced naked around Jean's bed and he would have found some excuse to go to another woman. You are a beautiful woman. You could have more children!"

Marian felt her face flame with embarrassment. "Claire watch your language. We are in a public restaurant and I would appreciate your not talking about me dancing around any man's bed naked."

"Oh all right, but it's true."

"Finish your lunch, I need to get home."

"I will, but I still think there is more going on inside that devious mind of yours regarding Louis Fournet. I just don't think you're ready to admit to it, even to yourself."

Marian glanced away from the table and ignored her sister's comment. She would not admit or deny anything else Claire said about Louis Fournet. No matter how much she ignored her attraction to the handsome man, she knew she was losing the battle. Even though they argued the other night, his apology had stunned her . . .

For the first time in more years than she cared to admit, she found a man attractive. She wanted him and that both infuriated and tantalized her. But she wasn't willing to marry any man again. Especially not the handsome Mr. Fournet, no matter how much he apologized.

CHAPTER NINE

Louis looked up at the house on Josephine Street and gazed at the mansion with its white columns and iron grillwork, which reminded him of Europe. He wondered again why Jean would give up Marian and all of this to live a lie with two other women? Marian was beautiful and witty and more strong-willed than any woman he'd ever met. Their verbal sparring both challenged and excited him. Even when things were tense, there was something about her that beckoned him like a siren to a sailor.

Marian hadn't shown up to the office today and after the way he'd left her the other night, he worried about her most of the day. Though he'd apologized that night, he felt as if she'd withdrawn to some unreachable place. On impulse today he'd bought her and the children beignets and brought her the latest financial figures. Anything to keep her trust and not arouse her suspicions during this time, while he worked to sell the business.

The sound of a child's laugh drifted on the breeze from the back of the big house. He walked down a flagstone path that led to a gate. A large crepe myrtle shaded him from the sun as he gazed over the top of the gate at Marian.

The sun glimmered off her white shirtwaist as he watched her pitch a baseball to her son. The boy swung awkwardly and missed the slow pitch. The daughter he'd seen at Jean's funeral chased after the ball, her braids swinging down her back. She scooped up the ball and threw it back to her mother.

Marian ducked her head to keep from getting hit from the child's throw.

"Momma, you're supposed to catch the ball not dodge it," the little girl said, laughing.

"Thank you, Renée, I'll try to remember that," Marian said picking up the ball. Then she gazed at her son. "Concentrate on how your coach told you to hold the bat, Philip."

The boy wrapped his hands around the bat and lifted it over his shoulder. "I am, but it feels funny."

"Give it time. It will get better," Marian reassured the boy.

She tossed the ball, the pitch going high and wide. Yet the boy swung, missing the ball by several inches.

Philip picked up the baseball and glanced at it as if it were defective. He then tossed the ball back to his mother who caught it. After the child repositioned himself, Marian threw the ball again, but this time Philip stepped too close and the ball connected with his forehead, knocking the child back.

Marian ran toward the boy, who dropped to the grass holding his head. "Oh my God, are you all right, Philip?"

"Ouch! You hit me," Philip said, embarrassment and hurt pride filling his voice.

Louis pulled the gate open and walked toward the trio, wanting to make sure that Philip wasn't hurt.

"Let me see your forehead. I didn't throw it that hard, so you couldn't have been hurt very bad," Marian said, her hand brushing back the hair from his face.

The boy scrunched up his face trying hard not to cry. "I want to quit. You can't throw. I can't hit. I knew it was a mistake to ask you to help me."

Louis tried not to laugh as Marian bent over a distraught Philip. The boy was not happy that his mother had hit him with the baseball.

"Momma," Renée said tugging on Marian's skirt as she noticed him coming toward them.

"Just a minute, Renée," Marian replied, her hand stroking her son's forehead. "There's not even a bump."

"It's that man," the little girl said.

As if she suddenly realized what Renée had said, Marian turned and glanced at Louis.

Their gaze met and he stared into her gray eyes watching as her pupils widened slightly. She looked beautiful, mussed from playing with her children. He swallowed. Whenever she looked at him with that warm, lazy gleam, he felt the world disappearing, receding, and he wanted to block out everything but the two of them.

"You're fine, Philip," she said, distracted, her eyes never wavering from Louis's face.

"Sorry to interrupt. You didn't come to the office today and I was worried. I thought I would bring you the latest financial numbers along with some beignets I picked up in the marketplace."

She rose slowly and for a moment he wasn't sure how she would react to his unannounced presence. He should have come through the front door, he should never have walked around to the back garden unannounced. But the sound of laughter had drawn him, lured him here, and when he'd seen her, he couldn't turn away.

She swiped a loose strand of silken hair away from her face. "Thank you. I'm trying to help Philip with his batting practice."

"She pitches like a girl," Philip said standing and dusting off his pants, while keeping a close watch on Louis and his mother.

Renée moved in closer to her mother, gazing at him in curiosity.

"You want to play?" the little girl asked. "I think brother needs someone beside Momma to throw the ball. He's not getting any better."

Louis laughed at the child's honesty.

Marian reached down and stroked her daughter's hair. "Renée, Mr. Fournet has other obligations. He just dropped by to give me some papers."

Louis winked at Renée and then returned his gaze to Marian. He'd thought of going to a club later tonight to sit and drink, listen to the music, and maybe argue politics, but he liked the idea of playing baseball. And he wasn't ready to leave, not before he'd proven to her he was sharing information about the finances of Cuvier Shipping. Not before he had a private moment with Marian.

"I'm not busy," he replied, with a slight shrug. "I can't remember the last time I played baseball, but I bet I could remember how to pitch. I'd like to play, Renée," Louis said gazing at the child. He glanced at Marian. "If it's all right with you."

"But—but don't you have someplace you need to be?" she stuttered, her eyes wide and questioning.

The bright afternoon sun shone on her rosy cheeks and Louis didn't know if her blush was from the heat or the fact that he intended to stay.

He picked up the bat and handed it to Philip, then glanced at Marian, his gaze serious. "There's no place I'd rather spend the afternoon."

She closed her mouth, seeming confused.

"Good," Philip said. "Maybe now I'll get some pitches I can hit."

Louis laid the beignets and the papers down on a bench and began to remove his coat and loosen his cravat, pulling the tie from around his neck and tossing the clothing onto the bench. He removed his cuff links and rolled up the sleeves of his shirt, past his elbows.

Louis turned his attention to Philip. "I watched you from the fence and noticed you were holding the bat too high. Here, let me show you."

Placing Philip's hands in the correct position on the bat, he then arranged the child's body in an accurate stance. "Now cock your bat back a little more like this." Louis stepped back and examined the boy's posture. "It's probably not perfect, but it's closer. It feels awkward but you'll soon get used to it."

Marian still stood at the center of the yard watching him warily. He walked toward her and took the ball from her.

"I'll pitch. You and Renée can be outfielders," he said with a laugh.

"I've never been one to play games. I think I should sit and watch," Marian said shaking her head.

"Oh no. A woman like you could use a few games in her life," he said, his voice husky and low. "Philip, don't you think your mother and Renée should play with us?"

"Nah, they're girls. Baseball is for men."

"Spoken by a child who has yet to discover women," he said low enough for her ears only.

"No," Louis said. "Me and Renée against you and your mother, Philip."

"Oh, all right, but Renée can't hit the ball and mother can't run," Philip said.

"Well then we're even," Philip acknowledged.

Marian stood there staring at him in shock. Finally she spoke, a slight smile on her lips. "You know, you just walked in here and suddenly you're staying and we're playing ball. Do you always take control?"

"Every chance I get. Besides, you have to admit that you needed some help. Philip could have been seriously hurt by one of your throws. I really am doing you a favor."

She laughed. "You're very sure of yourself."

"That's because I'm good at what I do."

"Humph," she said placing both of her hands on her hips. "I'm not going to challenge you on that one, because frankly I don't want to know what you're good at."

He winked. "You'd be surprised."

A blush stained her cheeks as they stood staring at one another. The thought of showing her just how good he could be slammed into his gut and he had to take a relaxing breath.

"Come on, guys, let's play ball!" Philip yelled getting impatient with the adults.

Renée had already taken her place in the outfield and chased a butterfly while waiting for the action to commence.

"Do you know how to use a bat?" Louis asked Marian.

"Only as a weapon."

"Hmm. That's something to remember."

She laughed. "Do."

The afternoon felt natural, as if they did this every day. After the atmosphere of Saturday night, it felt good to once again be verbally engaged with one another. He'd missed their skirmishes today at the office.

"Your son's getting impatient. I'll throw to him first and then we'll show you how to bat."

"I can hardly wait."

"Me, too," he said wondering if he could get away with wrapping his arms around her while he showed her the proper techniques of holding the bat.

Baseball had a way of growing on a man, especially when he was going to put his arms around a tempting woman like Marian, who challenged him mentally and physically. And for this moment he refused to consider the consequences of the growing attraction he felt for her.

Marian looked around the dinner table and watched her children chatting with Louis about their recent baseball game. For the first time in years, a man presided at the dinner table and a strange feeling had taken up residence in the pit of her stomach.

She gazed at the dark-haired man, her eyes lingering on his mouth as she reflected on the brief kiss he'd given her. That kiss had left her sleepless for several nights as she remembered the feeling of his lips covering hers. His drugging, demanding kiss had left her knees trembling, her stomach fluttering, and her mind rioting with questions.

"Momma, can we stay up until Mr. Fournet leaves?" Renée asked, bringing Marian back from the memory of Louis's kiss.

Marian glanced at Louis, wanting him all to herself.

"We need to discuss some business after dinner, Renée, so I think you had better go up after dinner."

"But I'm not sleepy," the child said.

"Tonight is bath night, you will certainly be sleepy after that," Marian said, knowing the child would be in bed asleep within minutes of getting out of the tub.

"We'll play ball again another day, Renée," Louis said, soothing her daughter.

"Do you play dolls?" she asked.

Louis smiled. "I've never played dolls. You'll have to show me."

"It's not hard," Renée informed him. "Even boys can do it."

"It's a girl's game and men don't play with dolls," Philip said, exasperated, clearly embarrassed by his sister.

"You don't know that!" Renée said, her voice filled with irritation.

"Don't forget your manners," Marian said quietly. "You are at the dinner table."

Both children hushed, but when Renée thought Marian wasn't looking, she stuck out her tongue at her brother.

"Renée, one more and you'll leave the table," Marian warned.

"Yes, ma'am."

When they finished eating, Marian sent the children upstairs to the maids to help them with their baths, while she and Louis retired to the sitting room.

"Would you like a brandy?" she asked Louis.

"Thank you, yes," he replied taking a seat on one of the small settees in the room.

Marian poured him a brandy and herself a sherry and handed him his glass.

She sat in a chair across from him, quietly studying

him, knowing she needed to apologize for her outburst the other day, but not wanting to spoil the cozy atmosphere. She twisted the glass in her hand, suddenly feeling quite nervous. For the first time that day they were alone and she knew she could no longer postpone the apology.

"Louis, before we start going over the figures, I need to apologize for my behavior the other night. I'm sorry for my outburst. I was wrong to accuse you of—of not telling me. . . ."

She ran out of words and sat back against her chair watching the way his eyes seemed to warm as she'd spoken.

Louis's mouth pulled taut and he shook his head. "No, Marian. I should have told you everything regarding the business. That's why I brought over the newest figures tonight for you. I wanted you to see I'm honoring my promise to you."

She nodded and couldn't help but smile. "You said you would do better, so I promise that I too will work harder to make our partnership succeed."

Louis leaned toward her, his hand reaching out and grasping hers. Just as he started to say something, Renée knocked on the door and called. "Momma, I'm all ready for bed."

Marian jumped up, startled by her daughter's voice. There was no doubt that Renée had just taken the quickest bath ever for a small child. Marian took a deep breath, gazing at Louis, and then slowly rose. "I'll return in just a few moments."

As she went out the door she took Renée by the hand, leading the child up the stairs, wishing somehow that her daughter hadn't chosen that moment to come into the room. Wishing that Louis had finished his sentence.

They walked into the child's bedroom and Renée

crawled into her bed. Marian leaned over and tucked her in.

"Goodnight, Renée," she said, kissing the child's cheek.

"Do you like Mr. Fournet?" Renée asked, hugging her mother close.

"He's my business partner, honey."

"Oh. Could he be our new Daddy if we asked him to?" she asked.

"No, dear," Marian replied, not wanting to go into any other details.

"Why not? Doesn't he like children?"

Marian tried not to feel frustrated by her daughter's questions. "Mr. Fournet likes children. But usually when people marry they are in love."

"Don't you love him? Aunt Claire said we are supposed to love everyone."

"There are different kinds of love. Marriage requires a special kind of love. Now it's time for you to go to sleep."

"Oh, all right. Night, Momma." The little girl turned over and snuggled deeper into the covers.

"Goodnight, sweetheart."

Next, Marian went to her son's room and knocked on the door before she opened it.

"I came to say goodnight," she said, as she glanced at her boy.

"Goodnight Momma," he said, lying in bed, reading.

"Go to sleep soon," she reminded him.

He nodded. "That was fun today with Mr. Fournet. Ask him to come back soon."

"I'll ask him. Now get some sleep."

"Okay, goodnight."

"Goodnight."

She closed his door. Her children liked Louis and

that gave her a warm feeling, but not warm enough to marry him, she thought with a smile. She hurried back down the stairs to her waiting guest.

"Sorry; they're in bed now. We shouldn't be interrupted again."

"I'll just go over these figures and then I'll be on my way," Louis said.

"Would you like some more brandy?" she asked.

"No, thank you."

She wanted to resume the atmosphere they had made before she left the room. Somehow she wanted to hear what he had been about to say. She sat down in the chair, wishing she had the nerve to sit beside him on the settee.

Her eyes lingered on his lips, remembering the feel of them against her own, wanting to taste them once more. She glanced away, trying to clear her head of her exciting thoughts. Their relationship was a business one, and yet her fantasies of him were more intimate and revealing than her dreams had been for many years. She had to stop this nonsense. If she continued she would be like a wanton woman for thinking of Louis this way.

"Here are the latest numbers that I have," he said handing her a balance sheet that showed a listing of debts and credits.

The figures seemed to blur before her eyes as she breathed in the musky male scent of Louis as he leaned close. The image of him rolling up his shirtsleeves to play baseball with her children this afternoon came to mind and she blinked to clear her vision.

"As you can see the new business is still down, but I'm confident that should correct itself soon," Louis said leaning close.

With a resigned sigh she leaned her head back against

the chair. "I'm sorry for putting you through all this just to prove to me that everything is going well with the business. My worries have kept you from entertaining one of your lady friends tonight."

He sat back against the settee. "I don't mind. I enjoyed playing with you and your children today."

"Well, I know that's all they talked about while I was tucking them into bed. Renée was falling asleep as I closed the door. And Philip—I've been so worried about him—he told me he had a good time today." She paused. "That's twice you've done something really nice for my children. Thank you."

"I like kids."

"Then why aren't you married with a couple of your own?" she asked.

He shrugged and appeared ill at ease. "Just haven't found anyone since my first wife died; I wanted to be with her forever."

Marian stared at Louis, not quite sure he was what he appeared to be. Yes, he reminded her of Jean, but he was different. Any man who truly wanted children like Louis proclaimed, would marry the first woman he found, would he not? What was the real reason he avoided marriage?

"Tell me what was so special about your wife that you cannot find in another woman?" she asked. As soon as the words were out of her mouth she regretted them. "I'm sorry, it's really none of my business, and I shouldn't be asking you questions like this."

He gazed at her with a curious look upon his face. "No, I'm simply surprised. You're the first woman who has ever asked." He took a deep breath. "My wife and I grew up together. She was my best friend, and when I returned from college, I knew I wanted to marry her."

He reached for the brandy decanter that sat on the

table between them and for a moment Marian feared he'd said everything he had to say about the subject. But then he continued.

"We had a traditional wedding and lived at Belle Fournet, our family's plantation. Six months after we married, Anne found she was expecting our child. We were so happy and she spent her time redecorating the old nursery."

He sipped from his glass, his eyes distant and filled with pain as he reminisced.

"Anne was a small woman and when it came time for the baby to be born, she labored for two days before the baby came, stillborn." He paused, glancing down at the amber liquid in his glass. "She never recovered. Eight hours later, I lost her too."

He took a big gulp of brandy. "I lost them both."

Marian sat there stunned, her heart aching for him, knowing his clipped speech was a result of the pain he still felt.

He shook himself and sat up straighter on the settee. "I'm sorry, that wasn't what you asked. You wanted to know how Anne was different from most women I meet." He shifted around restlessly on the settee and then stood up. "Can't really say."

"I shouldn't have asked. It's just that if you want more children, you should marry."

He stared at her over his brandy glass. His brows rose and he released a deep sigh.

"Now you sound like my father. I don't need someone else encouraging me to find a wife," he said, his words resigned.

Marian smiled, trying to ease the seriousness of their conversation. "I like your father. As for finding you a wife, I am the last person who would push or encourage anyone into marriage."

Louis laughed. "No, I think not."

The clock chimed nine o'clock and Louis drained the rest of his brandy and sat the glass down on the table. "It's getting late, I'd best be going."

Marian felt a sense of disappointment. She'd enjoyed his company, though the hour was late.

"I'll walk you to the door," she said.

The afternoon had been fun and the time spent talking about the death of his wife had been revealing. She couldn't remember a more enjoyable time spent with a man. She couldn't remember a man who intrigued her more than Louis.

They walked through the house, the ticking clock echoing through the stillness almost in rhythm with the sound of their shoes against the wooden floor.

When they reached the door she glanced at his lips, so full, so inviting. If they kissed again, would it be the same as before or more breathtaking?

She licked her lips, her mouth seeming to go dry, her lungs feeling as if they wouldn't expand. She wanted him to kiss her. She wanted just once more to test if that wondrous feeling had been a mistake or if she really could experience passion once again. Maybe she wasn't as immune to sexual ardor as she originally thought?

"I enjoyed today," he said gazing at her, his blue eyes dark.

"Me, too. Thank you for helping Philip, and for bringing the beignets and the report."

He nodded. "My pleasure."

Louis took her hand and Marian felt dizzy with expectation. But then he touched his full lips to the back of her hand in a pleasant kiss that left her disappointed and tense with longing. She wanted so much more.

Clearing her throat, she raised her chin in a haughty

manner, so he wouldn't realize her disappointment at the simple press of lips to the back of her hand.

Her face felt stiff as she smiled.

"Well then I guess I'll see you back at the office tomorrow?" he said raising to his full height.

"Yes, tomorrow," she said breathlessly.

"Yes. I'll see you then," she said.

He walked through the door and she closed it behind him with a lonely click.

She leaned against the door and touched the back of her hand to her lips. What was wrong with her? The man was her partner and she had no business wanting to explore sensuous desires of the flesh with him.

But then never before had she gazed deeply into a man's eyes and wanted to feel his hard body beneath her hands. Or imagined how a man looked beneath his clothes and dreamed of him carrying her up the stairs and taking her.

This fluttery breathless feeling of anticipation whenever Louis was around, she'd never experienced before. Frankly, it frightened her.

She wanted to cry, but the tears had long ago dried up. Jean had obviously been repulsed at sharing her bed. What made her think Louis would find her any different?

CHAPTER TEN

Marian sat at her desk trying to focus on the customer files she had pulled, unable to think of anything but the man across the hall.

The last two nights she'd spent tossing and turning in bed, restlessly, her dreams filled with his image. She'd gone over every detail of the afternoon they'd spent together. Her imagination must be playing tricks on her to think he gazed with more than just friendship in his eyes. Yet something in his looks left her hot and restless.

Sighing, Marian glanced blindly at the scattered papers before her. With little experience with men and unable to perpetuate Jean's interest in their marriage, she doubted her ability to discriminate between a flirtatious glance and a friendly hello. Her observations of the other sex could not be trusted. What made her think any man would be sending her flirtatious looks? After all, sitting behind this desk, few men would think of her as a woman, let alone an attractive one.

Creole women had run businesses in New Orleans for hundreds of years, but the Americans frowned on their women doing anything other than taking care of the family. Yet in a way she was taking care of her family by preserving the business for her son and supporting them.

And though Louis's family was Creole, he made it clear that he had adopted the American way of thinking that a woman's place was in the home. Perhaps he viewed her behavior as too masculine to find her attractive?

Footsteps alerted her that someone approached. Henry came into view, but turned toward Louis's office.

"Excuse me, Mr. Fournet, you have a visitor up front."

Marian stared across the hall at the man her thoughts centered on. Another visitor? Another woman?

Louis glanced up from the papers on his desk. "Who is it?"

"A Mrs. Evette Simone."

Marian gritted her teeth hearing the name of the well-known widow, renowned for her flirtations. Rumors said she often took a lover, though Marian didn't know if this were fact or just gossip. Still she couldn't help but feel a twinge of jealousy at the woman's daring courage to live the way she wanted, without the restrictions of propriety.

Louis laughed and shook his head. "Bring her back to my office, Henry."

"Yes, Mr. Fournet," he said, and trotted off to do his boss's bidding.

Louis looked up and caught Marian staring at him. He smiled and nodded in her direction. She tilted her head in acquiescence and then quickly returned to her papers.

Another woman. She wasn't jealous. She wasn't—just irritated.

"Louis!" the widow called when she saw him.

He came out of his office to greet her in the hallway, their bodies turned toward each other, giving Marian a clear view.

Mrs. Simone's voice seemed cheerful, her pouty lips turned up in a come-hither smile.

Marian couldn't resist watching as the widow greeted him taking both of his hands in her own. She pulled him close as she pressed her lips to his cheeks. She leaned back, not releasing his hands and gazed at him.

"Mon chèr, I've missed you. What woman has stolen you away from me?" she said, her voice velvet huskiness. "I will have my servants toss her to the 'gators if she's stolen your heart away from me."

The woman flirted with Louis in a confident and coquettish manner. A stylish hat sat at a flirtatious tilt on her head, her dark hair hidden beneath the wide brim. Her clothes were the latest fashion and prominently showed off her curvaceous figure. Marian felt a twinge of envy.

"Evette, you know that if my heart were available, it would belong to you. But, alas, I have no heart," said Louis.

She reached up and patted Louis's cheek with her hand. "You lie, Monsieur, too easily. Don't think that you fool me. I hear how easily you break women's hearts."

Louis shook his head, taking her hand and placing it in the crook of his elbow. He gazed down at her upturned face. "It's all untrue. These women make up stories about me. I would give all women up for you, if I could."

"Oh please, I know better," she said as they walked through the door.

He shut the door behind him, effectively cutting off the rest of the widow's response. Marian turned back to her papers and sighed.

How would it feel to be able to greet men as if you were bestowing your presence upon them like a gift? To look them confidently in the eye and flirt with them in an obvious manner? Why couldn't she be so confident?

Perhaps because no man had ever wanted her in such a fashion.

She wished she were in Louis's office and could watch their interaction. She wanted to see how the widow flirted with Louis, take notes, and practice coquettish behavior on Louis, to see if he would react to her the same way.

Was she crazy? She needed less of Louis Fournet and his rakish personality, not more. She must never fall in love or marry a man like him again. Too much charm with so little substance had proved detrimental when she had been foolish enough to give her heart away before. Yet he was someone she could practice her attempts at flirtation on.

The sound of laughter drifted through the door and she felt a stab of envy. Right here in the office he flirted with one of his many women friends, while she sat across the hall straining to hear like a pathetic old maid living vicariously through others.

How would it feel to have a man respond to her the way Louis had responded to the widow? How powerful to know that she could tempt men and banter with them in such a way that they tripped all over themselves. Was there a school where women learned the art of social banter and flirtation? Could Marian attend special classes that taught her the art of seduction and temptation? Would she graduate with a degree in enticement?

Could any of this have helped keep her marriage from deteriorating to the point that her husband had sought other women?

She sighed. Maybe if Jean had stayed home enough for her to attempt seduction and charm, their marriage would have lasted. Or maybe his lack of desire for her would have brought the end quicker.

She frowned at the closed door. What *were* they doing behind that door?

It was none of her business!

With that thought, she jumped up and slammed her own door. She didn't want to think any more about what Evette and Louis were doing. She didn't want to think about how the widow might be seducing Louis. Marian had a business to run and a family to support and she didn't need any of the distractions Louis's women presented. After all, he wasn't her man.

Thirty minutes passed. Marian kept her focus on the new accounts she intended to retain. Anything to keep her mind busy and not think about the office across the hall.

A knock on her door interrupted her and she glanced up. "Come in."

Louis stuck his head around the doorframe. "Are you busy? I'd like to introduce you to someone."

She took a deep breath, not really wanting to meet the widow, but not sure how she could politely refuse.

"Who?" she asked, pretending she didn't know, the smile on her face feeling forced.

Louis pushed the door the rest of the way open and the widow swept in, holding out her hand. "Mrs. Cuvier, I'm Evette Simone, thank you for seeing me. It's a pleasure to meet you in person."

Marian stood and walked around her desk to greet the widow. "Thank you."

"I have a lot of respect for a woman who has ensconced herself in a man's world. I know you're in mourning, but I'm giving a small dinner party next Friday night and I would love to invite you to be my guest." She turned toward Louis. "Louis, you wouldn't mind escorting Mrs. Cuvier, would you?"

Louis glanced at Marian, his brows lifted, questioning. "I would enjoy being your escort to the party, Marian."

She looked from Louis to the widow, wanting to say no, but suddenly very curious about Evette and her dinner parties. "Yes, I'd be delighted."

"Wonderful." The widow held out her hand again. "I look forward to seeing you Friday night at my party."

"Thank you for the invitation," Marian replied.

"You're quite welcome." The widow turned to Louis and reached up to place a goodbye kiss on his cheek. "I would ask you to save your flirtations for me, but I know that's impossible. I'll talk to you later."

Louis smiled. "Always."

"Goodbye," Marian called as the widow swept out of the room almost as quickly as she had entered.

As she walked down the hall, they could hear her heels tapping against the wooden floor in a steady rhythm. The scent of her perfume lingered in the office, a pleasant flowery scent. Marian felt like an awkward girl compared to the woman who had just left.

"So what do you think of the notorious widow Simone?"

Marian shrugged as she gazed up at Louis expectantly and tilted her head to one side. "She's beautiful and seems very pleasant."

"She is," Louis responded.

Marian sighed, the sound almost whimsical as she

gazed off in the distance. "I wonder what men find attractive in a woman like that? I'm not being critical, I'd like to understand what men find fascinating about certain women."

Louis begin to laugh.

She turned and stared at him. "Why are you laughing? While I've been here there seems to be a steady stream of women through your office, and all of them appear confident and sure of their womanly appeal. Is this why you're attracted to these women?"

"I'm sorry, Marian. I'm laughing because you're the only woman I know who would try to search out the reason why men find women attractive."

He took a step closer to her, the smile on his face somehow tender.

Marian refused to budge though she wanted to run back behind the desk to have as much furniture between them as possible.

"Let me try to explain. Men are attracted to women for different reasons. With some women, it's their smile. Could be the way they laugh, or the way they look, or what they say to you. Most of the time, it just happens and you're not even aware of their allure, until you realize you can't seem to get that woman out of your mind."

"Is that the way it is with you?" she asked, her voice coming out in a breathless rush.

He moved closer, reaching out to push a tendril of hair away from her face, his eyes large and dark. "Sometimes."

Marian swallowed, her throat feeling tight and constricted. "Are you attracted to the widow?"

"Evette? She's beautiful and charming, as well as witty. I enjoy bantering with her. Just as I enjoy flirting with you."

"Me?" she interrupted suddenly feeling very uncomfortable.

"Yes. Don't you enjoy flirting? Most women enjoy trifling with a man and testing their womanly wiles."

"I—I've never been a flirt. Jean and I never 'bantered.' And I certainly don't think I have any womanly wiles," she said, the palms of her hands beginning to perspire.

Louis nodded. "Jean wasn't very bright when it came to women. He seemed not to notice what was right beneath his nose, because you definitely have womanly wiles. Very nice ones too."

"Oh?" Marian raised her chin and gazed at Louis with interest. The conversation had taken a definite personal turn. Somehow she had to get it back on more familiar ground, where she felt less exposed. "Wiles are not physical. Wiles are to entice or deceive.

He grinned. "I know. Entice is what I meant."

She shook her head. "I'm hardly enticing."

"I disagree," his voice was deep and sure and sent tremors through her body.

She felt her face flush and she thought she could hear her heart pounding. The conversation had definitely gotten personal again.

And then she asked the question that had bothered her almost from the day they first met. "Do you notice the women around you, all the time?"

"Pretty much."

She pursed her mouth. "Then I would have thought you would be attracted to a woman as lovely as the widow."

"I didn't say I wasn't," he said watching her. "Evette is beautiful, but she's the type of woman who will never marry again. And I usually expect more from a woman than I think she could give me."

"What do you expect?" Marian asked risking the conversation turning personal again. But she had to know.

"I like a woman who greets a man and makes him feel welcome and accepted. Whose attention makes him feel special, like he's the king of the world and she's his queen." He stepped in close and cupped her face in his hands, tilting her face up toward him. Marian took a deep breath and felt as if the room seemed to recede from the edges of her vision.

"I like a woman who laughs easily and isn't afraid of getting mussed." She swallowed, feeling as if her throat were the size of a single thread.

His voice dropped lower. "I like the way a woman's eyes sparkle when she's excited." He ran his finger down the bridge of her nose. "The way her nose is gently turned up at the end and she raises it ever so slightly when she's angry." His fingers continued their path down her face to her lips. "The way her lips are soft and subtle and made for kissing. And the little sighs that come from between them when she's complete."

His thumb felt rough against her lower lip and she could scarcely breath. He was going to kiss her. She knew it, just as surely as she knew her next breath was just a heartbeat away. He lowered his mouth—then she heard Henry calling his name.

"Mr. Fournet?"

Louis stepped away from her immediately, breaking the spell that circled them. He swore, and then gazed with longing at her, taking several deep, long breaths and shook his head as if trying to clear it.

He glanced at her once again, his face a worried frown. The spell completely broken. "Excuse me."

He walked from the room, his step sure, once more in control, but when he reached the door, he glanced back at her with one last look of longing.

Marian sank down into her chair and released a heavy sigh. She wanted to cry. His intention had been to kiss her and she'd longed for that kiss, ached for the feel of his lips against hers.

She glanced at the doorway through which he'd disappeared feeling as if the walls were closing in on her. She needed to get out of here. She needed fresh air.

They had been mere seconds from pressing their lips together. She grabbed her reticule, jumped up from the chair and all but ran out the door. God, she'd desired that kiss more than anything she had ever wanted in her life.

What was wrong with her? All she could think about was being in his arms. Foolish, very foolish indeed.

Marian jumped into her carriage, leaving the office behind.

"Take me to my sister's house," she demanded.

She needed to speak with Claire. The questions and the doubts had to end and Claire was the only person she trusted to help her decide what to do.

At thirty years of age, she had needs. Too many years had passed since she'd been with a man and the last times with Jean had been less than memorable. Suddenly her body refused to be ignored, screaming for attention every time Louis entered the room, she wanted him. No longer could she deny her curiosity, if being intimate with Louis would satisfy her.

She'd never in her entire life thought of being loved this way. Why now? Why had this man awakened her sleeping body?

When the carriage pulled to a stop, Marian jumped out and all but ran to her sister's door. She pounded on the door until her servant opened the portal. "Is Claire at home?"

The servant looked startled to see her.

"No, ma'am. She's spending the afternoon at the Dupree's residence. She asked that the carriage pick her up at three-thirty."

"Tell her driver not to bother. I will pick her up in my carriage and bring her home."

At three-twenty, Marian sat outside the Dupree's home waiting for her sister to appear. She took her fan and tried to cool herself in the stifling carriage, but the summer air hung heavy, the clouds bulging with moisture. At any moment they would burst, releasing the sweet rain.

If only they could cleanse this desire from her and leave her in peace. But her mind demanded answers for her injured self-pride. Was she really so undesirable?

Finally Claire came out the door expecting to see her own carriage. Her eyes widened in surprise to see Marian and she hurried to the waiting carriage.

"Good Lord, Marian, what's wrong? Is one of the children ill?" she asked climbing up into the carriage.

"Everyone is fine. Well, everyone but myself." Marian took a deep breath and released it slowly. "I had to speak with someone or go mad."

"What's wrong, Marian? You're worrying me. You look tense."

Marian shook her head, laughing. "I am. This is just difficult to speak about."

"No one has hurt you?" Claire asked suddenly fearful.

"No. I need to ask you a very personal question."

Claire looked stunned. "You drove out here to ask me a question?"

"Yes." Marian paused and looked at her sister, needing the truth. "You've never told me directly, but several years ago I heard rumors that you had taken a lover."

"I hardly think that's any of your concern," Claire said defensively.

"I'm not condemning your actions, but rather need your advice." Marian took a deep breath and released it slowly. "I want to take a lover."

Claire settled back against the cushions of the carriage and smiled at her younger sister. "Dear God. I'm shocked to hear you say that. But pleased." She laughed. "I've often thought that a lover would be good for you."

"Really?" Marian said, surprised.

"Yes, you should have taken one years ago."

"I couldn't, not while I was married to Jean. But now I have so many questions about myself, Claire, that I want resolved. Though I don't have a clue as to how a woman lets a man know she's interested in sharing her bed with him!"

The carriage bounced over a pothole just as a loud clap of thunder echoed in the streets of the French Quarter. "Oh dear, I think we're in for a shower."

"Good, the driver can't hear our discussion and you can tell me how to seduce this man I'm interested in," Marian said in a rush. "I don't know where to begin."

Claire grinned at her sister. "May I inquire as to who you've taken an interest in?"

"It's hardly a secret. Louis Fournet, who else could it be?"

"Louis?" Claire asked. "But he's given you so much trouble since Jean died. Are you sure of this, Marian?"

"He's the only man I spend my time with nowadays."

"You're certain you're ready to make him your lover?" Claire asked. "He is quite versed with the ladies. I don't want you to get hurt."

Marian sighed and heard the first drops of rain hit the top of the carriage. "I must know if Jean searched out two other women to marry because of me. Because I lack some quality. I need to know if I am a desirable wife and lover, or if the problem was Jean's."

Claire shook her head. "You know my thoughts on your dead husband, though I understand your need to know your abilities as a woman. But what about Louis? How will he react to all of this?"

"I don't know. He's obviously bedded lots of women and possesses a casual attitude toward them. Although I could never treat lovemaking in such a callous manner, I have no intention of making any demands on him. I'm not looking for anything permanent. Just a lover for one night. Just someone to help me see if I'm . . . desirable. He's the only man I know well enough to consider."

"You're certain of this, Marian? You know if you do this it's going to be hard to face him every day in the office afterwards. Are you sure you can do this?"

Marian glanced out the window at the rain that cascaded from the sky like a waterfall, pouring down on the earth. She watched as people scrambled to find shelter, splashing as they ran through puddles.

A woman of the streets stood beneath a street lamp letting the water trickle down her face and over her clothes. She danced a sensuous dance in the pouring rain, her skimpy clothing clinging to her curves in a way that was both erotic and enticing. Marian longed to be as free, so seductive and alluring that you were certain of your beauty.

For just a moment Marian wanted to join her in the rain dance, as the prostitute turned her face toward the heavens letting the rain cleanse her.

If only Marian could wash away the self-doubts, the years of marriage and Jean's subsequent betrayal had bequeathed her.

Marian returned her gaze to the inside of the coach and her sister. "I must find out if I'm a normal, healthy woman or doubt myself the rest of my life."

"Dear God, I never realized how badly he hurt you until this moment," Claire said softly to her sister.

Marian glanced down at her hands folded tightly in her lap, remembering their near kiss.

"For the first time in my life, I want a man and I don't know what to do." She glanced up at her sister, tears pricking the inside of her lids. "Tell me what to do, Claire. How can I show Louis I want to sleep with him?"

Claire rubbed her hands together gleefully. "Oh Marian, this is going to be so much fun. We'll plan the seduction together and believe me, dear Louis will be unable to say no."

Louis hurried down the street to meet Evette for dinner that evening, wondering why he had agreed to this meeting. They were friends and often joked about becoming lovers, but had never taken that next step. Somehow he understood they were meant to be only friends, as their expectations in life were different.

He walked into Antoine's Restaurant and saw her waiting for him.

"*Chéri*, I begin to think that you had found someone else to dine with tonight," she said giving him a sultry smile.

"I'm sorry, Evette. A problem at the office kept me," he said, his mind picturing Marian and the way he'd last seen her.

The memory of her standing there in shock, trembling, ready for his kiss, haunted him still. Becoming involved with Marian could be dangerous. When he notified her of a buyer for the business, she would hate him. Kissing her sweet full lips would only fuel her revulsion when she realized he'd sold her out. Still her mouth tempted him, during working hours, but especially when she haunted his mind in the middle of the night.

"That problem wouldn't be a young widow who sits across the hall from you, would it?" Evette asked candidly, jerking him out of his reverie.

Before he could answer, the maitre d'hôtel approached. "Your table is ready."

"Thank you," Louis said, and took Evette by the elbow.

The man pulled out her chair and seated her. Louis sat across from her, flipping out the tails of his tail coat as he sat.

"Could you bring us two glasses of Bordeaux?" he told the waiter.

"Yes, sir," he said, and disappeared.

Evette glanced across the table at him, the corners of her mouth turned up in slight smile, her brows lifted. "You did not answer my question."

"Sorry, we were interrupted. No, Marian is not the reason I'm late tonight. The Captain of one of our boats that was due to leave today has gone missing."

"Oh, the trials of the working man."

Louis waved her words away. "It's been taken care of and now I'm here to spend the evening with you."

She smiled and opened a delicate fan to fan herself. "I'm glad."

An awkward silence seemed to envelop them as Louis

sought for something to say, while his mind was filled with thoughts of Marian.

"What did you think of Marian?"

"I think she's very beautiful and much too young to remain a widow for long," she said watching him carefully.

"She claims she will never remarry."

Evette nodded her head. "It's understandable for her to feel this way. To face the scandal that has been forced upon her with Jean's murder would certainly sour one against the idea of forever after. Maybe Jean was a terrible lover and she's never experienced passion."

"What do you mean? She was married and had two children," Louis said thinking that was unlikely.

Evette smiled and leaned forward, her voice barely above a whisper. "Yes, but just because you have intimate relations with a man, does not mean that he has shown you the fires of pleasure. Many women never experience *le grand orgasme.*"

Louis glanced around at the tables around them. Dear God, had anyone heard her? "Evette, are you really saying this to me?"

"Why not?" She reached over and slapped the back of his hand with her fan. "You're not a school boy, so quit acting like one. You should know this is true."

"The idea of her and Jean together is sickening," he said, as the waiter set their drinks down.

Though he knew it was ridiculous, the thought of Marian disrobing for Jean left him angry. Though she bore him two children, Jean's mistresses had received better treatment than Marian and that bothered him most of all.

He glanced across the table to see Evette watching him. "Why are you looking at me that way?"

She smiled. "I think things have changed while I was away. Somehow I get the feeling that you are different."

He frowned. "Give me a couple of weeks and I'll be myself again. With Jean's death, a lot of things changed."

"Yes, I see that." She sipped her wine. "I also heard they arrested one of the wives for his murder."

"I hadn't heard. I met them all at the reading of the will. Layla Cuvier seemed to be in shock at that time. It's hard to believe such an innocent looking woman could kill. She's hardly more than a child."

"No, I do not believe it," Evette said.

"Her servant told the police that Layla gave Jean laudanum at night to help him sleep. She had the opportunity to poison him," said Louis.

Evette shook her head. "Spoken like a man. Think about this, why would she kill her only source of income? Now she has nowhere to go."

"Even if she found out he was already married?" Louis questioned.

Evette nodded. "The woman was wandering the streets when they found her. No woman chooses that kind of life. Not even a wife who has to put up with a husband she detests." Evette took a deep breath. "I tell you, they arrested the wrong person."

"Marian told her she could continue to live in the house in Baton Rouge. Why would she wander the streets of New Orleans?"

"According to my source down at the police station, the authorities would not let her return to Baton Rouge and the hotel kicked her out. No money, no home. She's been sleeping wherever she could find a place."

Louis shivered. "I wonder if Marian knows her plight? I'll need to tell her as soon as possible."

He pulled out his pocket watch and noticed the time,

the urge to talk to Marian overwhelming. Evette had tickets for the opera and they had only an hour to get there. He frowned. Maybe he should consider skipping the opera tonight?

"What if we miss . . ."

She stiffened and her eyes grew large. "Don't say it!"

He stopped. "I was going to ask you if we had time to run by Marian's house and let me tell her."

"Marian again." She gazed at him quizzically. "I think dear friend, that you are much more interested in the Widow Cuvier than you are letting on. I think your affections have changed and you are not quite aware of this new fondness."

Louis didn't say anything. Could she be right? He was all too aware of his attraction to Jean's widow, but he also realized any tryst would be impossible, especially after he found a buyer for Cuvier Shipping.

Though lately he'd begun to notice that she seldom left his thoughts and the realization bothered him.

He reached across the table and grabbed Evette's hands. He could still play the rakish flirt. "Evette, my affections are still my own. Though I must admit a certain fondness for a very beautiful widow, known for stringing men along."

She gazed at him, still frowning. She lifted her chin. "Keep talking and you may yet manage to salvage the evening. Though I don't believe a word of the pretty lies you're telling me."

Louis lifted her hand and pressed his lips to her skin. "Your intelligence and wit, along with your friendship, are why I continue to see you."

She laughed.

The words were true, but still he couldn't deny that

part of him wanted to find some excuse to leave and go to Marian. To tell her how the police had found Layla Cuvier wandering the streets. But would Marian care or was his need to discuss Layla's troubles just an excuse to see Marian and finish what they started in her office this afternoon?

CHAPTER ELEVEN

On Friday of the following week, Louis knocked on the door of Marian's home to drive her to Evette's dinner party. Anxiety twisted his insides at the thought of the coming party. More than once, Evette had expressed the opinion that Louis seemed more than just attracted to Marian. And while he admitted he admired the widow, his infatuation was merely a physical thing that he experienced with many women. Why should Marian be any different?

Intelligent, beautiful, witty, and strong, she'd attracted him like no other. Yet lately, he couldn't seem to get her out of his mind.

The last time he'd been to the house on Josephine Street had been to tell her of Layla's arrest for Jean's murder, but the police had already informed Marian.

The door swung open and he gazed in at Marian, looking radiant in a low-cut gray silk dress that reflected the color of her eyes, showing her enticing cleavage. He couldn't help but stare at her, openmouthed.

"Do I know you?" he asked.

She smiled. "Of course you do, silly."

"I don't believe we've met. I'm here to pick up Marian Cuvier. You must be her younger sister."

Marian laughed and then spun around for him. "Claire and I did a little shopping for tonight."

"I see that." He reached over and kissed her cheek, the sweet seductive smell of magnolias tempting him. "You look beautiful."

She blushed. "Thank you."

"I didn't expect to see you answering the door. Where are your servants?"

She smiled. "I gave them all the night off."

"Who's watching the children?" He glanced down at his hand. "I brought Philip a new baseball. I thought I might get a couple of pitches in with him before we left."

"Sorry. Claire took Renée and Philip to stay at her house overnight. I'm the only one here." She opened the door wider. "We're still early if you'd like to come in and have a drink."

"Thanks, but no. But let me leave this baseball here. I don't think Evette would be pleased if I started to pitch the ball at her party."

"Good idea," Marian said stepping back to let him in.

He stepped inside and laid the baseball on the hall stand in the entry way, as Marian moved close to his side.

He gazed down at her, noting her hair was gathered loosely in a clasp, the dark curls cascading past her shoulders. Tonight was the first time he'd seen her hair loose and her face looked younger, softer, and more feminine than he'd recalled.

She walked past him into the den and turned out the gas lamps. When she came back into the entry hall, she picked up a gray silk shawl that matched her dress. He helped her place the silk folds around her shoulders, a sudden rush of protectiveness toward her catching him off guard.

"If you're ready, I think I am," she said.

With no lights burning in the house, a dark quietness penetrated the atmosphere. He cast a worried glance around the shadowed hallway. "Maybe you should leave a light on?"

"I considered it, but I just hate to leave a lamp on when there's no one at home. If you don't mind, I thought that when you brought me back, you could come in while I lit the gas lamps."

"All right," he said. He could understand why she would not want to come into a darkened house alone, but it seemed strange that she'd let the servants off for the night.

They walked out the door and Marian turned the key in the lock and slipped it into her handbag.

"You know Evette only lives three blocks away. There's a cool breeze tonight, if you'd like we could walk instead of riding in the buggy."

"I didn't know she lived so close. That sounds lovely."

Louis took her hand and placed it in the crook of his arm and they set off at a leisurely pace, strolling down the street, taking care to stay away from any puddles left from an early afternoon shower.

"Who does Mrs. Simone invite to these dinners?"

"All kinds of people. Her parties are usually entertaining and the people interesting."

They crossed Josephine Street and turned on Magnolia. "I've missed going to parties. When I was a girl, Claire and I went all the time. But once the children were born, I never attended many parties."

"But Jean liked parties," Louis said.

She turned her big gray eyes on him and smiled, her rosy lips full and inviting. "Let's not talk about Jean tonight. I want to have fun and when I think of him, pleasure is not what usually comes to mind."

He chuckled. "All right, I won't mention his name again this evening. Let's have a good time."

Louis didn't blame her. In fact, he wanted nothing more than to spend the evening with her. They didn't have to go to Evette's party, he just wanted to be with Marian.

Again, he felt physical attraction to Marian that he didn't know what to do with. Well, that wasn't exactly true, there was one thing he wanted to do, but he was desperately trying to keep the thoughts and images of Marian, the business partner, in check. Tonight he was her escort for the evening, and tomorrow he would return to trying to sell the business she clung to. Being with Marian would only complicate a difficult situation. For just a moment he felt a sense of guilt tinged with sorrow, but he quickly pushed the feeling away.

Strolling down the street, they came upon a puddle that stretched several feet in front of them. It was deep and muddy enough to ruin the hem of Marian's dress and too wide to jump. They stood there a moment staring at the pool of water.

"My dress. What do we do now?" Marian asked.

Louis glanced around trying to find a way around and saw mud in all directions. "There's only one thing we can do."

He bent down and scooped her up into his arms.

"Louis," she exclaimed and then started to laugh, her voice bubbly in the evening air. "Put me down."

Her dress fluttered in the breeze exposing her lacy drawers and he wished the breeze would blow the hem of her dress higher. Just enough to give him a glimpse of her long graceful limbs. Quickly, she pushed the skirt down, covering her feminine undergarments.

The evening shadows loomed as he stepped across the puddle and stood her gingerly on the ground again, his arms feeling particularly empty as he released her. What was it about this woman that kept him in a constant state of awareness? Still, she wore pretty pantaloons and he had caught a glimpse of a trim ankle.

"I had no coat to throw across the water," he said grinning at her as if he'd just rescued the princess.

She shook her head and laughed again. "I've never been carried across a puddle before. Thank you, Mr. Fournet, for being such a gentleman."

"My pleasure, ma'am." Feeling her in his arms, the sweet smell of magnolias, and her satiny skin against his more than rewarded his efforts.

They weren't far from Evette's, yet he wished they could avoid the dinner party. So seldom were they alone and he enjoyed the times when it was just the two of them.

He liked the way she laughed and the way her eyes twinkled when she teased him. For more than a week, he'd found himself watching for her, waiting, hoping to catch a glimpse of her, and have her glance at him from across the hall. Sometimes he felt as if they were dancing, mirroring each other's moves, circling one another, waiting for that moment when they would move into each other's arms.

They arrived at Evette's home and a servant ushered them through the entry hall into a room where a large wooden staircase spiraled to the next floor. A crystal chandelier hung suspended from the ceiling, the lighting soft, and music played under the sound of talk. They were led into the main room of the house, where a small crowd of people gathered, listening to a man playing a piano.

"Mrs. Cuvier, I'm so glad that you came," Evette said, coming forward to greet them. She turned her attention to Louis, grabbing both of his hands and reached up and kissed his cheeks. "As always, a pleasure, *chéri.*"

She stepped back and released his hands. "Please help yourselves to a drink and join the others. We're still waiting for a few guests, but we should eat soon."

A servant approached them with a tray of drinks and Louis handed Marian a glass of champagne.

"Thank you. Do you know many of these people?" Marian asked Louis, as she gazed about the room filled with men and women dressed in the latest fashions. He nodded to someone he knew.

"Yes, most of them have been to other dinner parties Evette has held," Louis said watching her.

Marian sipped her champagne and gazed up at him. The light shimmered from her smoky eyes with a glint that hinted at mischief. "Do you mind if I ask you a personal question? If you wish, you can tell me it's none of my business."

He watched her expression, wishing he could kiss the upturned corners of her mouth. "All right."

"Are you and Evette just friends or something more that's none of my business?"

Comforted he could answer her question without offending her, he took Marian by the arm and led her toward a loveseat in the corner. "We're just good friends, nothing more."

"Friends are nice to have," Marian said, a relieved

expression on her face, though why he didn't understand. She had nothing to fear from Evette. They sat down on the loveseat and sipped their champagne. "You know, we really should mingle."

"Later," he said not wanting to share her for some reason. He picked up one of her loose curls and ran the soft dark lock of hair between his fingers. "I don't think I've seen you with your hair down before."

"No. This is the first time in years I've worn it loose."

"So you decided to let your hair down tonight?" he asked. "Is there something you're not telling me? A particular gentleman you wish to pursue?"

She smiled up at him her eyes twinkling. "I'm not the pursuing type. That's you. Though I've recently decided that I need to change. I need to become bolder, go after more of what I really want."

"Oh really," Louis said surprised, noticing the flirtatious air that suddenly surrounded her. "I thought you were already doing that with the shipping company."

"Yes, I guess I am," Marian acknowledged. "But there are other areas of my life that I've neglected. Areas that are just as important."

"Like what?" he asked curiously.

She leaned closer to him and whispered in his ear, her soft breath tickling him. "I've decided to take a lover."

Louis gasped just as he took a sip of champagne. He started to choke.

"After all, I am a widow, I can do that now."

Louis sat coughing, trying to catch his breath, unable to speak, only stare at Marian. My God, was she serious?

Marian pounded him on the back. "Are you all right? I guess I should have waited until you weren't drinking to let you know my plans."

"You are joking, right?" Louis said, as he gasped for

air, the image of her naked with another man causing him sudden discomfort.

Oh, God, he had to save her from herself. He was going to have to protect her from a lecherous man who would only use and abandon her.

"No," she said, her face an innocent mask. "I'm serious."

Before Louis could recover from the shocking news Marian had just delivered, Evette found them, her gown rustling as she bustled about. "Darlings, there you are. Everyone is here now, so we're going to the dining room. Louis, I've seated Marian next to you. Take good care of her."

She hurried off to hustle more people toward the dining room.

Louis, who could finally breathe again, stood and helped Marian to her feet. Who could she intend to seduce?

Jean had been dead for almost three months and already she was searching for someone to take his place. Yet, she hadn't said remarry. She specifically said she sought a lover. So why was Marian suddenly interested in a man's touch? Could Evette's theory be true, that she'd never experienced passion?

He took her by the arm and they walked into the dining room. He seated her at the table, his mind cataloging all the men who worked at Cuvier Shipping, their customers, and the men he met at Jean's funeral. None of the candidates were worthy and the thought of her with another man left an unpleasant taste in his mouth.

He leaned close to her ear and whispered. "So just who are you planning to seduce?"

She smiled at him, her gray eyes sparkling in the candlelight from the table. "Now that, dear sir, is something a lady does not disclose."

Louis stared at her stunned for the second time that evening. For a moment he couldn't move. Could her refusal to answer him mean that she intended to seduce him?

The blood seemed to drain from his limbs into one area of his body, the area that didn't need to be reminded of the beautiful woman sitting at his side.

Who was he kidding? He'd wanted Marian for months now and suddenly it seemed as if he might be going to get his opportunity. Tonight.

The reasons for her dismissal of the servants and the children's overnight stay at Claire's suddenly became clear. Everyone was conveniently gone so they could have a night of passion. If he went back to the house on Josephine Street, he could probably make love to Marian. Hadn't he been considering this for weeks? Suddenly he knew he wanted this more than anything. He wanted Marian.

The thought tantalized him, and left him hungry with desire. Part of him wanted to run out the door and take Marian now, while another part of him warned of the complications this could create. He pushed the thought aside, he wanted Marian.

He swallowed, his gaze returning to the woman who'd just given him something to contemplate during dinner. She sat there smiling coyly at him and suddenly he knew without a doubt. Yes, she'd decided to take a lover, but it wasn't anyone he didn't know.

She meant to seduce him.

"Eat quickly, Marian," he whispered. "Eat quickly, so we can leave."

On the walk home, tension wrapped around them like a cloak. Marian felt so aware of the man walking beside her, she could barely think. She felt like such an idiot for divulging so much information to Louis at the party. She hadn't meant to tell him that much, just tantalize him a bit. But the more she thought about the elaborate scheme she and Claire had hatched, the more ridiculous the plot seemed.

In fact, the closer the moment came, the more Marian just wanted to back out. Obviously she had never pleased Jean with their lovemaking. How did she know Louis wouldn't feel the same? What if Louis wanted nothing more to do with her? What if she couldn't go through with the act? Or what if she did?

Dear God, she was mad. A sane and rational woman would never consider intimacy with a man known for escorting so many different women. But that was exactly the reason she wanted him. No other man she knew would be suitable for her experiment tonight. Marian could be intimate with Louis without worrying about ties being forged between them. After all he did this with other women all the time. With him she could prove to herself that she was desirable.

When they arrived at the house, Marian fumbled in her reticule for her key, her hands shaking nervously. Oh God, what must she do now? Marriage had not prepared her for seduction.

He reached for her handbag and withdrew the key, placing the metal in the lock and opening the door easily.

They moved into the darkened hallway, awareness running like a taut wire between them.

"Thank you," she said.

He stepped up to her and before she could turn away, he pulled her into his arms and pressed her back against the door, his hardened body clearly indicating what he had in mind.

His mouth covered hers in the darkness, consuming her in an exciting, demanding kiss that left her clinging to him as he expertly savored her. His tongue parted her lips, searching, exploring her mouth as his hands slid down her torso. Just when she thought she would expire in his arms, he broke the kiss, his breath harsh-sounding in the darkness.

The doubts came rushing in and she wanted to tell him to hurry before she changed her mind.

With one hand he gently held her chin and turned her face back to his gaze. In the darkness she was unable to see the expression in his eyes, but she could feel the strength and power in his limbs. She leaned into him, absorbing his might.

"Do you want to do this, Marian?" he asked, his voice so deep and warm touched a chord deep inside her that left her hungry and wanting. Still pressed against the door, the dark house surrounding them, he touched his lips to the side of her neck. "Be certain."

Wherever his lips touched her flesh, she felt a tingle, causing her to shiver in anticipation. "I do . . . but I'm afraid."

His teeth found her earlobe and then his breath grazed her ear, his tongue sending more shivers through her, as her breath quickened.

"What are you afraid of?" he asked, taking his time, nibbling on her ear, his hands caressing her through the silken dress.

"I . . . I just am." She couldn't tell him the truth that she was so undesirable that her husband had not been to her bed in many years. "It's been such a long time," she finally said, pressing her breasts against his chest, feeling them crushed and aching against him.

He kissed her temple, her face, moving closer to her mouth, taking a lifetime to reach her lips. God, she'd waited what felt like an eternity to feel his lips again, and now, all she wanted for him to do was take her.

He released her and pulled her through the darkened hallway into the family room, with its comfortable sofas and tall chairs.

"Have you ever made love in this room before?" he asked, his voice low and breathy.

Stunned, she pulled back and gazed up at him. "No, of course not. Why?"

In the moonlight from the window, Louis stared at her as if he could see deep down into her soul. A shiver of anticipation went through her at his gaze.

"Because the first time I take you, I want no memories coming between us."

For a moment her breath ceased and whatever last bit of hesitation she'd had disappeared. Suddenly she wanted Louis more than anything. The implied promise of no memories was enough to convince her the time for hesitation was over.

"But, what if I—" she said, her breath coming in fast rushes.

He put his finger against her mouth. "Hush, Marian."

Louis slanted his mouth over hers, his lips covering hers and the kiss she had dreamed of for so long was suddenly upon her, whirling her away. The damp heat of his mouth engulfed hers and she gave herself to his expert mouth.

Was she doing this correctly? Did Louis feel the same sense of pleasure? Did he understand that she wanted to experience passion only tonight, that there were no promises for tomorrow?

He wooed her mouth, her body straining against his, aching for the promise of fulfillment, while slowly he tasted her as if the moon would never set on this night. Marian swayed against the rock hardness of his chest, her limbs sluggish, her mind swirling with numbing pleasure.

Maybe she wasn't giving him pleasure the correct way, but he certainly had no problem providing her gratification.

She dropped the shawl from her shoulders, letting it slide to the floor. She reached up to encircle his neck, holding on to him as if she were afraid she would fall.

With the silk shawl removed, the tops of her shoulders lay exposed to his gaze. His mouth left hers to explore the bare skin at his perusal. Her lips were bereft without his, and she sighed with regret, wanting only the return of that sweet plunderer to bring her delight.

This night of passion belonged to her and she reached out a tentative hand and pulled his mouth back to hers. She wanted to experience more of the way his lips explored her own, parting them, sending tingles to the tips of her toes.

He laughed, the sound deep and vibrant as his mouth covered hers once again, his obliging lips spiraling delight through her. His fingers reached for the buttons on the back of her dress and he undid them one by one, until his arms could reach no further. Releasing her lips, he placed both hands around her waist and spun her around. Pulling her in tight against him, her back fit snugly against the hard length of him. He moved his hips against hers, letting her feel his erection hard against her buttocks.

God, he did want her and she thrilled at the realization!

His lips traced the curvature of her neck, while his fingers began to work on the rest of her buttons.

"Do you like to be kissed here?" he asked, as his lips grazed the top of her shoulder.

"Or do you prefer it here?" he asked, kissing the bare skin along her spine.

Marian shivered. "There! There!"

"Here?" he said, his voice low and breathy, his hands still struggling with her buttons.

"Yes," she gasped, arching her back.

"Like this?" he teased, feathering a light kiss across her sensitive flesh.

"Oh, yes," she said, her voice almost a whimper.

"What about here?" he asked, kissing a little lower, pushing down her dress until a smoky silk pool appeared at her feet. Her petticoat followed, falling to the floor in a rustle of netting and lace.

She moaned her low and throaty response. Marian stepped out of her dress, and then stood with her back to him, in a lacy corset cover, her French drawers covered by her chemise, feeling exposed and vulnerable. Doubt crossed her mind. There was still time to back out.

He must have sensed her hesitation, because he pulled her tight to him, so that she fit snug against him, her back to his front. He feathered hot moist kisses, and his fingers skimmed her body, pausing when they reached her breasts.

Marian felt stirrings deep within her belly and an urgency for him to take her began to build.

"Louis, do this quickly!" she whispered in the dark.

He laughed softly, his breath sending shivers down her back. "We've got all night, Marian. I'm not going anywhere."

All night? What might he do that could take all night?

Desire curled inside her tighter and tighter, making her breathless with want for him. He pulled her corset cover over her head and tossed it to the floor where it joined her dress. She stood feeling naked and vulnerable. When would he back out if he found her unattractive? When would he tell her he'd changed his mind?

She wanted this so badly, but still fear mixed with her desire. She was determined not to give in to her fright, but to experience everything that Louis offered her tonight.

He took her hand and pulled her to the nearest settee where he sat down and placed her between his legs. Wearing only her corset, her French drawers, and chemise, she watched him reach for her stockings. Slowly he pulled down first one stocking and then the second one, caressing each leg as he removed the silk from her limbs. That simple caress left her muscles feeling like liquid, hot to the touch.

His hands glided up her stomach not stopping until he found her swelling breasts. He held her breast in his palm like a precious piece of gold and then placed his mouth on the pebble-like kernel that stood up through the material.

Lovingly, he suckled her breast through her chemise, until she thought her knees would buckle beneath the onslaught of pleasure. When he released her, she sagged against him, gasping for air.

The corset cinched her ribs and her waist, pushing up her full breasts to spill over the top of the whalebone.

"Hmm," he said, gazing at her appreciatively in the almost dark. "Let me remove this thing from you."

He turned her around to untie the strings of her corset and she realized that soon she would be naked before him. A shiver of fear went through her, but she pushed the doubt from her mind.

He released her corset and then tossed the torturous piece to the floor. She stood in her chemise and drawers, her nervousness beginning to build. Was she mad?

In the darkness she heard the rustle of clothing and

knew he must be removing his own clothes. She pictured him naked in her mind and her pulse accelerated, wishing she could see him in the darkness. Knowing it was mere moments before they would be joined.

For the first time in her life, at the risk of her reputation, she was taking action to find out if she were indeed a woman desirable for lovemaking and she wanted this night more than anything.

Tonight, this moment was her chance to learn about herself. If she really were a desirable woman. In the last few months Louis had become so important to her and it felt natural to be here with him at this moment.

His hand gripped her drawers, when she stayed him again.

Dear God, wait, was all she could think.

"Wait," she said suddenly, fear overwhelming her.

He kissed the top of her head. "Oh, Marian I've wanted you for so long."

"Me? You wanted me?" she asked, her breath coming in little gasps.

"Yes, you," he said, and as he lifted her, she felt his nakedness as he carried her to the sofa. He sat her down and then his mouth covered hers once again. The anxiety that had almost overwhelmed her disappeared under the onslaught of his lips against hers. His tongue swirling and building a need that she'd long since forgotten.

Years had passed since her last lovemaking experience and she couldn't remember this mounting pleasure, the pulsating desire and onslaught of emotion.

She felt dizzy and flushed and parts of her body were more alive than she could remember. And now she wanted him to hurry to reach the end of the race, but Louis moved at the slow pace of a field hand on a hot summer day. Lazy and slow, each caress building until her body trembled with readiness.

He released her lips, pulling her chemise over her head, and tossed it into the darkness.

His hand found her bare breast and she arched her back giving him easier access. She cried out as his tongue sought her nipple and she grasped his head holding him still.

This time when he pushed down her silk drawers, she helped him and soon the garment landed on the floor with the rest of their clothing. Soon she lay sprawled on the sofa, naked and waiting. He lay on the edge, his body half covering hers, their naked skin touching from chest to toe.

"God, you feel so good," he whispered in the darkness, his breath a feathery caress across her flesh. "So soft, so smooth."

She felt his heated flesh pressed against her, strong and vibrant and oh-so-ready to take her.

Tentatively she ran her hand down his back, lightly tracing his ribs with her fingertips. He shivered and she grew bolder. Reaching down to touch his passion, kissing the curve of his neck she stroked him, half waiting for him to tell her to stop, that no longer did he want her caresses but instead the only sound that came from his mouth was a moan of pure pleasure. Amazing, how a single sound can make you feel joyous, can confirm you are a woman who can rouse a man's passion, and build your own excitement to new heights never before attained. An expanding desire centered between her thighs left her wet with anticipation.

She was no virgin and she knew what happened next, but still she had never experienced this restlessness, this sense of need, but still he lingered, caressing her breasts, his tongue ravishing her. She was almost past the point of wanting him inside her.

"Louis . . ." she gasped, trying to convey her sense of urgency.

"Yes?" he asked, his voice raspy.

"Please—," she said, arching her back toward him.

"Is this what you need?" he asked, his hand trailing down to cup her feminine mound.

His finger parted her folds and delved inside her, spinning a magic spell that left her to claw at the edge of the sofa.

"Yes," she gasped, as he pushed her to new heights of pleasure that touched every part of her. "Please, Louis."

He moved between her knees and entered her in one swift movement, filling her to the hilt. She welcomed him into her body, wrapped her arms around him, moaning her pleasure into his shoulder.

With each stroke, all the years of feeling so inadequate, unfeminine, and rejected, disappeared, releasing Marian from doubt. Louis wanted her, he'd said so and she could feel him inside her, loving her. Warmth reflected from his blue eyes and an intense intimacy she'd never experienced before showed in his gaze as he stared at her. Passion overtook her and she lost herself in his gaze.

She felt so natural with him, so complete and she clutched his back, her hands moving down to grip his buttocks as he filled her. With each thrust Marian felt a sense of renewal, of rebirth and the burgeoning sense of herself as a very desirable woman.

With each stroke Louis showed her the meaning of pleasure between a man and a woman. And she realized she was complete, she was whole and somehow at last all right.

A tightening spiral of pleasure built within her, a feeling so intense she couldn't remember experiencing anything quite like it before. In the moments of shattering contractions and releases, her mind tumbled out of control, and she cried out her pleasure, just as she felt Louis swell within her and heard him cry out her name.

They lay there recovering, locked in each other's arms, their breaths slowly returning to normal when Marian felt the prick of tears behind her eyelids.

She swallowed and blinked trying to hold them back, but there was no stopping the uncontrollable flow of tears once they started down her cheeks.

"Marian, I . . ." he froze, and then rolled to his side and put his hand on her cheek, feeling the dampness. "My God, you're crying. Are you all right?"

"Yes. You healed me."

CHAPTER TWELVE

Louis held Marian, stroking her soft back gently. "What are you talking about, healing? What do you mean?"

She sniffed. "We promised not to mention his name. I don't want to spoil this night."

"I don't care, Marian. Just tell me. Why are you crying?"

"Nothing." She reached up and caressed his face. "You are wonderful. I've never experienced anything like what we just shared."

She laid her head on his shoulder and entwined her limbs with his. The feel of her soft flesh against his aroused and confused him all at once. He felt protective of her and only knew he didn't want to hurt her.

"Then why are you crying?" he asked again.

"Jean and I, we didn't share a bed for months, sometimes even years."

Stunned at her confession, Louis swore. No wonder she hated Jean.

"After the birth of Renée, Jean seldom came to my bed, even after being away for months at a time. I tried to talk with him on several occasions about why he avoided me, but he never gave me the same reason. I guess I took his rejection personally. I begin to believe he no longer found me attractive."

"Oh, Marian," Louis said holding her tightly in his arms. "You *are* attractive, you're an intelligent beautiful woman."

She started to cry again and wiped her eyes with the back of her hand. "I'm sorry, I never meant to tell you all this and I certainly never thought I would become upset talking about our lovemaking problems. It's just that since Jean's death I've wondered if my lack of attractiveness is the reason that he searched out other women."

Louis shook his head. "You're not thinking like a man."

She leaned back and he could feel her gaze upon him in the dark. "What do you mean?"

"Men who cheat on their wives don't need a reason. They cheat because they want to." He paused, his hand stroking her hair, the sweet perfume of magnolias rising from it.

"Is this the reason you wanted to seduce me tonight?" he asked, suddenly realizing it wasn't loneliness that drove her into his arms, but something else that he feared to hear.

In the darkness her voice trembled. "Jean's deception has been eating at me for months, probably even years. I decided to find an answer to the question that nagged at me."

Louis kissed the top of her head. "You still haven't told me why."

"I . . . I wanted to see what part I played in the break-up of my marriage. I needed to know if I was normal."

"What do you mean, normal?" he asked.

"I needed to see if I was attractive enough to seduce a man. I needed to see if I'm a normal woman," she said.

Louis froze for a moment, his mind reeling from her confession, feeling stunned. What they just experienced, she had initiated this to reassure herself that nothing was wrong with her? She wanted to test her abilities as a woman in bed with a man she'd never been with before? And she'd chosen him?

"Why me?" he asked, suddenly curious, not at all expecting her to respond.

"Because . . . because you're so good with women and because I needed someone that I knew."

He lay with her in his arms, silent. This had never happened to him before and he didn't know whether to feel angry, sad, or pleased as hell that she'd chosen him. All because she needed reassurance of being a desirable woman!

Saddened, he realized the pain of Jean's deception went deeper for Marian than he'd realized.

"I don't know why Jean didn't make love to you. Mad is the only word to describe him, if he didn't find you attractive." Louis kissed the top of her head, holding her tight. "God, Marian. He's dead. He doesn't matter any more. You're alive, you're beautiful, and you just about drove me crazy tonight. Bury Jean and leave him behind."

She reached up and kissed his mouth hard and Louis felt himself responding once again to her body. Her lips released his and she gazed deeply into his eyes.

"Thank you, Louis, but you don't have to be kind. I understand that you're used to women more sophisticated in these matters and . . ."

"Marian, I'm not being kind. You were everything a man could want. You are everything I want."

His lips plundered hers making her his, not Jean's. Louis lost himself as he felt her naked and wanting against him. It was true that he couldn't remember enjoying a woman more. No one since his late wife had aroused his passion to such heights and even Anne had never made him feel so much.

So what would he do now?

Come Monday, could they return to the office and look at each other in the same way again? Could he sit across from her without remembering her soft whimpers and the way she melted in his arms. But did he really want to?

Louis watched as Marian's bedroom slowly lightened with the promise of a new day. Sometime during the night they had moved upstairs to her big bed and made love into the early hours of the morning.

When she drifted off to sleep, he'd lain there and watched her, unable to slow his continuous thoughts. For the last three hours he'd gazed down at her sleeping form, wondering what to do.

The passion they aroused together stunned him. Still in shock from how good they were together, he wanted nothing more than to make love to her again and again.

So what now? Every day he would have to face her, remembering her wrapped around him, wondering when she would find out about his attempts to sell Cuvier Shipping. And God, when she found out about him trying to sell the business, she would hate him even more than Jean.

Louis didn't want to cause her more pain than she'd already had, but he still needed this new business. And he only knew one way to get everything that he wanted. Marriage. He'd been considering matrimony again with the right woman and Marian would be an excellent choice in more ways than one.

He wished he didn't have to deceive her about selling her portion of Cuvier Shipping, but . . . maybe he wasn't looking at this correctly. Maybe he didn't have to mislead Marian into selling if he could convince her to marry him.

Marriage would give him control and eventually she would accept his decision to sell Cuvier Shipping. Together they could build his new sugar mill. All night long he'd looked at the different ways he could obtain what he wanted and have Marian too, not wanting to settle for anything less than having both the new business and Marian.

Dawn crept in through the window, an unwelcome portent of a new day. Soon the servants would be returning as well as the children. He should be going, before the sunlight exposed them and burned away their midnight ardor. Before her neighbors realized he'd spent the night and made her even more scandalous.

Would the passion they felt last night remain this morning? Or would it be as fleeting as the dawn mist?

He leaned down and began to nuzzle Marian's neck. She was soft and beautiful, and he loved the way she responded to his kisses, stretching in her sleep, rolling over and surrounding him with her naked flesh.

Her eyes opened and he smiled into the depths of her sleepy gray gaze. "Good morning."

She returned his smile. "Good morning. What time is it?"

"It's still early, probably around six."

"Hmm. The servants will be here at seven." She closed her eyes as if to go back to sleep.

"I know." He trailed his finger down her silken shoulder, wishing there was time to explore her body once again. "Marian, wake up we need to talk."

"I am awake," she said, opening her eyes sleepily and gazing at him.

"I've lain awake all night thinking about us. About the business, your children, wondering what would be best for all of us."

Her eyes widened. "Why?"

"It's going to be difficult working together after what we've done. I mean, I don't want to be slipping around trying to find a moment alone with you, when the servants and the children are around."

Marian sat up, her hair tumbling about her creamy shoulders, her nipples peeking out from beneath her tousled dark locks. A frown gathered between her brows, her gaze suddenly wary.

"I think we should get married," he said. "I know I'm not doing a very good job of asking, but would you marry me? Would you be my wife?"

Silence filled the room for a moment as she stared at him, her eyes wide with shock. She glanced away and pulled the sheet up to cover her nakedness, her expression filled with distress. Several moments passed before she looked at him, still frowning.

"Marriage? Why are you doing this?" she asked. "This was supposed to be for only one night."

"What? What are you saying?" he asked. He'd just proposed to her and she appeared irritated. He'd asked her to be his wife and she didn't appear the least bit excited.

She faced him, her smoky eyes flashing as if she were angry.

"You have all these women traipsing through your office and you want to marry me?" She laughed, the sound sarcastic. "I've told you repeatedly, I have no intention of ever remarrying. I only wanted one night, not a lifetime."

"I thought you would be happy if I asked you to marry me. How can you want just one night? We could be together forever."

"Forever is a fairytale," she said, her voice rising. "I chose you because I knew you didn't want forever, either. So why are you doing this? Can you tell me that you love me?"

Louis paused, staring at her. He hadn't considered love, last night. He'd thought only of the shipping business and his desire for Marian. But if those three little words would make her feel better and convince her to marry him, then yes, he could say them.

"Yes, I . . . I love you, Marian. I want you to be my wife, because I love you. That's why I asked you to marry me."

Marian jumped out of bed, enraged. "You thought about those words just a little too long." She grabbed her robe and wrapped it around her nude body. "You're acting isn't convincing, Louis. Why would a man known for seducing women suddenly want to marry me after one night together?"

"It's more than sleeping together!" he said jumping up from the bed and striding toward her nude.

She moved to within inches of him, her face flushed.

"Why couldn't last night just remain one passionate night? That's all I wanted. I don't want to get married."

"Good women are supposed to want to be married the morning after! What's wrong with you?"

"What's wrong with *me?*" she asked her voice rising. "After spending most of my life married to a man who didn't want to make love, I just wanted one night. Nothing more. I don't want to be tied to a man. I want the freedom to make my own choices, work at Cuvier Shipping, and earn my living."

She paused and gazed at him. He could feel her eyes upon him searching out his face and he suddenly felt uncomfortable. "What's wrong?"

"Cuvier Shipping . . ." she said, her voice dying away. "Are you trying to get control of the business? Is that why you're asking me to marry you?"

"Of course not, Marian," he lied, knowing he'd miscalculated once again and now he looked a fool. He'd let the night affect his thinking and should have realized she would recognize his ploy to acquire the business.

She glared at him, her face flushed, her eyes wide with anger, her body shaking, madder than he'd ever seen her.

"Why did you have to ruin last night, Louis, by offering to marry me? I just wanted one night of passion and now you've tainted the memory by asking me to marry you." She seemed to run out of steam. "Get dressed and get out."

Later that morning, Marian watched from the window as the carriage arrived with Claire and her children inside. God, she dreaded facing Claire. How much should she tell her sister? Wonderful night, fantastic lovemaking, until he'd ruined the night by proposing?

How many women turned down a marriage proposal the morning after being so intimate with a man?

Once he'd left this morning, she'd thrown herself into cleaning Jean's old bedroom. The time to purge her life of Jean's personal belongings and put him in the past had come.

The midnight's moonbeams had touched and healed her, while the morning sun's glare left her disturbed and disappointed that Louis could be such a cad. To think he would deliberately marry her just to get his hands on Cuvier Shipping!

Now doubts crept in like spring ants crawling their way through cracks. If he would propose to gain control of the business, should she believe he had really accepted their partnership? And was the proposal just another lie he wanted her to believe for his own reasons?

Marian pasted a smile on her face and smilingly opened the front door, happy to see her children home again.

"Momma," Renée said, running up the walk to fling herself into her mother's arms.

"Hi, sweetheart. Did you have a good time?" Marian asked hugging her daughter to her, the child's body feeling comforting and uplifting.

"Yes. We played Old Maid and I won. I stuck Philip with the old maid two times. He got mad at me." She leaned back and looked up at her mother, her arms still around her. "What did you do?"

"I went to a dinner party with Mr. Fournet. Then today I've been cleaning out your father's room," she said.

"Oh," said Renée and stared at her mother for a moment. "What are you going to do with Papa's things?"

"Today you and Philip can go through them and pick out what you want and the rest we'll give away to charity," Marian told her daughter.

"All right," Renée replied in a subdued voice. "It's going to be strange not seeing his stuff."

"You're right," Marian acknowledged.

Philip and Claire walked up. "Hello, Mother!"

"Hello, son. Did you have a good time?"

Philip glanced at his younger sister. "It was all right. What's to eat?"

"I smelled lunch a little while ago. Go check the kitchen."

Philip started toward the kitchen, the smell even now drifting on the breeze.

"Me, too!" Renée said, running after her brother and leaving Marian alone with Claire.

"Well?" Her sister smiled at her. "You look a little peaked this morning. What happened?"

Marian shrugged as if it meant nothing. "The evening was lovely."

"And?" Claire said, her face lighting up into a grin.

"I'm really tired."

"That's usually a promising sign that someone didn't get enough sleep the night before."

Marian shrugged. "Come into the parlor where we can talk."

She led her sister into the small room not certain what she intended to tell Claire. She'd have to tell her sister something or Claire would never let her have any peace, but the night had been intimate. She didn't want to discuss the way Louis pleasured her until she cried out his name. Some things were private. Some things hurt too much to remember.

After Claire walked in the door, Marian closed it firmly behind her. She turned and faced her sister. "I'm tired and I really don't want to discuss the details of last night." Marian took a deep breath. "But I will tell you this much. We came back here after dinner last night and, yes, we made love."

Her sister smiled and then she frowned. "You're all right aren't you? He didn't hurt you?"

Marian shrugged and walked away. "I'm fine. Actually last night was really good."

Claire took a seat on the couch. "Then why aren't you happy?"

"I'm fine, really. It's just that before he left this morning we had an argument."

"I see. Then you're not upset about what you did with Louis?" Claire asked Marian, her eyes questioning.

Claire took a seat on the settee.

"No. I didn't expect what he said to me this morning. I don't know. In some ways, I'm more confused than ever before," Marian acknowledged.

"Did you at least get the answers you were looking for?" Claire asked.

Marian paused in her pacing of the floor and smiled wryly at her sister. "Yes. And I've spent the morning cleaning out Jean's bedroom. It's time to put that man out of my life. He's dead and I must go on."

A sigh escaped from Claire as she brushed a speck of lint from her skirt. "That sounds very good. Do you consider last night a success?"

Marian stopped her pacing and frowned. "I enjoyed being with Louis. The dinner party was fun and he is a fantastic lover. But . . ."

She could feel the tears coming, pricking her eyelids. She shook herself and turned back to Claire, regaining control. "Anyway, last night was great, but this morning everything came apart."

"I see. But as long as you're all right, and you don't regret what you've done . . ." Claire said, her voice sympathetic.

"No, I don't. Louis helped me realize a lot of things about myself. Jean never spoke to me about why he was unhappy or why he didn't want to share our bed. Last night proved to me that I'm attractive and I can have normal relations with a man. So my marital problems weren't all my fault."

"Good," Claire said, studying Marian closely. "Are you going to see Louis again?"

Marian bit her lip in consternation. She glanced at her sister reclining on the settee, her skirts spread about her. She'd asked herself this same question several times this morning, and at first her response had been an emphatic no. But later, the voice of doubt kept rising up asking, What if his proposal had been sincere? What if she were wrong about his ulterior motive? What if she'd accused him falsely?

No! He acknowledged he'd lain awake all night making plans. She suspected he'd been plotting how to get complete control of Cuvier Shipping and came to the conclusion that marriage seemed the easiest answer. No she didn't have any real proof. How do you get proof that a man was lying? But her instincts told her his motives were less than honest. She didn't know what, but something wasn't right.

"I'll see him at work each day," she finally responded.

"That's not what I meant and you know it."

Marian gave a half smile. "I know. I just don't know if I can answer your question just yet. It's doubtful I'll ever do anything with him again, but just the same, I'm not ready to say never."

Claire smiled. "Then don't."

"I'm not ready to say never, but then, I'm not ready to agree to be his wife or anyone else's, for that matter."

"His wife?"

"Yes, he asked me to marry him."

"Oh my!" Claire said surprised. "This is quite a shock. No wonder you're upset. I certainly didn't expect Louis to propose."

"Me neither," Marian said with a sigh. "But it would be a nice and tidy way for him to gain control of Cuvier Shipping.

Louis didn't like the way he'd left Marian's house but he didn't know how to change her mind. He'd underestimated her and should have realized she would recognize his reasons for marrying her were false. His thoughts had centered on his desires, not love, but that didn't mean it wouldn't eventually come. People married for business reasons all the time. She'd made him seem evil for considering the idea of marrying her. Eventually she'd tire of being involved with the business and miss spending time with her children. What would she do then?

Most of the time he could charm what he wanted from a woman, with little or no consideration for her feelings, until this morning.

But Marian was not as easily persuaded. She recognized he wasn't sincere and yet somehow leaving her upset and angry this morning troubled him. Confusion seemed to fill his mind, not knowing what he really wanted the most, Marian, Cuvier Shipping, or that damn mill he was so intent on acquiring.

He'd never been good at honesty, but last night she'd been warm and sincere and this morning he'd lied to her, though it wasn't a total lie. He wouldn't mind being married to Marian.

And why would she marry him if he *were* honest with her about his reasons for the proposal? Not a single reason came to mind. So he lied and tried to somehow convince her that he wanted to marry her because he loved her.

Coming from his lips the words rang false even to his own ears. He had shuddered at the sound of the lie clanging like a gong between them. He should never have attempted to persuade Marian to marry him for love. Yet most women would have jumped at his proposal without a declaration from the heart.

Marian had to be unique.

A knock interrupted his thoughts and he went to the door of the rooms he rented in the French Quarter.

He opened the door to see a messenger standing there and signed for the note. Breaking the seal he quickly scanned the message.

Dear Mr. Fournet,

I have a party interested in Cuvier Shipping. Please contact me at your earliest convenience.

Sincerely,
Stephen Hudson, Attorney

Louis stared at the missive, feeling more pressure than ever before. Someone wanted to buy the business. He could finally obtain his goal once he sold Cuvier Shipping! But first he had to convince Marian that he really desired to marry her.

How did you convince a woman she should marry you, when she recognized you for the obsessed, business-oriented bastard that you were?

A man serious about marriage found a woman he wanted for a mate and courted her until he expressed his undying devotion. Louis considered himself an amatuer at courting, a professional at seduction.

Even Anne, his first wife, he never really courted. Good friends all their life, they married young, very much in love, or so he believed. Now he wasn't sure he believed in love anymore. He tried to remember how he felt about Anne, but it seemed like one day they were happy, decorating the nursery, and then she was gone. He remembered feeling lost, like everything important had departed, leaving him alone.

No, he couldn't remember what love felt like. He just remembered the loss, the empty feeling of Anne's death, the guilt he felt that their marriage cost her her life.

With a sigh, he walked over to the window and stared down into the street. He still wanted to buy the mill but he needed Marian to sell Cuvier Shipping. Getting past Marian's barriers to gain control of the business seemed impossible. There could only be one solution.

Courting. How hard could it be to convince a woman he wanted to marry her? Seduction or courting, they were both the same game, though with different results.

Marian Cuvier was about to be swept off her feet and he intended to begin right after he spoke with the attorney.

CHAPTER THIRTEEN

Monday morning and Louis had not shown up for work. No one knew where he was and though Marian didn't want to admit it, she was beginning to worry. And that made her angry with herself for worrying about him.

How could she forget that he wanted to marry her just to gain control of Cuvier Shipping?

The clock in her office struck twelve and she glanced again across the hall at the empty office. Never known for his promptness, Louis had never blatantly not shown up for work. Could he be hidden away plotting his next attempt at taking over the business? Or could he be hurt, lying in a ditch somewhere?

Oh, where was he! She couldn't help but worry.

Outside in the hallway, a creaking noise drew her attention and she cocked her head to listen. There it was again, that same squeaky noise getting closer.

Marian stood and walked around her desk, going

to the door. Tentatively, she poked her head out and glanced down the hall. The sight shocked her and made her want to laugh, yet a sense of relief filled her. With a grin on his face, Louis strolled down the hall, pulling a little wagon filled with packages.

"Hello," he called cheerfully, making her want to wring his neck for causing her to worry needlessly.

She frowned, not ready to let him forget she was still angry and suspicious of him. She moved to go back into her office.

"Marian, wait," he called. "I brought us lunch."

She stuck her head back out the door, wondering where he'd been all morning, still not ready to put their conversation from her mind. "Whatever for?"

A cocky grin appeared on his face as he shrugged his shoulders. "I hoped you would give me a second chance. I knew you would refuse an invitation to lunch, so I brought the party to you."

Not ready to be alone with him, she shook her head. "You're wasting your time. I'm not having lunch with you. I have plans."

He glanced at her sheepishly. "If you're referring to your lunch with Drew, he had to cancel."

Her eyes widened. "What? You cancelled my lunch?"

"No. Something came up with Layla. Don't be mad at him. Layla's life is on the line," he said, a serious look on his face. Then he smiled and she felt the ice around her heart begin to melt. "In an effort to reconcile with you, I promise I've brought a very special lunch."

She raised her brows. "What, you're going to propose yet again?" she asked. "Have you forgotten I'm angry at you?"

He stared at her, his gaze unwavering. "If I thought your answer would be yes, then I would propose. But that last time, you pretty much crushed my pride and I'm not ready for a second go just yet."

She tossed him a dubious stare. "Your pride could survive being flattened by a train, so don't try to make me feel bad."

"Perhaps, but I hoped we could at least return to the way things were between us."

"That's doubtful."

"Well, I'm at least willing to give it a try." He grinned at her. "So will you have lunch with me?"

"You think you can just come in here and say a few charming words, bring me lunch, and everything will be all right?" She took a deep breath, though her fury seemed to be dying. "Well, you're wrong. I'm still mad that you thought you could try to marry me to gain control of the business. Do you think I'm stupid?"

"I have never considered you less than intelligent," he said standing in the hallway holding the wagon handle, not denying her accusations, which intrigued her. "Forget the proposal, forget about the business. Just have lunch with me."

"So you admit you were trying to marry me to gain control of the business?" she asked.

"I'm admitting nothing. I just want to have lunch with you and forget this damn business for a while."

The smell of hot fresh bread wafted through her office, tempting Marian. Her stomach growled, the sound loud in the silent room.

"You've got to eat," he insisted.

"I am hungry," she admitted. She looked at him to see his reaction. He smiled and she felt a moment of intense longing, followed by anguish. She wanted him even more today than before their night together. His smile was so disarming she needed to remember that what lurked behind those curled lips was a great deal of fun, not to mention emotional danger.

He waited, not saying anything, his face an innocent mask, his eyes giving her that promising gaze again that seemed to make her body come alive. Their liaison had been for one night only, she reminded herself. Not a lifetime, not even two or three nights. One night only and now that was over.

"I . . ." she hesitated. "All right. But it has to be quick. I have a lot of work to accomplish today. And I'm still upset with you."

He nodded, his eyes warm and understanding. "You can be mad at me as long as you eventually get over it."

Marian raised her brow. "That could take until the Mississippi runs dry."

"Yes, it could," he acknowledged, and pulled the little wagon into her office and shut the door behind him. "But I hope not."

She felt a moment of unease at the sight of that closed door, with just the two of them all alone together. She ignored him, determined not to let her guard down in his presence again.

When she glanced up, she gave him her best hostile look. "Why the closed door?"

"We need privacy for lunch," he said, with a shrug. "We could be discussing serious business issues or I might try to steal a kiss."

"And come back with a broken arm."

He laughed. "I'll keep that thought in mind."

"You do that," she said.

"Where do you want me to set up our picnic?" he questioned.

"Picnic?"

"Yes, we're having a picnic without the bugs."

"What did you bring?" she asked, her curiosity getting the better of her.

"I brought a feast."

He smiled at her and then turned to the wagon and pulled out a blanket, which he spread on the floor in her office. Next, he took out a large picnic hamper. He lifted the lid and pulled out napkins, silverware, dishes, and champagne glasses.

"Champagne?"

"Yes, champagne," he said.

"But we're working," she protested. "Alcohol is not going to take away my anger."

"We're having a picnic," he reminded her.

"Which is in an office," she replied.

He took a deep breath. "No, we're no longer in this office. We're out under a shade tree somewhere along the river, just the two of us. There's a warm breeze blowing and the heat makes us feel lazy. You put your head in my lap and we lay there talking all afternoon. Sometimes kissing, sometimes just holding one another."

She rolled her eyes. "Yes, we're under a shade tree somewhere along the river all right, but you're on one side of the blanket and I'm on the other. I'm still furious with you and you're asking for my forgiveness. I tell you, not until the sun rises in the west."

"I think I like my scenario better."

"You would."

He reached into another box that lay in the bottom of the wagon, covered until just this moment. He pulled the ribbon on the box, yanked off the lid and the smell of carnations permeated the air.

Stepping within inches of her, he handed her the flowers. "While we're gazing out at the river, I surprise you with flowers, hoping they will ease your disappointment in me and show you my intentions are sincere."

She glanced briefly at the bunch of flowers, struck by their beauty. He was definitely making it harder for her to stay angry with him. She gazed at the spread laid out on the floor before her. He'd gone to so much work just to make her happy. Never before had any man done so much for her and she could feel the ice slowly melting from around her heart. No wonder the man had women flocking around him.

This was his ploy. He was a master at seduction. He was a talented lover, a shrewd businessman. But what if she *had* been wrong about him? What if he'd been serious that morning when he'd asked her to marry him? After all, most women would have wanted a marriage proposal. They would have gladly said yes.

No, she couldn't have made that big a mistake. Louis wanted the business. She had to be on guard at all times.

"Thank you, they're lovely, though . . ."

"Don't say it. I know, you're still mad at me."

She smiled and laughed. "No, I have no vase to put them in."

Louis perked up. "Oh. Well, we'll find something."

He jumped up and found the water pitcher to put the flowers in, then hurriedly finished setting everything up. When the food was all set out, the champagne on ice, pillows for her to sit on, and the dishes all arranged, he took her by the hand and helped her to the oasis he had created.

"My, this is really nice," she said, and glanced up at him with suspicion. What was he up to besides trying to convince her to marry him?

He is a shrewd businessman. A master at seduction.

"Thank you." He poured her a glass of champagne and handed the glass to her. He tore off a piece of fresh bread and put it between her lips, feeding the soft warm bread to her. It all but melted in her mouth, so fresh and moist that she almost moaned.

Next he fed her some fruit, followed by cheese. She sat there and let him feed her bites of food as she gazed deeply into his eyes. There was something about being fed by another person who cared about you, that left you feeling special. And Marian at this moment felt very treasured.

Finally they ate the sandwiches he'd included in the basket.

"This is really good. Where did you get all this food?"

Louis shrugged. "I ran all over town this morning, finding it. I've also arranged for us to take the children for a boat ride on Saturday."

She turned and stared at him, doubts causing her suspicions to raise their ugly heads again. "Why?"

"Because your son told me the day I bought him the Italian ice that he wanted to go and it's also part of your training, my dear. Captain Paul is available and I thought it would be a good time to go." He frowned. "If you'd like to think of this as a business trip, that would be fine."

She stared at him, not knowing how to respond, but feeling more confused than ever. She recalled Philip's request to ride in one of his father's boats and her heart warmed at Louis's thoughtfulness toward her son.

He is a shrewd businessman. A master at seduction. The words echoed through her head.

"Why are you doing this? Why not just let us remain as partners?"

"What do you mean?"

"Why are you still trying to seduce me?"

His mouth was so close and she tried not to stare at

his full lips, so moist, so tempting, so delightful before her.

"Seduction is not the word I would use. I want to marry you and I intend to show you just how serious I am."

His lips covered hers and though she'd threatened to break his arm, she could not resist the touch of him any more than she could deny her thirst. How could one man be so tempting and maddening, all at the same time? His kiss felt wonderful and the lunch he'd gone to so much trouble over was a treat. No one else in her life had ever arranged something like this.

Louis was a shrewd businessman. A master at manipulation, the voice inside her head taunted her. A skillful lover who could make her melt, who could make her forget that she'd ever been angry.

She broke off the kiss and gazed at him, her stomach all fluttery. The velvety softness of his eyes made her want to throw herself in his arms and forget about the business and all the suspicions that clouded her thinking. But she couldn't.

"This doesn't mean that I'm no longer mad at you," she finally said, her breath coming in short little gasps.

"As long as you kiss me like that when you're mad at me, then everything will be all right."

She frowned. "I'm serious, Louis. I'm not going to marry you for any reason, so you can quite trying so hard to convince me that you want me."

"Well, I had thought of us just living together, but I don't think that would set a good example for the children. And I don't particularly want my children to be referred to as bastards." He paused for a moment. "You aren't against having more children are you?"

"No," she said without thinking and then shook her head. "What are you talking about?"

"Good, because though I promise always to treat your children as my own, I still would like to have a few more."

"Oh," she said staring at him as his words sank in surprising her. "Damn it, Louis!" she said jumping to her feet. "I'm not going to marry you, now or in the future. So quit this farce of trying to convince me you're serious."

This man was just trying to trick her into believing that he wanted to marry her. She pushed him away and rose to her feet. "It's after one, lunch is over and so is the picnic."

He reclined on the blanket, his head resting on one elbow, one knee propped up, watching her as she flitted around the room loading the picnic things into the wagon.

"Did I say something wrong?" he asked.

"No," she said putting their plates into the picnic basket. "You've said everything just right. Every calculated word has been said at just the correct moment and I almost fell for it a second time."

"What do you mean a second time? I haven't proposed yet."

She looked up from putting away the dishes and glared at him. "And you're not going to either."

"No, I wasn't, not today."

"Good." She closed the picnic hamper put it in the wagon, picked up the pillows and would have folded the blanket if she could have gotten Louis to move. But he just sat there watching her.

"I guess you'd like me to leave now."

"Yes, that would be nice." She stood gazing down at him, feeling so nervous. She'd almost succumbed to him a second time. Was she crazy? "Thank you for the lovely lunch. The flowers are beautiful and I enjoyed the picnic."

Louis gave her a lazy smile and she knew he recognized her nervousness. "You're welcome. But we didn't get to spend any time with your head in my lap, talking about our future."

"Our future should be discussed not under a tree, but in the office with our banker and our ships' captains."

Louis rolled to his knees and then to his feet. She watched as he dusted off his fine trousers and then glanced at her.

"Thanks for having lunch with me. If you're free for dinner . . . ?"

"No!" she said with an emphatic shout and then lowered her voice. "I promised the children we'd play games tonight."

"All right. I'll be right across the hall."

"If I need you, I'm sure I can find you."

"You want me. It's only a matter of time." He smiled and walked out, pulling the little wagon behind him. Though she fought the impulse, the sight tickled her, to see a big strong man pulling a child's toy.

Marian sank down into her chair and picked up her pencil. She tried to concentrate on the journal spread before her. Her hands began to shake badly.

God, yes, she wanted him. His touch was more potent than the strongest liquor, more intoxicating than the finest wine and somehow she had to resist the temptation he presented.

Marian glanced across the steamboat deck and watched Louis with her son.

Louis was a shrewd man. She'd dropped the businessman part, because though it fit him, she was quickly discovering the word shrewd described him.

She felt a pang of emotion seize her. Philip glanced at Louis so trusting that her heart ached for the child. He missed his father so much and though he appeared to be feeling better, there was a conspicuous absence of his friends around their house. At least he hadn't spoken of any more trouble, but then school had been out for the last month. The only time he saw his friends was for baseball games in the park.

She tried to remember when she'd last seen him play ball with his friends in their yard and couldn't remember. She would question him later.

"Momma, look over there at that island. Can we stop there?" Renée asked. She had been timid coming on board and even now she hadn't left Marian's side since the boat departed. The boat quickly slicing through the water, heading upstream had made the child wary, though Marian felt exhilarated.

"No, dear, we're going up river to some place Mr. Fournet knows."

"Will it be fun?" the child asked.

"I don't know. You'll have to wait and see."

"Renée," Philip called. "Come see this."

The child glanced at her brother and then at her mother, her reluctance to move obvious.

"It's okay," Marian reassured her. "Just be careful."

The little girl took one last look at Marian and then slowly ambled off toward her brother. Marian turned her attention once again back to the river and gazed at the shoreline.

Occasionally they passed large houses surrounded with fields of sugarcane, the green blades tall in the hot sun. Sometimes a field hand would glance up from his labor and wave at the boat. She stood watching the changing shoreline, her mind on the man who had picked her up this morning.

Now, he was trying not only to court her, but it seemed he also appeared to be working his charm on her children, which she didn't appreciate.

She felt his presence and turned to see him step to the railing beside her.

"So what do you think of one of your boats, Mrs. Cuvier?"

She gazed at him, noting the way the breeze ruffled his hair. "I think it's a typical steamboat."

"True, but they're a dying breed. If you'd like to, Capitan Paul said you could steer once we get past the sandbars on this part of the river."

"No, thank you. I'll leave that to the professionals," she said. "Where are you taking us today? Are we just out for an excursion on the river?"

"Yes and no. We're only an hour from Belle Fournet, my family's plantation, and Capitan Paul has a load for the White Castle plantation, which is just up the river. I thought that we could stop and spend the afternoon with my family."

"Your family?" Marian asked, surprised.

"Yes. The kids could ride horses and I could show you around Belle Fournet."

Marian took a deep breath and released it slowly. "Mr. Fournet, while I understand you're trying to charm me and somehow find a way to get me to marry you, I don't appreciate your enticing my children. If you harm them in any way, I promise you, I will retaliate in a most unladylike manner."

Louis frowned, his eyes flashing. "I would never do anything to hurt your children, Marian. That would be the worst thing anyone could do and I take offense at your even suggesting it."

"I'm just warning you," she said.

"Your worries are unfounded. I like Philip and Renée and would never use them to get to you," he said. "I will, however, do things I think they will enjoy."

"I can't argue with you for that. In fact, I appreciate everything you've done for them so far." She paused. "I guess I worry about how Jean's death has affected them and I'm very protective of my children."

"I understand."

They stood at the railing for several moments, neither one saying anything. The silence seemed peaceful and Marian enjoyed the feel of the breeze on her face.

"When we come around this bend, you can see Belle Fournet's landing. That's where we're getting off."

"Is your family expecting us?" she questioned.

"Yes, I sent word several days ago, after you agreed at the picnic."

As the boat docked, Marian gazed at the big house that sat at least half a mile from the river. The raised Creole plantation house stood off in the distance, the french doors on the second floor opened for the cooling river breeze.

"You never told me your family lived so well."

"Would it have made a difference?"

"No, though I would certainly hate to offend them in any way. Are you certain they will want me to visit them?"

"Marian, you don't understand the way of life along the river road. Everyone is welcome at Belle Fournet."

"I hope you're right."

A wagon pulled up to the dock, driven by a servant. "Mr. Louis, welcome home. Your mother said to tell you she's expecting you."

"Thank you, Leon."

"Mr. Fournet, I'll blow my whistle as I come around

the bend to let you know it's time to go. We should be back to pick you up in four hours."

"Thank you, Captain Paul," Louis said, and then turned to Marian. "Shall we?"

Marian gathered her children and they disembarked, stepping onto the dock and then crossing to the waiting wagon.

Louis helped Philip into the wagon and then lifted Renée up to sit beside her brother. He turned to Marian and helped her into the wagon, before climbing in beside her.

"How you been, Leon?" he asked the servant.

"Good, Mr. Louis. Your brother, he's been making some changes in the fields and they seem to be working. The sugarcane is looking even better than last year's crop."

"Good. How's the family?"

"Thanks for asking, sir. My son is going to be leaving for New Orleans to attend school."

"Tell him to look me up when he gets into town and I'll try to find some part-time work for him."

"Thanks kindly, sir."

They pulled up at the front of the big house and Marian heard the tinkle of wind chimes, soft and melodic in the breeze. Two huge oak trees shaded the front of the house, two matching staircases wound in a graceful curve toward the second story.

A beautiful, older woman stood on the second story verandah gazing down at them. Her dark hair was tinged with gray, her long neck graceful and proud. Marian knew she could only be Louis's mother. He took the stairs two at a time and when he reached her, wrapped his arms around his mother, kissing her cheek.

"Mon fils."

"Mère. Still the prettiest woman I know."

She laughed. "Still my son, the courtier. It's good to see you." She patted him on the cheek. "We miss you. The summer is upon us and you should leave that dreadful city and come home where it's clean."

"*Mère,* New Orleans no longer has the outbreaks of yellow fever it once had."

"Pooh! It's still not healthy, *mon fils.*" She released him. "Introduce me to your guests."

Marian slowly made her way up the stairs with Renée and Philip in tow. They stood quietly waiting, watching with interest as Louis greeted his mother. Somehow she'd never expected this big, strong man to care for his mother so much. His affection to her was a contrast to his usual callous ways with women.

"*Mère,* this is Mrs. Marian Cuvier, my business partner and friend," he said smiling at Marian.

"Nice to meet you," she said shaking her hand. She pointed to the land that surrounded the house. "Welcome to Belle Fournet."

"It's lovely," Marian said, in awe of the land and the house.

"Thank you. And who are these beautiful children?" his mother asked.

"This is Renée and young Philip, my children." Marian said proudly.

"We're honored to have you. Please come in."

In the Creole custom, she took them into the house through her bedroom, though she defied convention and led them into the parlor of the big house.

"My husband and other son, Edmond, will join us soon," she said. "Please make yourself comfortable."

Renée and Philip followed them, their eyes wide as they gazed at the rooms. They sat down in the parlor and a servant brought lemonade, which they sipped, their throats parched from the summer heat.

"I've sent a servant to fetch the men." She gazed at Marian. "Louis tells us that you've taken over your husband's part of the business."

"Yes, I've taken Jean's place," Marian said expecting censure from the older woman.

"Good for you," Mrs. Fournet said. "Creole women ran many businesses until the Americans came. Then it suddenly became *faux pas,* though the Creole women were excellent at controlling the family finances. Sometimes a woman has to take control of her own destiny."

Surprised by the woman's vote of confidence, Marian smiled. "Thank you."

"My son knows my feelings and I'm sure he must be very helpful in your work."

Marian tried not to laugh and managed to suppress her amusement to a grin. She glanced at Louis who looked sheepish and quickly changed the subject.

"Leon told us that the sugarcane crop is better than ever."

"Yes, Edmond has increased the production. Your father is very pleased with him." His mother reached over and touched Louis on the arm. "I must warn you that your father wants you to return home. Please Louis, listen to him, but do what pleases you." She glanced at Marian. "I only want my sons to be happy."

"When is he going to give up on me coming home and working under Edmond, *Mère?*"

She shook her head and gave a slight shrug to her shoulders. "He's a typical father. He wants both of his sons working the family business. He doesn't realize that one of them is as strong and stubborn as himself." She paused and laid her hand on Louis's arm. "You must do what your heart tells you to do, regardless of what your father says."

Louis leaned forward and kissed his mother's cheek.

"I don't want to work under my brother. I want to be in charge of my own company. He knows that's why I left."

"If you had children, you would understand his thinking better, Louis."

"I know he means well, *Mère,* but I'm not going to return to Belle Fournet, unless I'm working with the family in my own company.

Marian felt like they had forgotten her as they discussed the family situation as if she were not there.

"But what would you do, Louis? What kind of company could that be?"

"I have some ideas. When I'm ready to discuss them, then I'll let Papa know." He picked up his mother's hand. "Don't worry, *Mère.* Everything will be all right."

"Your father can be very stubborn," she said, and turned her attention to Marian. "I'm sorry, Mrs. Cuvier, for discussing such things in front of you, but my husband will be here shortly and well you know how protective a mother feels toward her children. No matter what their age, that feeling never goes away."

"I understand, Mrs. Fournet," she said, surprised at the way Louis reacted to his mother. She never thought of him as a man who would care deeply for his parents, but he obviously did.

This new revelation about him surprised her. Jean Cuvier had barely spoken to his mother and when she'd died he didn't appear to grieve. But then Jean had hidden so many of his emotions, she realized.

Heavy footsteps resounded outside the main room as his father strode into the parlor.

"Louis, you're home." His father came forward, tossing his hat onto the settee.

"Hello, Papa," Louis said.

"Mrs. Cuvier, it's nice to see you again. And who are these monkeys?" he asked glancing at Renée and Philip.

"Hello, Mr. Fournet. These monkeys are my children, Renée and Philip," Marian said, thinking how much Louis looked like his father.

"Ah! I bet you are bored silly sitting here with these adults. Would you like to go horseback riding?"

"Yes," Philip cried.

"Will the horse go fast?" Renée asked timidly.

"No, he's docile. Come now and I'll take you out to the barns."

The children jumped up, happy to escape the adult conversation.

Marian followed them. "I just want to make sure they're all right."

"I promised to show you around Belle Fournet. We'll go for a buggy ride and then come back," said Louis.

"Lunch should be ready in just over an hour," Mrs. Fournet advised. "Have a good time."

The hour sped by too quickly, with Louis driving her around the plantation, showing her the sugar mill process, and how the cane was cut and burned in the fields.

At the appointed hour everyone gathered around the family table. As they sat down to eat, Marian realized once again just how different Louis seemed around his family. He appeared relaxed, yet she sensed he was on guard waiting for his father's reproach. At the last second, a hurried Edmond joined them at the table.

"Marian, meet my older brother, Edmond."

"Nice to meet you, Mrs. Cuvier."

"I've heard a lot about you from Louis," Marian said.

"All good, I hope," Edmond said glancing at his younger brother.

"Of course."

Edmond smiled. "We did have some good times together." The man glanced at his brother. "Papa says the crops are better than ever this year."

"Yes, the weather has been excellent and so far the cane is looking very good. We could use another hand to help get the crop in," his father hinted.

"You know I will help you any time I can. I have my own business to run," Louis told him.

"Papa said that Mrs. Cuvier was helping to run your shipping business," Edmond remarked ignoring Marian.

"I am," she replied before Louis could answer for her.

"My life is in New Orleans," Louis said looking at his brother and his father.

"Your life should be here at Belle Fournet with your family. You're my son and you should be here working the land with your brother," his father said, his voice rising, taking advantage of the opening to express his frustration with his youngest son. Stunned, Marian watched as Louis defended his decisions.

"When the time comes I will return home and help with the harvest. But I have my own company in New Orleans, Papa."

His father turned to Marian. "I apologize, Mrs. Cuvier, but this has been a long standing argument between my son and me. Edmond is my oldest, but I always dreamed both my sons would work the plantation. But one of them runs away from his responsibilities to the family."

"I do not, Papa. I'm just not a planter. I find no pleasure in watching the cane grow."

"Who says you're suppose to get pleasure from the work? This is the way we earn our living," his father insisted.

Marian saw the tightening of Louis's facial muscles. She watched his eyes darken with anger and she suddenly felt sorry for him.

She turned to Mr. Fournet, needing to say something to help Louis. "Sometimes our children don't always follow the dreams we have set out for them."

He dismissed her comment with a wave of his hand, but the words suddenly resounded in her head and she wondered at them. Wasn't she setting up her own son in exactly the same situation? Would Philip want to inherit the shipping company or was there some other profession that he dreamed of, one she knew nothing of?

"Wise words, Mrs. Cuvier," Louis's mother said, and then turned her steely gaze on her husband. "I think this discussion should be continued after lunch, Mr. Fournet."

The older man started to reply, but then closed his mouth. "As you wish, Mrs. Fournet."

"Thank you," she replied with a nod.

Marian glanced across the table at Louis. She felt like a window had been opened and the reasons for some of his actions were clearly revealed. Cuvier Shipping was his escape from working under his father and brother. Without the shipping company he would have to return to working the plantation, which he clearly didn't enjoy.

So why then did he want to sell the business? What did he want to do if he no longer had the shipping company? Had she been wrong in assuming he intended to sell Cuvier Shipping?

CHAPTER FOURTEEN

Louis stood on the deck of the steamboat next to Marian, waving goodbye to his mother, a distant figure on the balcony of the house.

"I like your family," Marian said. "Your mother especially."

"*Mère* is the glue that holds us all together," he said quietly. "I should apologize for my father and brother's behavior at the dinner table today."

She turned to face him, her head tilted, her eyes questioning. "Do they often try to encourage you to return home?"

"Every trip. It's one of the reasons I don't come home very often. My father tries to convince me I should be home working the plantation like my brother."

She leaned against the railing of the boat, glancing down at the muddy waters of the Mississippi. "Yet, you seem to love them very much."

"They're my family. Just because we don't agree on

my choice of work doesn't mean I don't love them," he said wondering about her own family.

The wind teased wisps of hair around her face and he wanted to put his arm around her waist and pull her against him, shielding her from the breeze. But he resisted; her children stood close by, but more than anything he didn't know how she'd react.

The boat hit a whitecap on the water and bounced. She gripped the railing tighter, but didn't flinch as she returned her gaze to him.

"I can see that. My own family experience was different and Jean was never close to any of his people. It's odd to me that though you have conflict with your father, you appear to care about him."

"We're dissimilar, but that doesn't mean I don't love him." Louis shrugged and turned back to face the water. Nothing about his life had turned out like he'd planned. And his father's disappointment ate like a cancer at him.

"You yourself told my father that children don't always follow the dreams parents have for them. What if Philip wants to be an architect instead of running a shipping company or what if Renée decides to become a teacher?" he said pushing away the thoughts of how selling the business would hurt Marian.

She frowned. "I know. As the words came from my lips they awoke me to my own prejudices as a parent."

He gazed out at the flowing river and wondered how he would be as a father. He still would like to have children someday, he thought, and glanced at the woman beside him. If he were going to marry her for the business, he needed to get back to courting her, but somehow the day spent together had changed things between them. Their friendship and working relationship seemed more intimate, more personal than just the act of trying to convince her to marry him for profit.

"So what path are you following, Louis? One moment you want to buy my part of the shipping company and then the next you want to sell the business? What are you trying to do?"

Her words yanked him from his thoughts, spiraling alarm, taking him by surprise as he gazed at the woman standing at his side. She was the only other woman besides his wife that he had taken to meet his family. What prompted him to take Marian and her children to see his father in such an intimate setting? He'd let her see a side of him that very few people ever saw and now because he'd let her into this part of his life, he'd given her the ammunition to question his motives. Questions he felt he owed an answer to, yet feared answering.

"If I were free to do what I wanted, I would own my own business. But it would be something that I could do to help my brother and father. That way I would still be involved with the family business, but I would be in control of my own destiny."

"Can't you do that with the shipping business? Aren't we hauling their refined sugar to market for them?"

"Yes." He gazed deep into her green eyes. "But this is Cuvier Shipping, not Fournet Shipping. Not even Cuvier/Fournet Shipping. Jean got into financial trouble and that's the only reason I own part of the business now."

Marian's eyes widened at this knowledge. "Jean told me you were an investor who bought into the business."

"I did, when he was about to go bankrupt."

Marian turned and faced the front of the boat, the wind blowing tendrils of her hair. "Sometimes I think I would be better off selling Cuvier Shipping, just to get rid of the bad memories of Jean that seem to come with this business."

Louis jumped at the opening.

"You know I'll buy you out right now. You could have a fresh start in life with the money."

Marian considered his comment for a moment, her face thoughtful, her eyes squinting in the sunlight. She tilted her head sideways and gazed up at him. "But how would I support my family? Are you going to pay me enough for us to live on the rest of our lives? Enough for me to put Philip through school and give Renée a season? Or will I be forced to remarry just to keep my children and myself from starving in several years?"

Louis frowned, unable to respond. A month ago he would have leaped at the chance to convince her that everything would be all right, but now suddenly he couldn't lie to Marian and tell her that her fears were ungrounded. Her concerns were realistic.

"You're not answering me, Louis."

He turned to face her, his eyes taking in her interested expression. Very little slipped past Marian and certainly she'd noticed his sudden lack of response.

"No one can promise anything, Marian. I don't know if I could pay you enough money to make certain that you could live the rest of your life on the proceeds from the sale. Maybe you could buy into another business. Whatever you decide, I would suggest that you consider your options very carefully."

Just call him the biggest idiot in New Orleans. He'd just forfeited an excellent opportunity to persuade Marian to sell the business. He wondered if he'd told her too much.

She smiled at him and touched his arm. "Thank you."

"For what?" he asked, feeling the soft warmth of her hand on his flesh. She thought he was being considerate.

She didn't know the business was in the final stages of being sold. That any day now, he was going to have to sit down, tell her the truth, and ask for her signature.

The thought depressed him and left a bad taste in his mouth. He didn't like what he was becoming.

"For being honest with your response. I appreciate it."

The sudden urge to kiss her almost overwhelmed him. He wanted to pull her into his arms and feel her body against his own. He wanted to hold her and reassure her that he didn't want to hurt her, yet his pride refused to let him give up the idea of getting the business of his dreams. And owning a mill and working for the family business again would certainly make his family happy.

How could he force her into the situation she feared? But how could he continue doing a job he despised each day? And how could he give up doing a job that would make him look good in his father's eyes?

But most of all, how could he live with himself knowing how he had hurt Marian?

Marian sat in her office going over the latest shipping manifests, her mind focused on the afternoon spent with Louis's family. The time together had informed her on many of the reasons for Louis's behavior. Like a small boy, he seemed to crave the approval of his father and even a need to outdo his brother. Were all men this way and she'd failed to notice, or was she more observant regarding men's motivations since Jean's betrayal?

Determined to finish this stack of work before leaving today, her eyes returned to the papers before her. Louis had already left for the day, saying that he had an errand to run. Several days had passed since their trip to his family's home, and they had returned to the easy atmosphere they enjoyed before being intimate with one another.

Though she couldn't help but think of that night every time she glanced at him, remembering the way his broad shoulders felt beneath her hands, the way he smelled, and the taste of him upon her tongue.

Since that night he had not made any overtures toward her. He'd not even touched her. And while she was grateful in one regard, another part of her missed him. Her sense of loneliness had awakened like a sleeping giant, roaring for attention. Now she craved his touch and his body next to hers, but even more she yearned for the sound of his laughter and the way he could make her smile.

For the first time in her life she enjoyed being with a man and that amazed her. Louis hid his caring soul behind his teasing nature, but she knew from watching him with his family that feelings ran deeper in him than in any man she'd met before. Her thoughts of him being like Jean had not accounted for the man he hid from public view. He cared profoundly about the people he loved, and she wondered what it would be like if he felt concern for her in that same manner.

Quickly, she pushed the thought away. She was not going to become involved with a man again. After Jean's death she'd promised herself she would never marry. Yet now the words rang hollow and she wondered at their emptiness.

The sound of shouting and running footsteps drew her attention away from her thoughts.

Jon came running into her office, gasping for breath, his chest rising and falling in panic. "Mrs. Cuvier—the dockworkers—have gone on strike and they're marching this way. A nasty mob is on its way to the office, Captain Paul sent me to warn you to get out."

"What?" she said, stunned. "The workers are striking? Why? No one's told me they were unhappy!"

The young boy looked sheepish. "Ma'am they've been upset for months. Since before Mr. Cuvier . . . passed on."

Marian grabbed her reticule, intending to follow Jon, a thousand thoughts floating through her brain.

"No one told me. Did Mr. Fournet know of this?" she asked, anger swelling within her. Could this be one of those details that he'd somehow forgotten to mention to her?

"Yes, Ma'am. He met with the workers several weeks ago."

He'd known for weeks and never told her? Why didn't he tell her or was this just another one of those details that he'd forgotten to mention? Marian slammed her fist down on the table making the young man jump. "Is he never going to understand!"

The boy jumped with surprise. "Uh, understand what, Ma'am?"

"That I am to be informed on all decisions," she said laying her reticule back down on her desk.

"Ma'am, we better be going. This mob is carrying torches. The police have been called, but the workers are likely to harm you and burn this place down."

Burn Cuvier Shipping? Then what would she do? How could she support her children, and Philip would not only have no father, but he wouldn't have the inheritance she was so desperately trying to hold on to for him.

But Jon was worried they could harm her. Could she

somehow talk an angry mob out of their destruction? She had to try even though she knew she was putting herself at risk. She had to try for her children's sake. Without the income from the shipping company they would be nearly penniless.

She only hoped her children didn't lose their mother, since they'd already lost their father.

Marian glanced up at him, suddenly seeing the fright in his eyes. "You go on without me, Jon. I'm staying. I'm the only one who can calm them down."

"Oh no, ma'am. You can't do that. We've got to go!"

She stood up and smoothed her skirt, rehearsing in her mind what she was going to say. What would calm a crowd of striking dockworkers? Why wasn't Louis here to face this angry mob he helped create?

"Jon, how long do I have before they arrive?" she asked ignoring his attempt to persuade her to leave.

"Less than five minutes, Ma'am, that's why we need to get going. There's no time for trying to talk them out of this. They're feeling real mean."

Marian came around her desk and moved past Jon and out the office door. He followed her.

"You're going to stay, aren't you?" he said, astonished.

"Yes, I am. But thank you for warning me. You're free to go."

"What kind of man would I be if I left you to face this mob alone?"

She smiled at him. "Probably a very smart one."

"Come with me, Mrs. Cuvier. It's too late and it's not your fault."

"No, it's not my fault, but I've got to clean up this mess or be blamed for the consequences. I could leave, but I'm going to stay and do everything I can to save

Cuvier Shipping." She sighed and marched down the hall to take on this unpleasant task. Louis never mentioned trouble with the unions. Why?

When Marian reached the front office, only a few employees remained, cleaning out their desks and then hurrying out the back door.

"Mrs. Cuvier. We thought you had left." Henry said coming out of his office.

"No. I'm not leaving, Henry."

"You don't understand. These men are mean."

"Can you tell me what they're upset about?"

"It's been almost ten years since they received a pay raise. They work seven days a week and they'd like to have a little time off. Most of them are barely keeping their families from hunger. They're tired of it."

Marian frowned. "Why haven't we given them a pay raise?"

"In the five years I've been here, Mr. Cuvier never gave pay raises."

Marian swallowed. "So they must think that I'm a rich widow who has everything."

"Yes Ma'am, I'm afraid so."

"God, how am I going to get out of this one?" she said.

"Just give them some concessions. Give them one day a week and holidays off. And if you can afford it, a small increase in pay. That's all," Henry said sympathetically.

"Why didn't Mr. Fournet give them an increase in pay?"

"Mr. Fournet offered them holidays off, but nothing else. He told them the business couldn't afford a pay increase."

She stared off into space, her finger tapping against

her lower lip. Their earnings had dropped considerably during the period right after Jean's death, but the figures she'd seen recently showed they were beginning to rise again. No, they couldn't afford a huge increase in pay for anyone.

"When was the last time we increased the cost of our shipments?" she asked.

"It's been years. We're the lowest in the industry. That's why our business has grown so in the last few years."

She glanced at him surprised at this news since Louis had said he got into the business because it was in financial trouble. "Then how could the business be in financial trouble the last few years, if it was growing?"

The man's face turned a telling shade of pink and he glanced away from her and then back. "No disrespect to your late husband, Ma'am, but Jean took a great deal of money from the business for his own personal use. If you understand me."

Marian stood there for a moment, stunned. She knew he was telling her the truth as she'd seen where Jean had withdrawn cash from the business. And she also knew that money had been used to support two other households besides hers.

The rage she thought she'd put behind her at her dead husband's betrayal once again flared, leaving her shocked at how many lives his evil actions had touched. Determined to show the workers that Cuvier Shipping's owners were caring, she suddenly knew what she had to do.

"Then we'll increase the cost of the shipments and give our workers a raise," she said resolutely. "I can understand why they're upset."

The man smiled. "For a woman, you've got a good deal of business sense. I like you, Mrs. Cuvier."

She smiled. "Now if I can only convince our workers not to burn the place down."

He frowned and tilted his head. "I hear them coming."

The sound of angry shouts coming closer chilled her. "I guess it's time to see if I'm persuasive." She glanced at the man. "Henry, if it gets bad, get out of here. It's me they want, not you."

He shook his head. "No, ma'am."

She smiled. "Then we just have to hope it's going to turn out well."

"Mr. Fournet is not going to like this at all," he said, gazing at her worriedly.

With a shrug she begin to walk toward the door. "Mr. Fournet should have been here. At the very least, he should have told me about this months ago. Damn him!" She gasped. "I apologize. I don't usually swear."

Laughing nervously he followed her. "I know. But that tells me you're pretty scared."

She nodded. "Very."

Outside the voices grew louder. She glanced at Henry, the gray of his hair shimmering in the dim light. Taking a deep breath she realized he would be of little help to her if things became ugly.

Outside the voices were chanting, "Give us a raise!"

"I guess it's time," she said, her voice shaking, her knees knocking.

"Yes, ma'am," he said, his eyes compassionate. "They'll be surprised to see you. You can settle this."

He pulled open the front door, stepping tentatively out onto the concrete stairs that led into the building. A hundred or more men filled the street, some carrying torches, some holding signs, and others just shouting.

She stood on the stairs waiting for them to give her a chance to speak, wondering if they would or if this was a pointless exercise.

Finally, a man approached her, his face red with anger as he glared at her. For a moment she didn't think she could face him as the men cheered him on. She swallowed and took a deep breath. If she ran, they would probably destroy the building. She had to stay.

"We've come to tell you that we're on strike until our demands are met!"

"I understand that you're upset," she said nodding her head. "Did you recently speak with Mr. Fournet about your requests?"

"Yes ma'am," he said with disgust. "It was a waste of my time."

"What did he tell you?"

"He said that there was no way that the company could meet our requests for a ten-cents-an-hour raise. He did concede us holidays off."

Marian frowned, thinking that after so many years without a pay increase, their demands didn't seem unreasonable, yet it would increase the company's costs. "Your name, sir?"

"Richard Vanderhorn, ma'am."

She nodded her head and glanced at the crowd, noticing they seemed to have grown quieter as they watched her. Yet their expressions were not friendly and if she didn't offer them something, maybe they would tear her limb from limb and burn the building. And how could she blame them after what Henry had told her?

"Mr. Fournet is right in telling you that the company could not afford to give you a ten-cents-an-hour increase in pay. But I am willing to raise the cost of our shipments, which will in turn give us the money to give you a five-cents-an-hour increase. Plus, I'm willing to give you holidays and Sundays off."

The man stared at her for a moment in shocked surprise, then quickly recovered and asked, "You can't give us ten cents more an hour?"

"Not without raising our costs higher than the other companies in the area. If we do that we threaten the very existence of Cuvier Shipping."

He scratched his head, thinking over her response.

"Of course, that's with the condition that your workers return and finish loading the boats today. After all, I know we had several cargos due to go out this evening."

"If we accept your conditions, will we get another pay raise anytime soon?"

"I've been told about what's happened in the past and I promise you I will do my best to make sure that you're given regular pay increases. I will meet with you and two of your co-workers to determine a fair way to give increases in the future," she said meeting the man's intense gaze, refusing to show weakness.

He rubbed his chin and nodded his head. "Seems fair. How do I know you won't change your mind?"

"Will a handshake suffice for our agreement or do you want it in writing?" she asked raising her chin.

"I think a handshake will do," he said.

They shook hands and the crowd grew silent. Marian breathed a sigh of relief. "Now Mr. Vanderhorn, I expect you to disperse this crowd and somehow get them back to work."

He grinned. "Your business is what feeds their families, but the time for a pay raise had long since passed."

Marian nodded her head. "I agree."

She watched the man hurry down the steps and begin speaking to the crowd. Her knees felt so weak she feared she would collapse. She turned and went back into the building where she found the closest chair and sank into it.

Louis haad conveniently forgot to tell her about the strike. They could have lost everything and then what would she have done? She started to shiver uncontrollably.

Louis drove his carriage recklessly toward the docks, so afraid of what he would find. While at the attorney's office regarding the sale of Cuvier Shipping, he'd been told the dockworkers were marching on the company.

The image of Marian's face appeared before him and he urged the horses faster. The workers would tear her apart if they got their hands on her and it would all be his fault. He had hoped to sell the business before the labor problems became an issue. Now all he wanted was to get Marian to safety.

His heart pounded in his chest and he took the whip to the horses urging them faster. Panic rode him hard as the carriage sped around a corner and rocked, almost tipping over. Louis didn't even flinch as he focused on reaching his partner.

There were no crowds, no shouting angry men as he pulled the horse to a halt in front of Cuvier Shipping. An eerie quiet surrounded the building.

Louis jumped out of his carriage, tethered his horse and then took the stairs two at a time. Fear sent him running in the front door, glancing around wildly for Marian.

She stepped out into the hall and glanced up staring directly into his eyes. Fury darkened her eyes and sparked their smoky depths.

"The crisis with the dockworkers is over, Louis," she

said. "But you have a much larger fiasco on your hands right at this moment."

He hurried down the hall and took her by the arm. He pulled her into her office and into his arms. She stiffened. "Thank God, you're safe. Are you all right? I hurried over as soon as I heard. I was so worried. What happened?"

She pulled out of his arms and glared at him. "Tell me Louis, did you know the workers were about to go on strike? Is this one of those details that you forgot to tell me? Another one of those business decisions that both partners need not know about?"

He threw up his hands in the air, his words spilling out in a rush. "Marian, I never thought it would go this far. I didn't believe they would strike."

"Have you forgotten to tell me anything else, Louis? I need to know, because I promise you I won't be so understanding next time." She placed both hands on her hips, her voice shaking with fury. "I could have been killed by those men today."

"I know. I'm sorry, Marian. I should have told you, but I didn't believe they would really go on strike. You were new to the company and I didn't want to worry you." She turned to face the window and stood looking out the glass. He walked over and put his hands on her shoulders.

"How can I trust you, when I keep finding you've not told me what's going on?" she said, her voice shaking with anger.

"You're right. You have every right to be angry with me. Believe me, Marian, I've never been that frightened for anyone before." He squeezed her shoulders and then whirled her around to face him. "I hurried as fast as I could to get here. Thank God, you're all right!"

She gazed up at him, her gray eyes searching his and

then she sighed and leaned her head against his chest. "Call me a fool, but somehow I believe you. I think this time it really was unintentional."

He smoothed his hand over her hair, loving the feel of the silken strands beneath his hand. "God, I've never been so afraid."

"They wanted to burn the place down. I didn't know what to do," she said with a weary sigh.

She shivered in his arms and he tightened his hold on her. Remorse filled him as he realized he'd left her here to face that angry mob all alone. "Why didn't you leave?"

"I wanted to, but I couldn't." She sighed. "Someone had to stay and try to stop them. With you gone, it could only be me."

He was the biggest damn fool. He'd risked her life because of his stupid sense of pride and wanting to own his own business. When would he put an end to this constant struggle to achieve this goal?

"How did you stop them?" he asked trying to keep her in his arms. She felt so good, so right in his embrace.

"I gave in to their demands, but not to everything that they wanted. I gave them only a five-cent-an-hour raise, with holidays and Sundays off. I also agreed to meet with them regarding creating a pay increase schedule."

"How can we afford that?" he asked.

"We'll have to increase our shipping rates," she said. "I know it's not the best solution, but given the time, it was all I could do."

He put his finger beneath her chin and tilted her head up to gaze deeply into her gray eyes. "I don't care. I'm just glad you're safe. I wouldn't have cared if you gave them Cuvier Shipping."

His lips covered hers in a fierce and demanding kiss,

fed by fear and hunger. He'd come close to losing her and somehow until that moment he hadn't realized just how much she'd come to mean to him.

Until this afternoon, Marian had been an interesting woman who intrigued him and now he realized just how much he needed her. How much he desired her.

She leaned into his kiss, responding with the press of her body against his hardness, gripping his shoulders like a vine clinging to life. She moaned in the back of her throat, the sound heady and thrilling, as he gripped her buttocks through her skirts, pulling her even closer to him.

The sound of someone clearing his throat as he walked past her office had them jumping apart.

They looked at one another, their expressions locked in a stunned gaze. The kiss they'd just shared left Louis reeling.

Their one night of passion, he feared, could possibly be made of the stuff that lifetimes were created from. And suddenly he realized he was in more trouble than even he knew how to elude.

Two days later, Marian sat beside Renée, reading a book with her daughter when her servant, Edward, walked in the room. She glanced up.

"Yes?"

"A Layla DuChampe is here to see you," he said.

A tremor of fear swept through her. What did the woman accused of Jean's murder want with her? While she didn't know if the young woman had actually killed Jean, she didn't want her visiting them at home.

"Renée, Momma has to see someone. Why don't you run upstairs and play with your dolls for a while?"

The girl frowned. "Why can't I stay?"

"Because this is grown-up talk. Now go on upstairs and we'll finish reading later."

"All right," she said, her face drawn in a pout. The little girl trudged up the stairs, expressing her dislike by stomping on every step.

Marian stepped into the entry hall where Edward had left Layla standing. Most of their guests he would have shown into the parlor, but obviously he knew of Miss DuChampe and had left her standing in the hall.

"Miss DuChampe," Marian said, her voice coolly receptive.

The young woman stood there looking nervous, with a canvas bag in her hand. Marian recognized the worn sailor's bag as Jean's.

"I'm sorry for coming without sending you notice, but I feared you wouldn't see me."

"Yes, I understand," Marian said, not denying that she would have refused to see the woman. There was no reason to see her again and, though she felt sorry for the young woman, she wanted nothing more to do with her. Just as she wanted nothing more to do with Nicole.

She held up the bag. "I've brought you some of Jean's things that I thought you might want back. Or at least his children might someday want. I had my servant send them from Baton Rouge."

Marian took the bag out the girl's hand, a feeling of gratitude at her thoughtfulness making her uneasy. She didn't want to feel a sense of obligation toward the girl. Layla had slept with Marian's husband. A husband who hadn't wanted his own wife. "Thank you."

Marian knew she was being rude though somehow she couldn't seem to help herself.

"Could we sit and talk for a moment?" Layla asked. "I know you don't want to have anything to do with me. But this may be my only chance to explain my side of things to you,'' Layla said, her voice strong and sure.

Marian frowned. ''I'm not sure I want to know your side. I'm trying to put the past behind me. Jean is dead and I'm ready to move on with my life.''

''At least you have your life. Mine could end very soon, so I'd like to at least attempt to tell you what happened,'' Layla said, her voice insistent as she stepped toward Marian.

Marian felt a chill go through her at the girl's solemn acceptance of her likely fate.

''Let's go into the parlor where we can talk privately. I'm trying to protect my children as much as possible from hearing the details of their father's deceit. Already, my son has been involved in fights at school and I just hope this all ends very soon.''

''I understand,'' Layla said, and followed Marian into the parlor.

Marian shut the door behind them, pointed to the loveseat and then took a seat across from the girl in the wingback chair. Normally, she would have offered her guest something to drink, but she wanted Layla to leave as quickly as possible.

They sat there awkwardly, staring at one another. Layla glanced around the room, her hands folded in her lap shook slightly. She turned her gaze to Marian. ''You have a nice home.''

''Thank you.''

Layla sighed. ''I want you to know I did not kill Jean. I could never deliberately harm another person. I could not do it.'' She took a deep breath. ''Also, I didn't know that he was married. I never loved him and didn't want to marry him.''

''Then why did you?'' Marian asked leaning forward,

the girl's comments angering her. Why did she still feel anger, when she herself had not loved Jean for years?

Jean's betrayal was more about Marian's pride than love, she suddenly realized. By ignoring her as his wife, she felt less valued and that had hurt. Then, finding out he had married two other women magnified the pain of his disregard.

"My father arranged my marriage to him. It seemed that Cuvier Shipping had taken away all of my father's business, causing him to go bankrupt. Jean acquired Father's company with the agreement that he would marry me."

"But if your father knew Jean, surely he realized Jean was already married. Granted I didn't go out much, but I would have thought people would know of Jean's wife and children."

Layla shifted uncomfortably on the couch. "My father asked and Jean told him that you died of yellow fever and that the children moved to Virginia to be with your family."

"What a liar!" Marian said. "And your father believed him? What if you and Jean had run into someone we both knew?"

"Jean would never let me travel with him or leave the city, except for this trip, which I could not understand." She paused reflecting for a moment, then shook her head as if to clear it. "My father died several months ago, so he never learned of Jean's lies."

Silence filled the room as Marian contemplated this new bit of information regarding her former husband. "You know, the sad thing is that he ruined so many lives around him with his lying ways."

Layla nodded. "I know it looks very bad for me. Many people believe I killed him. I hated him and never wanted to marry him.'' She lifted her chin. ''No matter what, I would never have harmed him.''

''But who could have killed him?'' Marian asked. ''Someone did.''

''I wish I knew. He was poisoned. Someone had to have done it in the night.''

''But didn't you give him the laudanum? Isn't that why they suspect you?'' Marian asked.

Layla glanced down. ''Yes. I often put laudanum in his nightly drink to avoid being . . . intimate with him.'' She looked at Marian and shivered. ''I'm sorry, maybe you enjoyed being with him, but I despised the act. I couldn't stand him touching me any longer.''

''I would never describe Jean as a kind or patient lover.''

Layla shivered with revulsion. ''I never want to have a man touch me again.''

Marian wanted to tell the young woman that not all lovers were like Jean, but decided to keep that piece of information to herself. Layla's feelings were reminiscent of her own emotions regarding Jean. Yet the woman's words again confirmed her beliefs that the problem was with Jean and not with herself. She hoped someday Layla would learn this lesson.

''Layla, just remember that every man is not like Jean. I know it's hard to realize that at this time, but there are a lot of good men in the world who would never treat a woman the way we've been treated.''

She shook her head, her expression bleak. ''It won't matter. I'll never get the chance to find out about them. If I'm convicted, I will receive the death penalty and I will hang.''

Silence filled the room as Marian gazed at the young girl, sympathy swelling within her. ''I'm going to hope that somehow the real killer is found and you are released."

"I hope so. Right now I'm not holding out any hope. It's so much easier for the papers to condemn me, than to think that someone else could have done this."

Marian shut the door behind Layla, her heart swelling with sympathy for the young woman. She seemed so resigned to her fate and that troubled Marian more than anything. How could she just accept the fact she was going to die, if she were innocent?

And if she didn't kill Jean, then who did?

Suddenly the urge to find her children and hug them close overwhelmed her. She wanted to protect them, keep them safe from the winds of change and trouble that seemed to be whirling around them since their father's death.

Marian picked up her skirts and hurried up the stairs to find her babies. She opened the door to Renée's room and found the little girl curled up asleep on her bed, her dolls spread around her. Marian felt her heart swell with love at the sight of her child sleeping so trustingly, and as Marian gazed at her daughter her resolve strengthened to keep her safe.

Closing the door, Marian continued down the hall to Philip's room, realizing she hadn't seen the boy since breakfast this morning.

She knocked and opened his bedroom door. At first glance it appeared to be in order, but then Marian noticed items missing. His favorite hat that his father brought back for him, a teddy bear he hadn't yet given up, and his father's picture. Then she saw a note lying on his bed. She walked over to the bed and picked up the piece of paper, a sense of fear overtaking her. As she begin to read, her heart leapt within her chest and she gasped.

Mother,

I don't like living here without Papa. I don't like what the children say about him and you. I'm going to France to find Papa's family.

Love,
Philip

Marian ran out the door, screaming for her servants. Philip had run away!

CHAPTER FIFTEEN

For the last two days, Louis had done nothing but think about his reactions to Marian facing the strikers. The last time sheer terror struck him like that was at Anne's death. The feelings caught him completely off guard and he'd spent days analyzing them.

At first Marian had been a thorn in his side, an easy target to help rid himself of Cuvier Shipping. First she'd been an adversary and then she'd become his lover and now . . . God, now he feared the feelings that gripped him with such power. After more years than he wanted to remember, he now cared about a woman.

The thought scared him and warmed him at the same time. He'd been trying to convince Marian to marry him because he wanted control of the business, but now his reasons for wanting her were so much more than the business. Yet if she found out about him arranging the sale of Cuvier Shipping, she would hate him.

The buyer for the business was ready to conclude the

deal. They were waiting for the final signatures and the sale would be complete. Yet he hesitated, knowing how much this business meant to Marian and her children, and how much she meant to him.

If she found out, she would never forgive him. Yet for the last two days he had struggled, knowing he should tell her, should be honest and give her the choice of what she wanted to do. He felt torn between his own selfish desires and Marian. He'd dreamed so long of owning his own business, yet he wanted Marian too.

For the last two days he had gone over and over in his head how he could have both Marian and the mill, yet every time he'd found no solution. The buyer was waiting for the final papers to be signed and Louis knew he couldn't keep him in limbo much longer. Sooner or later she would have to be told and her signature acquired.

Time was running out on Louis. Very soon Marian would want nothing to do with him, unless somehow he convinced her to marry him. They were getting along, she'd even kissed him back in the office after the strike. Maybe now was the time to ask her to marry him again. Maybe this time she'd say yes and he could rush her to the altar.

Louis picked up his hat and pushed it onto his head. He left his small apartment in the French Quarter and walked down the street to the livery stable where his buggy was kept. In a matter of moments they hitched his horse and brought the buggy to him.

As he passed down Bourbon Street, past the bars and the restaurants, he realized he couldn't wait to see Marian. He slapped the reins against the horse's back, picking up speed. In just a few minutes Louis turned into the Garden district where Marian lived.

A young boy walked along the roadway, carrying a

small suitcase. As he passed the child, Louis recognized Philip, Marian's son. He pulled the buggy over to the side of the road, tethered the reins of the horse, and hurried to catch up to the boy.

What did he need a suitcase for? Especially this late in the evening and alone?

Finally, he sauntered up beside the boy. "Hello there."

"Hi," Philip said sullenly. "I'm not going back."

"Where are you off to?" Louis asked, ignoring his remark.

The boy frowned at him suspiciously.

"France. To live with my Papa's family," he said, his eyes dark with unshed tears.

With all the change and turmoil in the young boy's life recently, Louis realized he was running. Marian probably knew nothing of the child's whereabouts.

"France is very nice, I hear. You've got a long trip ahead of you. And your Mother gave you enough money for your ticket, did she?"

The boy glanced up at him his eyes widening and Louis knew he hadn't even thought of how he would pay for his passage.

"No, but I'll work my way across," the boy replied. "Or maybe I'll stow away."

Louis fought to keep a straight face, knowing that to the child his pain was serious and he felt compelled to help Marian's son.

"I wouldn't stow away. If you get caught, they'll toss you overboard." Louis pulled out his money clip and peeled several small bills off. "Here, take this. It's a little money to get you started."

"Thanks," Philip said pocketing the bills. "You're not going to try to take me back?"

Louis shook his head. No, he wouldn't force the boy

to go back, just help him to reach the conclusion that it would be best to return home. And he wasn't going to leave here without him.

"A man's got to follow his dream," Louis replied.

"Yeah," the boy said, not as certain as before.

"Your Mother will be upset about your leaving."

Philip shrugged.

"She and Renée will miss you."

He shrugged again, not saying a word, his young face drawing together as if he were in pain.

Louis remembered the fight Philip had gotten into at school and doubted the children made his life any easier now. Adjusting to his father's death and the news surrounding Jean's demise couldn't be easy for the child.

They continued down the street, the suitcase banging against Philip's legs.

"It must be hard to lose your father. You met my father, the old goat is still around and I'm glad." Louis observed the boy carefully, and said, casually, "But yours is gone and I'm sorry about that. Other kids often don't understand what it's like to lose a parent. Especially a father."

The boy kept walking and nodded his head. Louis thought he saw him wipe away a tear in the fading sunlight.

"Kids don't talk about your father and mother the way they do mine," said Philip. "Everyone laughs and says he married all those women. They call them the Cuvier Widows. I don't believe my friends. My papa wouldn't do that." Philip glanced up at Louis, his green eyes accusing. "They're also talking about you."

"Me?" Louis asked stunned. "What are they saying about me?"

Philip's child's face drew together in a scowl. "They're talking about you and my mother."

Maybe he and Marian hadn't kept their romance such a secret after all. "You know your mother and I work together for the business now."

"Yes, I know. Most mothers don't work. They stay at home," Philip said, his eyes dark and accusing, like the kid wanted to cry but refused.

"Not all mothers. Your mother is determined not to let your father's death interfere in your welfare, so she went to work in your father's business. She's really trying to look out for you, Philip."

Louis watched the child consider his words carefully.

"But what's she doing with you?"

Halting on the street, Louis looked at the child who awaited his response. "I don't know what the kids are saying about your mother and me. I'll admit that I think your mother is a beautiful woman. I'll also admit that in the last month our business partnership has changed. I like your mother, Philip."

"So you two have been kissing?"

His question startled Louis.

"Did someone tell you they saw us kissing?"

"Well, were you?"

Louis thought for a moment wondering what to tell the kid and then decided to be honest. "Yes, I've kissed your mother and I'll kiss her again if I get a chance."

The boy considered this for a moment and then frowned up at Louis. "So you like her now?"

"Very much," Louis told the boy honestly.

The boy nodded his head and then suddenly became cheerful. "Do you think I should go to France?"

Louis felt a sense of calm overcome him and he smiled at Philip. "Yes, I think you should go to France, someday, when you're older."

A small smile of relief lit Philip's face. "Would you take me home?"

"I'd be happy to take you home," Louis said.

It took them about ten minutes to get to the house on Josephine Street. Purple and orange rays streaked across the sky, bathing the home in a warm glow as they pulled up front.

"I wonder if she found my note?" Philip asked.

"We'll find out together," Louis said smiling at the boy trying to ease his discomfiture.

"She's probably going to be mad," the boy said climbing down from the buggy.

"Maybe not," Louis said. "Let's go see."

He carried Philip's small suitcase up the sidewalk to the door. Philip opened the front door and stepped inside, and Louis followed him.

"Mother?" he called.

Claire came round the corner, her eyes wide with gratitude. "Is that you, Philip Cuvier?"

"Yes, Aunt Claire. Where's Mother?"

She glanced at Louis standing in the entryway holding Philip's suitcase, and then returned her attention to the boy.

Claire dropped to her knees and wrapped her arms around him, hugging his small body to hers. "Thank God, you're all right. Your mother has gone to the police station to ask for their help in locating you."

"Oh!" he said dejectedly. "I guess she found my note."

"Yes, sir, she sure did." She glanced up at Louis. "Did you find him?"

"We sort of found one another," Louis said.

"Philip, you worried your mother terribly," Claire scolded.

"I'm sorry."

"Go upstairs, young man, and wait for your mother. She should be home soon."

"Yes, Ma'am." He hung his head and started toward the stairs. He turned back and glanced at Louis. "Thank you, Mr. Fournet. Let's play baseball soon."

"It's a deal, Philip. Get some sleep."

"Goodnight."

Louis watched the boy disappear up the stairs, his heart going out to the child. He needed love and support, not to be made to feel guilty for running from the scandal of his father. He waited a moment longer to make sure that Philip was out of hearing and then turned his full attention on Claire.

"Don't be too hard on the boy. He ran to get away from the scandal of his father. The kids are teasing him about it and he needs the adults in his life to understand. Tell Marian I brought him home."

He walked out the door, not giving Claire a chance to respond.

Marian opened the door of the big house, exhaustion and fear causing her to shake. The image of Philip wandering the streets of New Orleans alone brought tears to her eyes. She was so afraid for him.

It was her fault he'd run away. If she'd been there for him when he needed her, he would still be at home and not lost on the street somewhere. She was a terrible mother not to have realized the depth of her son's continuing grief at Jean's death.

Claire came running around the corner. "I'm so glad to see you! Louis brought Philip home."

"Thank God, he's back! Where is he?" she asked not giving Claire time to respond, but moving toward the stairs.

"He's upstairs, waiting for you."

She lifted her skirts and ran up the stairs hurrying down the hall. He was home! Flinging open the door, she burst into his room to see him, unpacking his suitcase, putting his clothes back in the chest. He glanced up at the sound of the door opening, his eyes troubled, his face downcast.

"Hi Mother," he said meekly.

She went to him and took him in her arms, hugging his small frame to her own. "Are you all right?"

"I'm okay. Mr. Fournet found me walking and brought me home."

Louis had found her son and brought him home. She felt a sense of relief and overwhelming gratitude for her partner.

"Philip, you scared me so badly. Why did you leave, son?"

He stepped out of her embrace. "You found my note?"

"Yes, I've been out looking everywhere for you."

He shrugged. "I get tired of everyone telling me how bad my father was. I miss him. I don't want the kids to make fun of him anymore."

Marian felt her heart plummet for her son. The urge to scream at Jean almost overwhelmed her, though she knew she couldn't reach him beyond the grave. But his selfish acts had touched more than her life, their children were affected by his immoral behavior.

"Oh, Philip, you'll always love him," she said trying to soothe her son and temper her anger at her dead husband.

"Yes," the boy said. "But how could Papa have married two other ladies? Didn't he love you, Mama?"

Marian sat down on the bed and pulled her son down beside her.

"I don't know why your father did this. I think he loved me as much as he could. We just have to go on and know that what he did is in the past and forgive him. We'll get through this Philip, I promise."

"The kids call the other women the Cuvier Widows," he said, his big green eyes sad.

"Yes, I know. The adults are calling them that also. Sometimes people say hurtful things and no matter what you do, it makes you sad," Marian said.

"I wish Papa were here and that none of this had happened."

"For you and Renée, I wish he were too, but we can't change the past, only move forward. Someday soon you'll look back and realize this is all behind you," she said leaning over and kissing his forehead.

Philip glanced down at his hands, his mouth drooping.

"What else is wrong, Philip?" Marian asked.

"Have you been kissing Mr. Fournet?" he asked.

Marian stared at the boy, her face feeling frozen. "Who told you that?"

How could he know about her and Louis?

"My friend Tom said his father saw you out dancing with two men," Philip said, his eyes not meeting hers.

"Yes, remember that night I went with Louis and I told you we were taking out our biggest client. Did he tell you I kissed Louis?" she asked.

"No. I just wanted to know."

"Would it matter?" she asked.

Philip gazed at her, his forehead wrinkling in a frown. "Depends."

She sighed. "I like Louis. Yes, I kissed him. Does that upset you?"

He smiled. "No. I just wanted to know. Louis told me this afternoon that he kissed you."

Surprised, Marian managed to hide her reaction from her son. "What else did he tell you?"

Her son shrugged. "He told me he likes you now." The boy smiled at his mother. "And he wants to kiss you again."

Marian shook her head, a warm feeling coming over her. "That's nice."

Dear God, was the man crazy? The boy had enough to trouble him without Louis telling him about them. "Promise me that you won't run away again, without talking over whatever is bothering you. I love you and I was frightened, Philip."

He glanced down. "I'm sorry. I promise to talk to you."

Marian felt a sense of relief, even if she knew that the boy could run away again. She'd found her son and he was safe. She hoped the troubles that sent him running were at least soothed if not yet solved.

"Okay, I think it's time for you to go to bed."

"Already?"

"Yes," she said, and walked to the door. "I'll come back to tuck you in."

"I love you, Mother."

His comment took her by surprise and filled her heart with love. Since he'd started to grow up, it wasn't often he said those three words. She blinked back tears. "I love you too, Philip. I'm glad you came home safe."

Louis sat reading the newspaper, relaxing after such a harrowing day, when a knock sounded at the door. The clock on the wall showed the hour to be late. Cautiously he opened the door to find Marian standing on his doorstep.

Fear seized him as his thoughts instantly assumed she'd found him out.

"What's wrong?" he asked.

"I came to talk to you about Philip," she said, her gray eyes worried.

Louis glanced down the darkened street and, seeing no one, grabbed Marian's arm and pulled her into his home and shut the door. She leaned against the door, staring at him with those smoky gray eyes. The urge to push her against the door and lean his body into hers almost overwhelmed him, but he resisted.

He released her and she glanced around the room nervously. "I came to thank you for bringing my son home. Philip told me what you did. I was so worried."

Louis shrugged. "He's a confused kid."

She nodded as she walked around his small living room glancing around at his very masculine furnishings. "He asked me about us." She raised her worried eyes to his. "Philip told me you said that we had kissed."

"I wasn't going to lie to him," Louis said watching her. He saw the pain in her expression and wanted to comfort her, ease her hurting. "I told him I kissed you and would do so again. He asked me if I liked you now and I said yes, very much."

She smiled at him, her eyes still worried. "You didn't say anything else?"

"No," Louis said with a frown. "Why would I?"

Marian shrugged and walked around the room, her hand lightly touching his books. "I don't know. He seemed all right with the fact that you and I were kissing, yet he ran away. He's still troubled about his father and his friends are teasing him about the Cuvier Widows." She paused taking a deep breath. "I'm so worried about him. I'm such a terrible mother, Louis."

"What makes you say that?" he asked.

She glanced at him her eyes troubled. "I didn't know about the way his friends were treating him. I thought since the fight at school, things had gotten better. I feel so bad for not helping him and now he's hearing gossip about the two of us."

He stepped toward her, his voice gentle and soothing. "People have been talking about me for years. And frankly you've been the center of scandal since Jean's death. You're not a bad mother, Marian, you've just been preoccupied with the business and didn't notice the absence of his friends around the house."

She rubbed her hands up and down her arms as if she were chilled. "But how could I do that to my son? My children have always been important to me." She paused, gazing at him for guidance. "What am I doing, Louis? I'm losing touch with my children, yet I'm trying to earn a living for them. I'm so confused about what's best for them, for me."

Louis walked over to Marian and put his arms around her. It felt so right, Marian so warm and tender in his embrace. The urge to protect and shield her filled him and he knew this was where he belonged.

"You're just worried because Philip was missing this afternoon. He's a good kid. He understands what you're doing, but he's struggling with the knowledge that his father betrayed his family and that everyone knows his father's shame."

"But how can I protect him? He's just a boy. He doesn't deserve to be treated this way," she said leaning her head against his chest.

His hand massaged her back in a circular motion, soothing her. "You can't defend him from life, Marian, no matter how much you want to."

She leaned back in his arms and gazed at him. "I know you're right, but he's my son. I want to keep all the bad things in life away from him. He deserves an innocent childhood and Jean has taken that away from him."

"I know. But he has you and his sister to help him through this difficult time." He paused. "And you're working to keep a business for him. You can't be all things to him."

She sighed heavily and returned her head to his chest. "Since that trip we took to see your family, I can't help but think that he may not want Cuvier Shipping at all. You don't want your father's business. What if I'm forcing my son into something he never wanted?"

"Then you sell it or you give the business to Renée. Whatever you decide, accept your decision and realize you are making the best evaluation you can at the time. Quit second-guessing yourself," he said tenderly, enjoying the feel of her in his arms.

Leaning back in his arms, her hand reached up and stroked his cheek with her fingertips. "Why is it that you always soothe me and make me feel good about the decisions I've made? How is that?"

He placed his fingers beneath her chin and lifted it up to within inches of his lips. Gazing deeply into her smoky gaze he felt as if he were lost in their depths. "Maybe it's because we're good together. Maybe it's because we complement one another. Maybe it's because I care about you more than any woman I know."

His mouth covered her parted lips seeking the soft, sweet recess of her mouth. Since the day that Marian came into his life, she had challenged him in ways that constantly kept him hurrying to keep up with her. Intriguing and interesting, she'd changed him. For only the second time in his life, he'd found a woman he could spend the rest of his life with.

He suckled her lower lip, teasing her mouth as his

hands molded her body against his hard one. She pushed back and stepped out of his arms to stare at him, her gaze wary. "This is not another one of your pranks? Not another one of your attempts to acquire Cuvier Shipping?"

"God, no. No matter what happens, never forget I care about you. I've never felt so much fear as when they said that you were there in front of those strikers all alone." He ran his hands through his hair; he should tell her about the sale, but not yet. He wanted and needed this moment with Marian. Not yet. Just a little more time.

"I was such a fool, Marian, for placing you in a position that put you in so much danger."

He ran his fingertips down her arm and when his fingers touched her hand, he skimmed them across her palm and then entwined her fingers with his. He drew her to him and this time she leaned her body into his, touching him in all the pertinent places.

"I want you so badly," he said putting his lips against her ear.

"God," she said, with a sustained sigh. "You drive me crazy with need."

Louis laughed, his lips brushing against hers. He'd tell her about the sale of Cuvier Shipping in the morning, just give him tonight.

Grabbing her by the hand, he began to pull her toward his bedroom.

"Where are we going?" she asked, her eyes shining with pleasure.

He raised his brows. "We're alone and you've told me I drive you crazy with need. Now I need you to show me."

Just as they reached his bedroom, he pulled her tightly

against him securing her hips with his. She felt his passion, her eyes widening in surprise.

She glanced at his plantation bed in the center of the room. "You do have good taste in furniture."

"I've dreamed of you lying in that bed. Now we're going to experience it," he said, as his lips savored hers once again, pouring out his passion, making her his. Her arms wrapped around his neck and she hung limply onto him, his fingers moving over the buttons on the back of her dress.

She clung to him, her hands reaching up to run her fingers through his hair. She gripped his head, pressing his obliging lips against her own.

Kissing had always been something he'd done mostly to lead his women to bed, but with Marian, he craved the taste of her. He longed for the touch of her sweet lips and he found in them his claim of absolute possession.

They broke apart and for a moment stared at one another, their breath sounding harsh in the darkness. Without a word they begin to shed clothing, hurrying to feel fevered skin against skin once more.

She turned around and he undid the buttons on her dress, his fingers shaking as he hurried. When all the buttons were freed, he tugged on the shoulders of her dress, which fell to the floor in a puddle of cloth. She turned to face him and he gazed at her soft curves outlined by her camisole, shadowy in the moonlight. He bent over to put his lips to the material and suckled her sweet bud, loving the way her nipple puckered in response. He laved her breast, holding it soft and heavy in his hand.

She pushed him away pulled her camisole over her head, standing before him in her pantaloons, corset, and chemise. She turned her back to him, so that he could untie her corset.

He hurried with the lacing, his fingers fumbling in his haste. And then he slipped the garment from her, followed by her chemise, and last her pantaloons. The pale moonlight streamed through the window exposing the supple gleam of her delicate back, and he pressed his lips along the soft curves. Shudders rippled through her as he worked his way up her spine to the top of her shoulders, where he gently nibbled on the long column of her neck.

She moaned and turned toward him, slipping her arms around his neck, pressing her breasts against him. His lips covered hers in a slow endless kiss as he gently propelled her backwards toward the big bed waiting for them.

How many times had he dreamed of her in this very bed? How many times had he pictured her naked and wanton between his sheets?

When the back of her knees touched the bed, he broke free of the kiss, his breath rasping with need. He stepped back and while she watched him, he removed his underpants and shirt. When he'd shed the last of his clothing, he moved toward her and pushed her down upon his bed.

His leg touched her smooth satiny leg and he couldn't help but think it felt so right to have her in his arms, in his bed. He covered her with his body, his hand caressing the side of her face, brushing back her hair.

"God, you are so beautiful."

She smiled, her hand reaching for the part of him that throbbed thick and unyielding.

Her hand closed over him, enclosing the fierce heat he felt building within his body and she stroked him, fanning the flames into a raging inferno.

He laid back and she half covered his body with her own as each long, slow stroke of her hand was a scalding caress that took him closer and closer to the edge. There was no guarantee of tomorrow, they only had this moment and he reveled in her touch, in the soft sighs of her excitement. Nimble fingers explored him, coaxing and probing his arousal as she clasped his erection within her fingertips.

Finally, when he could stand it no more, he flipped her to her back and put his mouth against her breast, his fingers seeking between her thighs. Gently he cupped her, stroking her moistness, wanting to give her pleasure.

Marian had made him realize his life was empty and meaningless. She had shown him the importance of family and honor. Her courage and strength had made him stronger and now because of her, he was a better man. No woman before her had ever made him feel so complete, so strong and yet so vulnerable at the same time. He pleasured Marian, needing to hear her cry out his name, wanting her more than anything he'd ever wanted in his life.

In the soft light he laved the pebbled kernel of her nipple. Soft sighs and murmurs came from her as he circled the hardened nub of her breast with his tongue. He pressed his hot flesh against the warm expanse of her skin, needing to get even closer to her, to be inside her.

"Louis," she gasped, her breath raspy, her voice husky.

"Yes, love?" he asked, his hand closing over her tremulous breast.

"Now!" she said, her lashes fluttering open.

He chuckled at her impatience and brushed his lips across her breast. He rolled until his body covered her own, careful not to press his full weight onto her.

But instead of giving her the satisfaction she craved,

he lingered, his lips covering hers in a long kiss that swirled him closer and closer to the edge. He wanted to prolong the moment, he wanted to resist as long as possible and give her more pleasure than she'd ever experienced, but it was becoming more than he could bear.

Breaking the kiss she begged, "Louis."

Louis couldn't wait another minute. He plunged into her slick body, the feel of her tight and snug around him, consuming him. Sensation whirled around him expanding his perceptions as he covered her lips with his own. He wanted to be inside her forever. He wanted to have her wake up with him each morning, and go to bed beside him each night. He wanted her with all his heart and being, until they were old and gray, until death separated them and eternity brought them back together again.

He needed her, more than he'd desired anything in his life and this moment, plunging into her warm body, he knew nothing would ever make him as happy as being with Marian.

"Louis," she cried, her body tensing around him. With each stroke, he sealed their fate until she clung to him, shudders racking her body, and his own climax came in a swift surge of power coursing through his body.

Together they clutched one another, letting the night soothe their racing hearts, their breathing ragged and choppy.

After several minutes of just holding one another, Louis slid down onto the bed beside Marian and pulled her tight against him, patting her gently. Feeling warm and responsive, her fear of lovemaking had disappeared.

He kissed her softly on the lips. "I meant what I said

earlier, Marian. I care for you more than anyone ever before. I want to marry you and spend the rest of my life at your side."

She paused, gazing at him, her eyes luminous in the darkness, her face rapturous yet contemplative as she stared at him. Minutes passed and Louis was beginning to fear her response.

"All right, Louis," she said. "I'll marry you."

CHAPTER SIXTEEN

It wasn't until Marian was in the carriage going home that the doubts begin to assail her. Was she crazy? She'd just agreed to marry the man who had done nothing but try to take the business away from her. Yet for the first time in her life, she felt happy. A sense of belonging enveloped her when she was in Louis's arms that she could never remember experiencing before.

In the last few weeks they both had changed. The last time he asked her to marry him, she'd known his declaration of love to be a lie. But this time, he seemed different and he hadn't mentioned the word love, only that he cared for her more than anyone ever before.

Men were certainly not good at expressing their emotions when it came to love and commitment. And while Louis did better than Jean, he still could use some improvement. But most important, he wasn't Jean.

Louis was a decent man, who cared about people, sometimes more than he should. He loved his family and treated her children better than their father ever had.

And though she'd promised herself never to marry again, she decided that Jean was not going to take away her happiness any more. She had let that man's actions influence her decisions for the last time. Yes, she'd vowed never to marry again to escape the pain and heartache that being married to Jean had brought.

But marriage to Louis would be different, because he wasn't like Jean. She trusted him, she loved him. And there was the biggest reason for saying "I do."

God, when had she fallen in love with the man? Could it possibly have been when he'd taken her to visit his family, showing a part of himself that she hadn't expected? Or could it have been during the pretend picnic when he'd tried to show her he was sorry for his blatant lie?

When had he broken down her defenses and claimed her bruised and battered heart? When he found her son and brought him home, giving her sister instructions to give the child love and support?

She put her hands over her face, massaging her forehead. Marriage to Louis would be good for her children. He could ensure their lives financially and be the father that Philip so desperately needed.

Louis had healed her wounded spirit and though falling in love with the man had never been her intention, she'd given her heart to him. And now she knew that though she resisted, she belonged with Louis.

The carriage pulled up in front of the house on Josephine Street and she glanced at the darkened windows of her home. Midnight had long since passed. How would her children react to the news she was marrying Louis?

Climbing out of the carriage she glanced at her servant, knowing that never before had she kept him out this late. "Thank you, Edward. I'm sorry for the late hour."

"It's all right, ma'am," he said, and clicked to the horses, driving the carriage around back.

She tiptoed into the house and climbed the stairs to each of her children's rooms. Slowly opening the door to Renée's room, she glanced in at the child. Curled safely in her bed, her daughter slept soundly. Marian tiptoed into the room, leaned over and kissed her cheek, love for her daughter swelling within her. Then she hurried out the bedroom and quietly closed the door.

Next she went to Philip's room and found the boy deep in slumber as she peeked in at him. The urge to protect him and Renée overwhelmed her and she thought back on the last three months of everything they had been through.

Her heart swelled at the thought of Louis and suddenly she felt certain of her decision. Yes, she would marry him and vow to stay with him until death did them part.

Marian sat in her office several days later, reflecting on how happy she'd been the last few days. Louis had come to the house and taken Philip to a baseball game, while she and Renée had gone on a shopping excursion. Then later they met at Antoine's in the French Quarter for dinner.

Her children responded to Louis as if he was a good friend and he treated them well, catering to them and spending more time with them than their father had. They were waiting for just the right moment to tell Philip and Renée they were marrying. But in the meantime, Louis came to the house for dinner every night and later while the children were in bed, they'd sat in the parlor and kissed until their lips were swollen and they were frenzied with desire. Then she'd sent him home.

Her heart warmed as she reflected on the way her life seemed to have changed in these last few months. Even before Jean's death she'd been unhappy, but now she felt almost giddy with joy. Slowly her heart and her mind were both agreeing that marrying Louis was a good decision and when she gazed at him, she knew deep in her heart she really did love him. But she had yet to whisper those three little words to him. She wanted to, but somehow every time fear seemed to clog her throat and keep her from saying them aloud.

A knock on her door jerked her out of her reverie and she looked up to see Jon standing in the doorway.

"Mr. Fournet is not here and a Mr. Stephen Hudson is here to see him. I wondered if you could talk to him," Jon said.

Marian nodded her head. "All right, bring him back."

Less than five minutes later an older gentleman with a scruffy-looking face entered her office.

"Mrs. Cuvier, I'm sorry to intrude. Maybe I should come back later when Mr. Fournet is here?" he said looking at her hesitantly.

"Whatever it is, I'm sure I can help you," she said.

"It's just that I didn't want to disturb you. Mr. Fournet informed me you were in mourning for your late husband."

She glanced at him oddly. Why would Louis tell him she was in mourning when he knew she'd hardly grieved the death of Jean?

"It's all right, Mr. Hudson," she said. "Please come in and have a seat."

"It's nice to finally meet you," he said walking in and

shaking her hand. "I was terribly sorry to hear about the death of your husband."

"Thank you," she said politely. "How can I help you?"

The man frowned. "Mr. Fournet told you that I'm the attorney handling the sale? Right?"

She knit her brow in confusion. "Sale? What sale are you referring to, Mr. Hudson?"

He took a deep breath his eyes widening. "Why the sale of Cuvier Shipping, of course."

"Cuvier Shipping?" Marian asked, in stunned disbelief.

"Yes, Mr. Fournet came to me and asked that I arrange to sell the business for you and him. I'm here to talk with you regarding signing the final papers."

Marian felt as if the world was suddenly ripped away from her and for a moment she sat there staring at the gentleman, her heart crumbling. She cleared her throat and reached for the glass of water sitting on her desk, anything to bring her back to the present and not the devastating black void his words had sent her spiraling into.

All Louis's words of trust and marriage and happily ever after seemed to rise in her throat, choking her.

That lying bastard had arranged to sell the business without her knowledge. His words of caring and affection rang empty and hollow in her heart, and she wanted to cry, but refused to let the tears come, knowing once they started, it would be hard to stop. There would be plenty of time for that later, but right now she must deal with his deceit.

"Mr. Hudson, Cuvier Shipping is not for sale."

"Are you certain?" he asked staring at her, his expression full of doubt and confusion. "Mr. Fournet said there was another business he wanted to invest in and he needed the money from the sale of the shipping company to start that business. He asked me to rush the sale."

Unspeakable rage filled Marian as she remembered his talk of wanting to start a business involving his father's plantation. Suddenly everything seemed to fall into place and she realized her earlier fears were correct. He only wanted to marry her for her signature and the subsequent sale of Cuvier Shipping. That tiny niggling doubt she'd felt concerning Louis had been right.

"Mr. Fournet owns only half of the business and I own the other half. I'm not interested in selling."

"He told me you wanted to sell your half, but he asked me not to bother you, since you were in mourning for your husband."

The bastard had whispered words of trust and affection and then intended to ask for her signature.

"How considerate," she said sarcastically.

"So what do I tell the buyers?" he asked, perplexed.

"You tell them there's been a huge mistake and that Cuvier Shipping is not for sale. It never has been for sale."

The man stared, his mouth open in shock. "I don't know what to say, Mrs. Cuvier. I'm sorry you had to find this out from me. Are you certain you don't want to sell? I have an excellent buyer who will pay well."

"I'm certain," she said feeling her strength slowly draining from her.

He sighed. "All right, I will go back to the buyer and tell them that there will be no sale."

"Thank you, Mr. Hudson," she said standing so he would get the message that their meeting was over. She could feel her composure beginning to crumble and she didn't want to break down in front of the man.

He stood and gathered his hat and briefcase. "Good day, Mrs. Cuvier."

"Good day," she said, and watched him walk out the door. She sank back into her chair, and her carefully constructed self-control disintegrated. She lay her head down on her arms and sobbed. Damn Louis for hurting her this way. Damn him for his deceitfulness and damn him for wooing her heart only to break it!

Louis opened the door to Cuvier Shipping and couldn't imagine feeling any better than he did right at this moment. Since Marian had agreed to be his wife, he'd made the decision not to sell Cuvier Shipping. He couldn't do that to his soon-to-be-wife. With the sale canceled, he would forfeit any chance of owning the mill for the time being, but he was willing to put his dream on hold for Marian and hope for some other opportunity later.

He walked into the office and greeted Jon with a smile. "Good morning."

"Good morning," the man said, not looking him directly in the face.

Louis passed Henry in the hallway and the man ducked his head and kept walking, refusing to meet his gaze. He passed one of the clerks and the man turned his face away from him and Louis felt like he had suddenly developed leprosy.

What was wrong with everyone this morning?

He walked into his office and set his bag down, his intention being to stroll over and say good morning to his soon-to-be wife. But before he could settle in, he looked up and saw her standing in his doorway.

"Good morning," he said, his voice trailing off. Her eyes were dull and swollen as if she'd been crying, her expression appeared almost hostile. "I . . . I was just coming over to say hello. What's wrong, honey? You look like someone died."

"Not someone, but something," she said, her voice even and cold. She shut the door to his office, the click seemed loud and fear trickled through him. Distraught didn't begin to describe the way she looked and an eerie feeling of apprehension crept through him. He wanted to run from the office, alarm at what she would say filling him.

"I had a visit from a Mr. Hudson this morning," she said, her voice shaky. "He came to see you and instead met with me."

"Oh, God," he said putting his hand to his head. His fears were being realized.

She ignored him. "He spoke with me about the buyers for our business that I didn't know was for sale."

"Let me explain," he pleaded, hoping she would listen. "I've been going to tell you for the last week and I just hadn't found the right moment. And then last night, I decided not to go through with the sale."

She took a deep breath, her chin quivered, but she quickly recovered. "Well you don't have to tell me anymore. I know."

"Please Marian, believe me, I was going to back out of the deal. I did this months ago. Right after Jean died."

"You've used that excuse once too often, Louis. It doesn't work anymore," she said.

Louis remembered their conversation after the strike when she had asked him if there was anything else he'd forgotten to tell her. But at the time, he hadn't realized he cared for her. He'd still been intent on deceiving her.

"I've already told Mr. Hudson that I will not sign *any* papers that sell Cuvier Shipping. Not now, not ever."

He shook his head. The fear that everything was lost almost choked him. She would never understand what had driven him to this point.

"Listen to me, Marian. I wanted to tell you so many times, but . . ."

She sobbed, but quickly gained control. "You knew how I felt regarding this company." She took a deep breath. "If you want out, then I'll do what I can to buy you out, but you are not going to sell this company without my knowledge," she said, her voice rising and gaining strength. "How dare you even try!"

He felt awful. All his fears slammed into him like a punch to his belly and he sagged, knowing she couldn't forgive him. "I understand. I didn't think anyone would buy just part of the business. I was wrong for wanting to sell all of it."

She took two steps toward him, her eyes flashing with fury. She slammed her hand down on his desk, causing him to jump with shock at her response. "How can you sleep at night for your lies? How could you do this to me, Louis? You lied and were willing to sell the business out from under me? What kind of person are you?"

"I'm a louse, okay? After you agreed to marry me, I decided I would back out of the deal, but I just hadn't done it yet. I hoped you would never find out." But inside he knew he hadn't backed out of the deal before now because part of him wished he could convince her to sell the business. Now his lack of action was going to rob him of the one thing worth keeping in his life: Marian.

"I don't want to hear any more of your lies," she said, her voice rising. "Everything you've said has been a lie and I believed you."

"No, Marian. You're wrong."

A tear slid down her cheek. "How can I believe you? How can I ever trust you again?"

"Marian, I promise you, that the only thing I've lied to you about is the sale of the business."

"You've never told me any untruths regarding the business before now? You've been completely honest?" she asked.

He paused for a moment thinking over the previous months and knew he'd never been completely honest with her. "I . . ."

"That's what I thought. You know, Louis, it hurt badly enough when Jean betrayed my trust. I thought I would never get over him. But now I see that your disloyalty is even worse." She wiped away a tear. "You've betrayed my love and that's something that Jean never had."

God, she'd said she loved him, but then she turned and walked out the office door, leaving Louis feeling as if someone had dropped a load of bricks on him. He lay in the dust hurt and bleeding, wishing for the end. He watched her leave and knew she'd just taken his heart with her and he might never get it back.

Marian cleared off her desk and then promptly left, not telling anyone where she was going. She needed some time away from the business, away from Louis, everything. She needed some time to resolve the questions that fogged her brain and made her feel crazy. She needed someone to surgically remove Louis and everything about him from her mind and her heart.

How do you replace someone who is constantly in your thoughts and repair the hole their love has left in your heart?

Marian sat in her carriage looking out at the city she

loved, not really seeing the people or the places, her mind still reeling with the implications of what had happened this morning. When the carriage pulled up in front of the house on Josephine Street, she wondered if she should sell the home that Jean and she had shared.

Since his death three months ago, had she taken any time to really reflect on her life and decide where she was going? In the past, she'd always taken the children to Virginia to visit her family, but this summer she'd spent her time at Cuvier Shipping, trying to make sure she'd saved the business for her son. But now she even wondered if saving the business for Philip was really worth her effort.

Climbing out of the carriage, Marian walked up the sidewalk to the front door and entered the house. She leaned against the wooden portal, wanting to cry now that she was home.

Claire rounded the corner. "What are you doing home at this hour?" Her eyes narrowed at the sight of Marian. "What's happened?"

Marian shook her head, the tears starting to fall and she knew she could no longer hold them at bay. "Louis . . . he's such a bastard."

Claire took her sister by the arm and led her into the parlor and shut the door. She sat her gently down on the settee and handed her a handkerchief. "What has he done now?"

For a few moments, Marian just sat and cried letting all the anguish she'd held inside her flow out through her tears. Finally after several moments her tears began to subside, and she wiped her face.

"I'm sorry. It's just that he asked me to marry him and we've been waiting to announce it to everyone."

"I would say congratulations, but somehow I don't

think you've told me everything. And I get the feeling there will be no wedding."

"Today, he was late coming into the office and Mr. Hudson, an attorney, came to the office to meet with Louis. Since Louis was not there he asked to speak with me."

She began to tear up again as she recalled the man's visit and the horrible look of surprise on his face when he realized she knew nothing about the sale of the business.

"He told me the buyers for Cuvier Shipping were awaiting my signature on the final papers and the sale would be complete."

"Dear God!" Claire gasped, her voice filled with shock.

"Louis has been trying to sell the shipping company," she said, her voice quivering.

"Did you confront him?"

"Yes and he said that he started the process of selling the company before I was involved, but that's his excuse for everything. He said that he decided to cancel the sale, but just hadn't gotten around to doing it," she said, her heart breaking as she realized the extent of his betrayal.

"Or he was waiting until you said 'I do' and then he could do what he wanted," Claire said quietly.

Marian started to cry again. "Of course he's been telling me how much he cares for me. And now I find out the truth. He didn't want me. He just wanted Cuvier Shipping."

"Oh, Marian, I'm so sorry," Claire said patting Marian's back. "What are you going to do?"

Marian wiped her eyes with the handkerchief in her hand. "I've not taken any time off since Jean died. I need some time with my children. I need some time away from everything to think. So, I'm going to go to Virginia for a few weeks."

Claire nodded her head. "That is a good idea. It would give you time to decide how you're going to work closely with Louis after everything that's happened."

The thought of going back into the office and sitting across the hall from the man who had lied his way into her bed was impossible. "I can't see him right now. I can't see him until I've gotten over falling in love with him."

Claire frowned. "That may be impossible."

"I can't work with him, knowing that I love him and that he's deceived me. I have to get over Louis before I can go back to work."

But how could she forget the man who had finally won her heart and healed her broken spirit? How could she forget the man who'd made her realize she was a desirable woman once again? How could she ever forget Louis?

CHAPTER SEVENTEEN

Two days passed, and Louis begin to wonder if Marian would ever return to Cuvier Shipping. Funny how at one time, he would have been overjoyed by her lack of attendance. But now he missed her. Despondent and miserable, he stared across the hall at the empty office, blaming himself. Everything had blown up in his face and it was all his fault.

He walked across the hall and stood staring into her office. Breathing deeply he thought he could smell the scent of her perfume lingering in the air. An ivy plant grew in the windowsill, a small bowl and pitcher of water stood in the corner with a dainty hand towel for washing. The feminine touches and tidiness made the room look more like a powder room than an office, but they were remembrances of Marian. And he feared he would never see her again.

With fierceness he'd never known, he could feel his heart aching, missing her desperately.

How could he have handled things so badly? How could he have imagined that she would agree to sell Cuvier Shipping? And why hadn't he been honest with her once he realized he wanted to marry her and spend the rest of his life with her?

Was he so blind that he couldn't see that he loved her? That he'd probably been in love with her for months now? When had he become the type of man who couldn't recognize love and was so selfish that he hurt other people just to get what he wanted.

How could being a mill owner be so important to him that he would sell out someone he loved? Guilt at his egotistical actions ate at him like a cancer. He was a fool to give up a woman like Marian for a mill, but the lure of owning his own business had driven rational thought from his head.

With a sigh he started to turn away when Henry came to the door.

"It's been awfully quiet around here without Mrs. Cuvier," he said, a sad tone in his voice.

"Yes," Louis said tiredly.

"Is she coming back?" Henry asked glancing at him uneasily.

"I don't know."

"We tried so hard to get rid of her at first and now since she's gone, we all want her back," Henry said, with a sigh. "Everyone misses her."

Something in the way Henry said the words irritated Louis. "Why does everyone think she's not coming back?"

Henry laughed nervously. "You. Closed doors keep people out, but sometimes voices raised in anger can be heard through doors."

"Damn!" Louis said running his hand through his hair. "So everyone knows how much of an idiot I am."

Henry gazed at him, his expression no longer friendly. "You said it, not me. Most of the men are pretty unhappy that you would try to sell us all out without so much as a word."

"It wasn't personal," Louis said.

"Tell that to the man who comes to work here every day to support his wife and kids," Henry said. "It's real personal to him, Louis."

Louis ran his hand through his hair. "I didn't think of the workers, Henry."

"That's obvious. Who were you thinking of besides yourself?"

Louis sighed and hung his head. "I certainly botched things badly. I love Marian and wanted to marry her, but now I don't think she'll have anything to do with me. She wouldn't even listen to my explanations the other day."

"You might try looking at it from her perspective, Louis. First Jean betrays her by marrying two other women and now you come along and lie to her about the business. I feel sorry for the next man who comes into her life, because she'll be looking to castrate him." He shrugged. "And I can't say that I blame her."

"I know I did her wrong, but I was going to try to fix everything. If only Mr. Hudson hadn't come and told her about the sale. I was going to back out, really."

"You're not getting the point, Louis. You never should have done this to begin with. You were partners with her and you've never acted like a partner in good faith. And I'm ashamed to say I helped you. Makes us both out to be bastards of the worst sort."

Louis didn't say anything. He just stood there absorbing Henry's words. Somehow he knew they were true and they made him feel contrite.

"You're right, Henry. I haven't been a good partner

to Marian since the day Jean died. I've acted way out of line." He sighed. "I think it's time I took a little time off to reflect on what I'm going to do with the rest of my life and discover just what kind of man I am."

Henry raised his brows at him. "And just where are you going to do this?"

"You're in charge of the business until Marian returns. I'm going home to Belle Fournet. I'm going home to decide my future."

Louis stood outside, leaning against an oak tree older than the states. He had been home for nearly a week and his father acted like he was home to stay. But Louis was still undecided as to what he wanted to do.

And he missed Marian fiercely.

He'd thought about her every day, he'd dreamed of her at night and through it all he had come face-to-face with the fact that he had behaved in a despicable manner. No wonder she hated him and probably never wanted to have anything to do with him again. He wanted her back but didn't feel like he could even ask for her forgiveness. He wasn't worthy of exoneration after the way he'd lied to her.

The evening shadows waned, the sun casting its last rays across the tall green stalks of cane. He liked coming outside at this time of day and enjoying the sunset, and the cool breezes off the river. He liked getting away from the family for just a little while to let his mind wander in different directions, seeking the solution that would be his future.

"Bet you don't get sunsets like this in New Orleans," his father said coming up behind him.

Louis continued to lean against the oak tree, refusing to give up the last rays of daylight.

"No, we don't, Papa. That's one thing the city doesn't offer."

His father took a drag on his cigar and exhaled into the fresh air. "Your mother won't let me smoke these things in the house, so I have to come outside if I want to enjoy my cigar."

"I think I can understand why," Louis said, thinking the odor was not particularly pleasant.

"So what are you doing home?" his father asked. "If you don't want to be here, why are you?"

"Because I have no place else in the world to be right now," Louis said, his tone angry.

"Are you moving home to work on the plantation?" his father asked.

Louis shrugged. "I don't know. I'm here for an undetermined time. Until I decide what I'm going to do with the rest of my life."

His father drew on the cigar and blew the smoke out in the fresh air. "There's an easy solution to that question. Stay here and work at Belle Fournet. We need you," his father said eagerly.

Louis turned to face his father, the frustration of his adult years spilling out. "Why? Why can't you understand that I don't want to work on the plantation?"

His father raised his voice to match his son's. "Because this is your home. This is your family and your place is here. There's plenty for everyone to keep busy."

Louis didn't know why he kept trying to make his father understand. Grown men did not appreciate being treated as if they knew nothing about what they were doing and were still the little boy they ran out of the barns.

"Edmond was the one that you wanted to run the business. He's the oldest and I moved on to find my own place in the world."

"Then why aren't you happy? You seem miserable since you've been home this time. Your mother is worried about you," his father said quietly in the darkness.

Louis shrugged and watched a shooting star fall from the sky. He remembered how when he was a boy he always made a wish when he saw a star fall. Now he wondered if any of them had ever come true. With a skeptic's mind, he made a quick wish.

"I've done something really foolish. The reason I came home was to reacquaint myself with the man I used to be," Louis said, not looking at his father.

"Sometimes a man makes a mistake and has to live with the consequences of his actions. Even when he doesn't like them," his father said and drew on his cigar.

"I tried to sell Cuvier Shipping without Marian's knowledge," he blurted out feeling like he was twelve instead of over thirty. He paused to let his father absorb the information. "I wanted so desperately to build a mill and work with you and Edmond milling the sugar crops, that I lied."

His father didn't say anything.

"I made decisions that were selfish and didn't concern myself with how they affected others. If I hadn't been so intent on owning my own mill business and more interested in leading the company I co-own, then the woman I love would have become my wife, instead of walking away from me and the business we own," he said staring off into the darkness at the red-glow from the tip of his father's cigar. "I can only blame myself and my selfish need to be in control."

A cricket sang his song of loneliness in the night air, as Louis seemed to sag even further against the tree.

His father looked at him and took a puff of his cigar. "Are we ever really in control of our destiny? Even at my age, I can plan for tomorrow, but I don't know what's going to happen." He paused. "The Mississippi may flood. Too much rain could ruin the crops or the price of sugar could plummet tomorrow, but your mother's love and companionship is what keeps me steady on my course. Pleasing her because of her steadfast love of me is what's built this plantation."

His father dropped the stub of his cigar to the ground and rubbed it out with the toe of his boot. "When I was a young man, I gave up my dream of going West not long after we met, because I couldn't leave your mother. I haven't regretted that sacrifice for one moment. Together we can face whatever life offers us and I dread the day that one of us leaves this world before the other one."

The sentimental words from his father shocked Louis and made him see his father in a new light. The old man could be gruff at times, but he loved his wife deeply and Louis felt a new sense of respect.

His father spoke again in the darkness. "It's been my dream that both of my children find a love as strong as ours. That your families be built on unbreakable bonds. That's why I continuously ask about the women you're seeing. I keep hoping you've found that special someone to grow old with."

"You know Papa, for so many years now I've dreamed of owning properties and businesses not understanding that I hadn't realized what really mattered in life. I'm ashamed of my actions and I'm embarrassed at the man I've become."

"You're my son. I've always been proud of you. I trust you'll do better," his father acknowledged. "So what are you going to do?"

"I'm going to become the type of man that deserves Marian. I'm going to put her needs before my own."

With startling clarity Louis saw the pathway to his own

future and he knew what he had to do. Suddenly he understood what he needed to do for Marian, for his own sense of pride. There was no guarantee she would give him yet another chance, but for his own self worth he had to show her he was sincere.

The two men stood there in the darkness, Louis clapped his father on the back and hugged him. "Thanks, Papa, you've given me something to think about."

Louis released his father and walked back to his room. Night had fallen and in the inky blackness he could barely discern the pathway, just like he could hardly see the road his future lay on. But the insight he'd received while watching the sunset was enough to give him a start. And while the moonlight might not light his way, he knew that the dawn would bring a new day and a new man. A man that would find his own way. A man determined to give up his selfish ways and be the man Marian deserved.

When he got back to his room, he sat down and wrote a letter to Drew, his attorney, giving him the necessary instructions. Then he wrote to Marian pouring out his heart and soul, praying that his words would show her just how sorry he was for his actions, knowing he had little chance of forgiveness.

Marian scurried around the room helping the servants pack the children's trunks when Edward came upstairs to tell her she had a guest. It had been over a week since she'd walked out of Cuvier Shipping needing to put some distance between her and Louis. Since that time, Henry had come to visit and let her know that Louis had also left town. He'd gone home to the plantation, leaving Henry in charge of the shipping company.

Marian trusted the man and knew he would make sure things were done right. In the meantime, she still intended to go home to Virginia, to rest near the pine trees, be comforted by her family, and let her spirit heal.

"Who is the visitor, Edward?"

"A Mr. Drew Soulier."

What was her lawyer doing here?

Maybe it had something to do with the trial or maybe something with the will. She hurried downstairs to meet him.

"Hello, Drew," she said coming into the parlor where Edward had left the man. Tall and distinguished looking, his dark hair matched the suit he wore, his green eyes were ever observant.

He kissed her cheek. "How have you been? You're looking beautiful."

"Thank you. I'm all right. I'm about to take the children home to Virginia for a few weeks and then I'll return and decide what to do about Cuvier Shipping."

They sat down on the settee in the parlor and he cleared his throat nervously, his brow furrowed.

"Before you go rushing off, I have some papers for you to look over." He took a deep breath and gazed at her steadily. "Has Louis been acting odd lately? Or has anything happened between the two of you?"

Marian glanced away, her hands clenched tightly in her lap. There was no reason for her to reveal everything to Drew. "Our friendship has always been rocky and lately it's been more strained than usual."

Drew frowned. "I must say his latest instructions shocked me." He shrugged, his large shoulders rising beneath his black coat. "He sent me a letter from Belle Fournet with instructions for me to draw up the papers giving you his part of Cuvier Shipping."

Marian gasped, her gaze locked on Drew. Had she

heard him correctly? "He's giving me his share of the business? Did he say why?"

"No, but he did enclose a letter to you," he said pausing as he gazed at her speculatively. "My instructions were to make sure that you knew it was a gift and that there would be no money exchanged. He said that Cuvier Shipping should belong to you."

"I don't understand." Marian massaged her forehead with her fingertips, trying to ease the ache that suddenly appeared. Why would he just *give* her the business? "Why is he doing this?"

Drew shook his head. "I don't know, he didn't explain his actions to me. Why don't you read his letter and see if there is anything there that tells you?"

He handed the envelope to Marian and she stared at it, afraid to open the missive from the man she still loved desperately. His handwriting scrawled across the front and she resisted the urge to hold the paper close to her heart. No matter what he'd done, her heart ached at the thought of him, and she missed him more than she thought possible.

She broke the seal and slowly pulled out the letter, the crisp white paper crinkling in her hand, the noise seeming loud in the silence. Unfolding it slowly, she began to read.

Dearest Marian,

What can I say that will make you ever truly believe anything I say ever again? I am not worthy of your love and forgiveness, and I realize the extent of the hurt and pain my actions have caused you. I would tell you I'm sorry, but I don't know if you would believe me. I would beg for your forgiveness, but I don't know if that's possible. I can only tell you that until you came into my life, I led a very selfish existence, thinking of only myself and my dreams. But you've shown me just how empty my life is, and how my dreams mean nothing without you by my side.

I know that words from me mean naught right now, so I want to show you how much I love you, how much your happiness means to me. I'm giving you my part of Cuvier Shipping. It is my gift to you and I hope it will fulfill your dream for you and your children. Along with the business, I give you my heart and my love, though they are only words to tell you of my affection.

All my love,
Louis

Tears trickled down her face as Marian finished reading his letter. What should she do now?

After Drew left, Marian returned to the parlor where she read the letter again. She wanted to believe him so much, but fear held her in its grasp more firmly than ever before. And if she made the wrong decision, she would have to live with the result for the rest of her life. That could be a long time and she'd already made one wrong choice regarding marriage and love. What if she made another?

She sat there remembering the way he'd been good to her children, the way he'd made love to her that first time, soothing her fears. She remembered how he'd finally begun to teach her the shipping business, the impromptu baseball game with Philip, the picnic in her office, the trip to his family home, and all the little things that made her laugh. From the very first he'd been kind to her, while lying repeatedly regarding the business. The business seemed to be his Achilles' heel and he'd just given it to her.

If it were possible, she'd sell the business and they could start something new, but that wouldn't be fair to Philip and she wanted so much to give the business to her son.

Claire entered the parlor. "Edward said you had a visitor. Who was it?"

"Drew Soulier, my attorney," Marian said staring into space, the weight of everything seeming to pile upon her, immobilizing her.

"Is everything all right?" Claire asked, concern filling her voice.

"No," Marian said, and handed her the letter from Louis.

Claire sank to the settee beside Marian and read the missive.

No matter how much Marian tried, she still found it hard to believe that he'd just given her the business.

"Oh, Marian," she said, her voice filled with sympathy. "What are you going to do?"

"He gave me the business, Claire. He outright gave me the business, which means he's sacrificing everything for me," she said, her voice filled with all the emotion whirling inside her.

"Is it legal? Can he just give you a business?"

"Yes, Drew assured me that everything was in order. That Cuvier Shipping is all mine," she said feeling so alone. "Louis's dream of buying the other company is gone. What do I do?" she asked Claire. "Do I just accept his gift or do I go to Louis?"

Claire sat silent for a few moments, her face contemplative. "I can't answer that question, Marian. You're the only one who can. But I will say that not many men would just give away a business they had invested so much in."

Marian nodded her head.

"I know," she said, her voice wavering. "He wants me back. I love him, but I'm so afraid."

"I think your fear is understandable. You've been hurt. You're afraid to gamble on a man who has not always been honest with you. But what does your heart tell you?"

"It wants to give him another chance. But I don't think I could take it if he hurt me again."

"So are you ready to crawl away and become a dried up widow who never risks her heart?" Claire asked. "What happens in five to ten years from now when the children are all grown up and you're alone? Will you regret not giving him one last possibility of love again?"

"Oh, Claire, I don't know." She took a deep breath and sighed. "I'm tired of being hurt by the men in my life. I need to believe that he will love me for the rest of our lives. I need to believe he will be honest with me."

"Whatever you decide, don't make the decision based on fear. Make your decision based on love."

Marian glanced at her sister suddenly. "Are we talking about me or you here?"

Claire's eyes filled with pain. "I don't want you to make the same mistake I made. Go to him."

Marian sat there on the settee, her heart aching with sadness. She loved Louis more than she'd ever thought she could love again, but she was afraid. Yet he wouldn't have sacrificed his dream of owning a sugar mill, if his love for her wasn't serious. But could she get over her fear of being hurt and accept his love once again?

The only way to find out the truth would be to go and speak with him. Drew said he was at Belle Fournet. She would go there and talk with him and see what her heart said to her.

"You're right. I can't go to Virginia until I've spoken

with him. Tomorrow, I'm going out to his parents' plantation. I need to see him and let my heart decide if I can trust him ever again. I need to see if I can give him one more chance to be honest with me," Marian said, slowly rising from the settee.

She was so afraid, but she knew her heart would never heal, unless she spoke with him and then she could decide whether to give love another opportunity.

CHAPTER EIGHTEEN

The sun glinted off the water as the steamboat chugged up the mighty Mississippi River to the dock of the Belle Fournet plantation. No one expected her, but she could see a wagon heading up the road that led to the main house. She'd only brought her damaged heart and she didn't know if this trip would heal the wounded organ or just deepen the injury.

"I'll be back in four hours to pick you up," Captain Paul reminded her.

"Thank you. I'll be watching for you," she replied, thinking that four hours was a long time to spend with a man when she wasn't sure of the outcome. The time span could be not nearly long enough or it could seem like an eternity, but either way, she was here for the next four hours.

As she stepped off the boat, the wagon pulled up to the dock and the same servant as before jumped down to greet her. "Hello, Mrs. Cuvier, I don't think the big house is expecting you."

"No, Leon they're not. But I'm here to visit with Mr. Fournet," she said, as he helped her into the wagon.

The drive to the big house seemed to take forever, and Marian sat, twisting her gloved hands in her lap, sweat trickling down her back from the hot afternoon sun. Part of her wanted the slow horse to hurry, while another part needed more time.

She couldn't help but wonder what she was doing here. Second thoughts seemed to attack her like a plague, though she remained outwardly calm. Her insides twisted nervously and she kept trying to remember the carefully worded speech she had prepared, but somehow the words deserted her.

Mrs. Fournet, Louis's mother, stood on the balcony staring down at her. As she disembarked from the wagon, Marian felt like a five-year-old child looking up at the woman.

"Mrs. Cuvier, what a pleasant surprise."

Marian climbed the stairs. "Mrs. Fournet, how nice to see you. I'm sorry for dropping in unannounced, but I must speak with Louis."

"I've already sent for him from the fields, dear. I thought that might be why you were here."

Marian felt the sweat seem to multiply as she realized there was no backing out now, and he would soon know she was here and wanted to speak with him.

"Come into the house and let me fix you a glass of lemonade. This sun will ruin your pretty skin, so let's get inside where there's shade."

Following the older woman through the door into her bedroom parlor, she motioned for Marian to sit in a nearby chair and though she was ill at ease, she did as the woman asked.

The woman gazed at her curiously.

"My son has been different since he's been home this time and I'm wondering if maybe the changes I see have something to do with you," the older woman said.

Marian gazed at his mother, wondering about her words, and then shrugged her shoulders. "It's hard to say. How has he been different?"

"He seems more serious and settled. Almost like he's lost his frivolous ways and finally become a man. Though I must confess he's in his thirties and has been a man for quite some time," she said, her mouth turning up in a smile. "Some men take longer than others to reach a certain maturity."

Marian returned her smile. "I don't know how I could have helped him to mature. For more than a week things have been strained between us and we've not spoken."

She nodded her head. "That explains a lot. You see, several nights ago, my husband came in from outside disturbed by a conversation he'd had with Louis, our youngest. Seems that Louis told him he had acted in shameful way trying to obtain his own selfish interest and had instead lost someone he loved."

"I . . . I don't know what to say," Marian said.

"My husband and Louis seem closer than ever since then. I've often worried that they would never breach the gulf that existed between them. I want to thank you for sending him home," his mother said. "He appears a stronger man and I think you're good for him."

"I didn't send him home," Marian said. "He made that decision on his own."

Just then the back door slammed in the house and she could hear Louis calling, "Mother, where are you?"

"In my room, dear," she called.

Louis pulled open the door and strode in, his white shirt clinging to him, his hair wet as if he'd dunked his head into water and then run his fingers through his hair. His pants were tucked into boots that had seen better days.

Marian gazed at him, her eyes filling with the sight of him and she thought he'd never looked more handsome than he did at this moment. His blue eyes returned her gaze and he went silent at the sight of her.

"Mrs. Cuvier has come to see you dear," his mother said. "Maybe you should take her for a walk around the grounds. That would give the two of you some privacy."

"Marian? Would that be all right with you?" he asked tentatively.

"Yes," she said breathlessly, feeling like a forty-pound weight sat on her chest. The urge to throw herself into his arms almost overwhelmed her, but she resisted.

She stood and they walked out the door, side by side, wordlessly, down the steps of the big house. When they reached the ground level, they strolled through the trees, away from the house.

"I'm surprised to see you here," Louis said glancing at her, his eyes wide with disbelief. "I guess you received the papers from Drew."

"Yes," she stopped and faced him. "Why did you do it, Louis? Why did you lie to me, then give me the business? I'm so confused now, I don't know what to do."

She watched him reflect on her words, his hand reached out to touch her and then fell to his side. "When I first met you, I thought that Jean had treated you so badly. I couldn't believe that he had betrayed you for two other women. It was wrong, yet you held your head high. I was amazed at your strength."

Louis ran his hand through his wet hair. "But you didn't deserve to be treated that way, and then I acted much the same way by lying to you. I'm not proud of what I've done. I felt the need to make it up to you in some way or be just like Jean. And that was the only way I knew how to show you I love you."

He wrapped his hands around her arms and held on to her. "You see you made me a better man. Working with you has changed me from being such a selfish bastard to a man who wants to be your husband, and Philip and Renée's father. Unfortunately, I had already set the wheels in motion to sell the business long before I discovered I love you. And then I waited too long to cancel it, once I realized that I wanted you, not the shipping company or even that damned mill."

She gazed at him, hearing the pain in his voice seeing the tears in his eyes, but she said nothing.

He released her arms. "For the first time in so many years I'd found something that made me happy and I can only blame myself for its destruction."

"Oh, Louis. I want to believe you, I really do, but I'm so afraid," she said in a quiet voice. "That's why I came here today to see if my fears were real, or if they were not."

He cupped her face in his hands. "Let me love away your fears, Marian. I promise you, that I will never willingly hurt you again. I love you and want you for my wife," he said, his voice breaking at the end.

She stepped away from him and walked a little way ahead. "Your mother told me you were different this trip, that she saw changes in you that she'd never seen before and she liked them."

"I came back to find how I'd taken the wrong path as a man. And discovered what I was missing in my life I'd left in New Orleans. I love you, Marian. Even if you never marry me, I'm asking for your forgiveness," he said moving to walk beside her.

She stopped and faced him, touching him on the

sleeve. "Louis, I came to you an empty shell of a woman and you made me flower. You taught me that I was beautiful, I was sensual, and I could do anything I set my mind to. You've made me stronger than I've ever been in my life and I love you with all my heart. I forgave you long before I came to Belle Fournet. Show me we were meant to be together."

She met him halfway and their lips met in a kiss that seared them together. Finally he broke the kiss. "There's nothing that we can't overcome together. I'm sorry for trying to sell the business and I promise to spend the rest of my days being honest with you."

"What about Cuvier Shipping?" she asked.

"It's all yours," he said and kissed her again.

Their lips sealed their love, creating more joy inside Marian than she thought possible. Finally they broke for air, panting, and happy to be in each other's arms.

"What are you going to do?" she asked breathing hard.

"My father has offered to help me buy the old mill and together we're going to build it into a profitable business."

"As long as you include me in your life, then I don't care what you do," Marian said, her voice husky, her arms tightly holding onto the man she loved.

"Always, my love. Always," he said and kissed her once again.

In the distance the sound of a steamboat whistle could be heard, but Marian didn't care. She'd found her place here in Louis's arms and together they would make their way back to the house on Josephine Street.

If you liked SUNLIGHT ON JOSEPHINE STREET, be sure to look for the next book in Sylvia McDaniel's *The Cuvier Widows* series, THE PRICE OF MOONLIGHT, available wherever books are sold December 2002.